PARANORMAL TALENT AGENCY

EPISODES 4-6

HEATHER SILVIO

Panther Books

Published in the United States by Panther Books, Las Vegas.

Correspondence to the author may be sent to:
heather@heathersilvio.com

Cover design by Sonia Freitas at Chloe Belle Arts
https://www.ChloeBelleArts.com

ISBN (Print) 978-1-951192-04-4
ISBN (E-book) 978-1-951192-05-1

BOOKS BY HEATHER SILVIO

PARANORMAL TALENT AGENCY

Lights, Camera, Action (Episode One)

Reset to One (Episode Two)

That's a Wrap (Episode Three)

An Unexpected Sequel (Episode Four)

Jumping the Shark (Episode Five)

The Season Finale (Episode Six)

NON-SERIES FICTION

Not Quite Famous: A Romantic Comedy of an Actress
on the Edge

Beyond the Abyss: Tales of the Supernatural

Courting Death

NONFICTION

Special Snowflake Syndrome: The Unrecognized
Personality Disorder Destroying the World

Happiness by the Numbers: 9 Steps to Authentic
Happiness

Stress Disorders: A Healing Path for PTSD

ACKNOWLEDGMENTS

Thank you to everyone who supported this series from its
original inception to completion.

Episode Four

An Unexpected Sequel

CHAPTER ONE

As the founder and owner of Landon Talent Agency, could I ever have predicted I'd make a deal with the devil? Okay, technically, Barbara Knollman was a low-level demon. But still. I'd agreed to do the demon's bidding and, if I wasn't yet entirely sorry for having made that deal, I definitely had regrets.

Now I sat in the overstuffed leather chair opposite the Councilwoman, my hands clasped in my lap, eyes downcast like I'd been called to the principal's office. Though, in a way, that was true.

"Robin, this has worked out perfectly," Barbara said. She stood at the window overlooking Main Street, immobile, her brown hair swept back in a tight bun. She returned to her chair behind the imposing solid wood desk and sat, her hands resting on its surface, talon-like fingernails displayed.

The effect worked. I swallowed audibly and Barbara chuckled. "You really wanted the supernatural underworld to be exposed?" I asked. A few months ago, a local pain-in-the-butt reporter revealed a crazy genie to be a serial killer. And then outed the lot of us.

Barbara smiled, her small sharp teeth drawing attention. "Yes. I did. I foresaw the path to my success. It included the exposure," she explained, tapping her manicured talons against the fine wood-grain.

"I'm not sure I understand what this has been about," I admitted in a small voice. My boss could see the future, but she kept her visions a secret. Even I didn't know what success she sought.

Barbara looked down on me, her minion. "You will. Everyone will." A demon posing as a 50-something year-old human, she also happened to be the unofficial head of the Las Vegas City Council. Technically that position fell to the Mayor, but Barbara held the actual power. Interestingly, although the paranormal underworld had been exposed, she had not. I wondered if she saw that in her vision.

My skin crawled as she stared at me, an ambiguous smile on her face. Now what? I waited. It would do no good to ask. After five years as her minion, I certainly learned my place. Maybe I used to be a witch, but today I was powerless and under her thumb.

"It's time for the next step," the Councilwoman stated. "You will shut down your agency."

I gasped. Shut down my agency?

"I want your full focus and attention. There is a being in town who must be eliminated."

Surely she doesn't mean—

"And you will eliminate him."

My jaw dropped open and I stared, aghast, at the demon. Close my agency and kill someone? I needed to buy time. "Who?"

"His name is Jackson McKee."

I waited to see if more information would be forthcoming. Nada. I risked her wrath. "Who is Jackson McKee?"

She gave me a withering look. "It doesn't matter. I need him killed."

I blanched at her tone and directive – and pushed back. "If I don't know what kind of paranormal being he is," I reasoned, "how will I know how to kill him?"

Barbara pursed her lips. "He's human, but with abilities."

Hmm. A witch like me? An empath like Catherine, that irritating fellow talent agent?

"So you can kill him like any other human."

I paled but nodded. Where was she going with this? "Okay. Where do I find him?"

"He's about to be a cameraman on *Forbidden Island.*"

I remembered receiving character breakdowns for actor submissions for that film and seized my opening. "Since it's a movie production, maybe it would make sense to keep my agency open so I have a natural in to get on set. After all, I sent actors to it."

Barbara stared impassively. I wasn't stupid. I knew she knew why I made my suggestion. She sighed. "Fine. Keep your agency open. I want him dead within the week."

I gulped.

She glanced down at the paperwork on her desk. I took that as my cue to leave and scurried out of her office, with nary a backward glance. I wasn't a killer. What could I do now?

CHAPTER TWO

The drive back to my office passed in a blur. I remained on autopilot while I considered my options. I was a glorified gopher for Barbara. That was it. She'd never asked me to kill someone before. Why would she ask me now? Could she have seen it in a vision? Surely not.

I zipped my black VW Jetta coupe into my designated spot outside the office building housing Landon Talent Agency but remained seated for a few minutes, my mind still buzzing. It wouldn't hurt to do a little digging, at least find out who this Jackson McKee was. Maybe he deserved to die.

The wind whipped against me when I exited the vehicle. I shuddered and pulled my beige coat tighter. Even in Vegas, December could be uncomfortably cold.

Who was I kidding?

I wasn't going to kill this guy.

I hurried into the two-story stucco building, took the stairs up to my locked office. I maintained a small enough agency that I didn't need to keep regular business hours or employ an assistant. I barely noticed the gray couches and end table with a lamp on it as I moved through the space. The office had come furnished. The furnishings did the job. I closed the door to my inner sanctum behind me and collapsed into my rolling chair, the one piece of furniture I had paid for. My butt needed to be comfortable!

My laptop quietly booted up, and I found my eye drawn to the only personal touch I'd added to my office. A picture of my childhood cat, Patches, his scraggly image in the frame I'd designed. The black, white, and orange stray had shown up one day and stayed with me for years, vanishing after the accident. I ran my finger along the edge of the wood. The painted images of blue waves, red flames, green trees, and white clouds represented the earth's magical elements. With a frown, I yanked my finger back, slammed that line of thinking to a halt, and focused on my purpose.

A niggling thought at the back of my mind told me *Forbidden Island* would begin filming tonight, but I wanted to confirm that. And the location. This might be one of those rare occasions when an agent visited a set. If Jackson McKee was a cameraman on the movie, unless he was shooting b-roll elsewhere, he would be there.

I sighed when I called up the production information. Mia Fynn was producing. She wasn't a bad person – well, nixie, actually, a water spirit – but we just didn't get along. To be honest, I didn't get along with anybody in this town. Yet another drawback of being tied to a demon. I shrugged. It was what it was. Although I was beginning to wonder if I could change that.

The cast list drew my focus. I groaned. Besides my actors, the Paranormal Talent Agency represented several others. Its real name was the Peterson Talent Agency, but once it started catering to the other-than-human acting crowd, the nickname stuck. I saw Catherine's boyfriend, Alex the half-incubus, on the list, as well as Evie, the vampire, and her human boyfriend, Ryan.

The possibility of running into any of them didn't thrill me. Barbara had sent me to cross paths with them enough in the past. I distinctly remembered the time Evie outed me as a demon's minion to Catherine; such a sarcastic vampire. And then (unfortunately, but accurately) called me out for not even knowing what my demon boss's plans were. My cheeks reddened at the unpleasant memory. Some things never changed; I still didn't know my boss's ultimate plan.

On the positive, I confirmed my belief that filming started tonight. I scanned for the address, saw it was near my Summerlin office. That was convenient. Checking my watch, I had two hours until night fall and call time for the shoot. Okay, this was good. I'd plan to be there, scope out this Jackson McKee.

And then what?
Kill him?

CHAPTER THREE

I tugged on the bottom of my fitted purple t-shirt, observing the frenzied activity on the set. Cones blocked off sections of the grocery store parking lot next to the park where tonight's scenes would be filmed. Despite the name *Forbidden Island*, the movie took place in Las Vegas. I hadn't read the script; something about the island being an analogy for the loneliness of living in a city surrounded by people but remaining apart. I wouldn't know anything about that.

Up ahead, set lights reflected off green hair pulled back in a ponytail. I inwardly sighed before heading in the nixie's direction. She turned at the sound of my footsteps. I didn't miss the downturn of her lips before she plastered a fake smile on her face.

"Hi, Robin, what can I do for you?" Mia Fynn asked, all fake-solicitous with her set visitor. Not that I was bitter.

"Hi, Mia. I wanted to check things out since I have a few actors on this movie."

Her eyebrows rose a fraction. She wasn't buying it, but I doubted she'd challenge me. "Of course, welcome," she said, her smile still not reaching her emerald eyes. "Let me know if you need anything." And with a small nod, she glided away.

I took in the controlled chaos. For anyone who's never been on a set, you have your director, assistant director, director of photography, camera folks, and actors (both lead and background, otherwise known as extras). Not to mention wardrobe, hair and makeup, and a bunch of others whose names I could never keep straight, even after five years in the business.

I spotted a portly gentleman hoisting a camera and decided to begin there. I crossed the park, passing in and out of the artificial lights, my sneakers making whisper sounds in the grass.

"Excuse me? I'm looking for Jackson McKee," I said to the back of the man carrying the camera.

He turned, a quizzical look on his face. "Jackson?" Confusion cleared from his blue eyes. "Oh, do you mean Jack?"

"Maybe? I've never met him," I confided. "I'm Robin Landon of Landon Talent. I was told to find him on set."

"Gotcha." He hefted his body in a circle, scouting the crowd. He stopped and pointed. "See that man by the

RED 8K." I scanned until I saw the man standing beside the expensive camera on a tripod. "That's Jack."

I nodded and smiled. "Thanks."

"No problem."

I considered the backside of Jackson McKee as I approached him. He had close-cut brown hair and wore an Imagine Dragons t-shirt stretched tight across well-defined muscles, over jeans molded to a very fine backside indeed. Heat suffused my face.

Not good, thinking naughty thoughts about the man I was supposed to kill. That sobered me instantly. I stopped about five feet from him.

"Hi, can I help you?" His chocolate brown eyes searched mine.

"Um," I rather eloquently responded.

Jackson McKee took a few steps toward me. "Are you okay? Do you need something?"

Only a few inches taller than me and probably late-twenties like me, he radiated coiled strength. He rubbed his jaw, my mind hearing the scrape of his fingers against the stubble, wanting to brush my fingers across it too. My eyes widened at this instant attraction.

Jackson's smile faltered. "Ma'am?"

Ma'am? What was I, his mother? I strode forward, hand outstretched. "Hi, I'm Robin Landon of Landon Talent."

His hand closed around mine and held a second longer than customary. His eyes searched my face again. What did he see in my brown eyes that had him so curious? I'd been told often enough through the body language of others that I was a humdrum plain-Jane. Instantly forgettable, someone once said. But Jackson didn't look at me that way. Not like a frump in jeans with her shoulder-length brown hair in an unassuming pony tail.

"Hello, Robin Landon of Landon Talent," he responded formally.

I burst out laughing.

Jackson released my hand and smiled. "What can I do for you, Robin?"

"I'm just checking out the set."

He stared at me. Yeah, he caught that the answer made no sense, given I had asked for him by name. He appeared to let it go. "Well, then, welcome to the set." He shrugged. "Did you want to see something in particular?"

You with your shirt off, my mind shouted. I blushed again. Good grief, this was ridiculous.

He smirked and I wondered if the blush was visible in the low lighting. Man, I hoped not. I wasn't sure how I expected this first meeting to go, but this was not it.

"Nope," I finally answered his question. "Just poking around." That, at least, was true.

"Okay. I guess let me know if you need anything," he said, uncertainty in his voice.

"I will, thanks," I responded brightly then turned before I shoved my foot any further in my mouth. Did I hear him chuckling as I walked away? What a great first impression. Wait. Why was I trying to make a good impression? That ran completely counter to my goal. I groaned aloud.

"Robin, are you okay?"

I sarcastically thanked the universe for increasing the awkwardness of the evening and turned to face Catherine Rodham. Her long blond hair curled down around her shoulders and her blue eyes expressed concern. Huh, that concern was new. Catherine and her Paranormal Talent Agency friends were always so rude to me. I didn't know how to answer her. Part of me wanted to blurt out the whole sordid mess. I sighed instead. "I'll be fine. Thanks."

If my genuine appreciation surprised her, she hid it well. "Okay, you seem off, is all," she continued.

I almost wanted to take offense. But, I worked for a demon. What did I expect? "I'm trying to get a handle on something," I said. She was an empath of a sort. A magical human lie detector, I'd learned. She'd sense if I lied.

"I know we haven't been friendly," she said, "but if you ever need anything."

Both of us looked shocked by her offer and I smiled. "Thank you. I appreciate that."

She nodded and moved away, her face still expressing uncertainty. She wasn't alone. She and her friends always just tolerated me. Maybe I could ask them—

I shut down that thought. Barbara would be none too happy if I involved anybody else. And she had spies everywhere. She'd find out, for sure. I let that possibility go. Permanently.

With unexpected clarity, a plan came to me. I searched the crowd for Jackson again. A thrill of desire snaked through me when I saw him. He was laughing at something a fellow crew member was saying. His perfect white teeth flashed in a captivating smile. I made my way to him.

"Hello again, Robin Landon of Landon Talent," he greeted me.

"Hi, cameraman Jackson McKee," I responded in kind. We both grinned.

"Would you like to have breakfast or lunch with me tomorrow?" I blurted out the question before I could talk myself out of it. I didn't know if this was a good idea, but it was all I could come up with. Get close to him and… what? I'd figure it out as I went.

His eyes widened in surprise. I braced myself for the rejection. "I would love to," he accepted and my jaw dropped open. "Did you think I'd say no?"

"Um," I shook my head, "I didn't know."

"Give me your phone." I handed it to him. He entered his information. "Send me a text so I'll have your number. We'll go to BabyStacks for brunch, if that works for you."

Our eyes met and I swore something flared. Desire? This was a dangerous path I'd started down. I ignored the foreboding now flooding through me.

"It definitely works for me."

CHAPTER FOUR

I kicked myself for arriving at BabyStacks so early. There was no traffic to speak of and I zipped along Buffalo Drive toward Desert Shores. My heart fluttered when I saw Jackson standing just inside the front door by the hostess station. I scanned the cozy restaurant décor, noting the red-brick-style flooring and natural wood and stone accents throughout. My eyes returned to Jackson. He again wore a pair of jeans and a concert t-shirt. How was he not cold? It was probably his uniform style. I smoothed out nonexistent wrinkles from my purple long-sleeved fitted shirt over leggings and boots.

"Guess I wasn't the only one eager for brunch," he quipped and I chuckled. "I've already put my name on the list. When I saw how early I was, I figured I'd go ahead and do so. That way you wouldn't have had to wait at all," he explained.

"That was very gentlemanly of you."

"I try."

We smiled at each other.

"Jack, party of two?" The hostess broke the spell. We followed her to a two-top table next to a stone wall. Jackson pulled my chair out.

"Thank you," I murmured. He took the wooden chair opposite. We watched each other as the hostess placed menus in front of us. "The hostess called you Jack. Do you prefer that to Jackson?"

A half-smile flitted on his face. "Normally I do, but I like the way you say Jackson."

"You do?" I asked with a flirty smile back.

"I do." His voice sounded huskier.

"Okay, then. Jackson." We stared at each other. I rubbed my lips together; his eyes followed the movement with interest. Okay, then, indeed! I opened up the menu.

"Have you been here before?" Jackson asked.

"I haven't. I assume you have since you picked it."

"I have, but it's been awhile. The pancakes are awesome, as you'd expect by the name."

"I'll have to try some."

After that scintillating exchange, the conversation lulled while we perused the menu and surreptitiously checked the other out. He still had his five o'clock shadow; it worked for him, highlighting the contours of his jawline and kissable lips.

Kissable? I inwardly rolled my eyes. Time to focus on why I asked him out. Not just because I found him sweet and insanely attractive.

"How long have you been a cameraman?"

"A few years. I tried acting first, believe it or not, and hated it."

"You hated it?"

"Turned out I didn't enjoy the audition process."

"I don't think anybody does."

"True. But I also didn't enjoy memorizing lines."

My brow furrowed. "Why did you want to be an actor at all then?"

He laughed, low and sexy. "I didn't, to be honest. A photographer told me I had the look for it and I thought it might be fun."

I echoed his laughter. "You definitely have the look," I said. An instant flush crept up my neck. He quirked an eyebrow. "I'm a talent agent. It's my job to notice."

He nodded, but the twinkle in his eyes told me he didn't buy my explanation.

"It's too tough a business if you aren't committed," I added.

"Exactly. I did, however, discover that I enjoyed watching the cameramen. So, I took some classes, did some student films, and ta da, now I'm a full-time cameraman. What about you? How long have you been a talent agent?"

My smile fell and I swallowed past the lump in my throat. How to explain that I got my agency by signing a pact with a demon?

"Hey, it's okay," he said with concern, reaching to take one of my hands in his. "We're just getting to know each other. If it's not something you want to talk about—"

I rolled my eyes, tried to laugh off the awkwardness. "That's a long boring story." I pulled my hand from his when the waitress appeared to take our order.

His eyes stayed on me as I purposefully kept my own on the waitress. She took the order and departed. I dropped my gaze to my lap. I needed to get this conversation back on track.

"Tell me about the others on set."

Jackson took my conversational redirect in stride and regaled me with his histories with various members of the crew. Slowly the conversation became loose and fun. So, of course, I realized it was time to make it weird again. I needed to remember my goal.

"Do you know Barbara Knollman?"

"The Councilwoman?"

"Yes, that's her."

He shrugged. "I know of her. I've seen her on *Entertainment Daily* but I've never met her." He tilted his head. "Why do you ask?"

"Are you sure?"

"Yes. Why?" He frowned slightly.

I needed to say something but my thoughts swirled in consternation. Why would Barbara want him dead if he had never met her? Could he have done something he wasn't aware of?

"Why do you ask if I know the councilwoman?"

I decided to provide part of the truth. "I sometimes do work for her," I started vaguely. "Anyway, she mentioned you the other day."

Understanding dawned in his eyes, but there was an undercurrent of something unreadable. He knew more than he was saying, I'd bet money on it. "That's why you were checking me out on set?"

"I wasn't checking you out," I disagreed. He grinned. "Okay, I was checking you out. But you were checking me out, too," I reminded him.

He laughed. "Yes, I was. I freely admit that."

"Why?" The question slipped out before I could stop it. Ugh. That sounded pathetic.

Again, the inscrutable expression, though his face quickly smoothed out. "There's something about you, Robin."

My jaw dropped open and I snapped it shut. This hunk of a man thought there was something about shy, unassuming me? That blew my mind.

Not that I had low self-esteem or anything, but I understood my strengths. Physical beauty wasn't one of them.

I redirected the conversation back to safer ground and the rest of the breakfast passed as expected. For the life of me, I could not understand why Barbara wanted this man dead. When Jackson walked me to my car and hugged me goodbye, promising to call, I made my mind up.

I would challenge the demon.

CHAPTER FIVE

"What did you say?" Barbara Knollman's icy tone clashed with her fiery eyes. Did I smell brimstone? I clamped down on my overactive imagination, ignored the acid burning a hole in my stomach. I lifted my chin and met her hard stare.

"You heard me." The calm in my voice amazed me. I willed my poker face to stay in place. "Unless you can give me a good answer to why you want Jackson McKee dead, I refuse to kill him."

The demon's red eyes slowly returned to their normal obsidian. Fathomless black holes, I sometimes thought. I withstood the urge to shudder. Barbara smiled, her small, pointed teeth unnerving as always. She stood and leaned over her desk.

"You are not in a position to refuse," she responded, her reasonable tone belying the steel beneath.

"Yes, I am," I retorted. "What's the worst you can do?"

Barbara lifted a single eyebrow.

My cheeks reddened. Well, yeah, she could probably damn me to hell for all eternity. I shook my head. "It doesn't matter," I insisted. "I'm not a killer."

"Now I'm confused." She retook her seat, the fabric of her pants whispering as she crossed her legs with deliberate slowness. "Either you aren't willing to kill him at all or you're only willing to kill him for a good reason. Which is it?"

Her saccharine tone chilled me. "He doesn't even know you," I redirected. "None of this makes any sense."

Barbara sighed, startling me. "Fine."

"Really?"

"Not that I owe you an explanation," she continued. "But my visions showed me that his death is necessary."

"For what?"

"For me to achieve my goal."

"What goal?" I couldn't believe how belligerent and demanding I was being. Did I have a death wish this morning?

"That is not information I plan on sharing." Barbara stared placidly at me, waiting for my response. I considered it for a half minute, made a show of considering my options.

"That's not good enough." I took a deep, steadying breath, which did not go unnoticed by the demon, who sneered.

"It's not?" Her tone remained light, but I didn't buy it.

"No. It's not. I refuse to kill anyone. For any reason."

She tilted her head.

"That wasn't in our agreement," I added, hoping to find an end-run around her demand.

"Are you sure, minion?"

I hesitated. No, I wasn't sure. I had been in such a low place when I made the deal. I didn't remember much about what I had signed in blood. That was bad, right?

"I gather from your silence that you realize the folly of refusing?"

Goosebumps rose on my arms. I opened my mouth. How much longer would I live after uttering this next phrase? "I do – and I choose to do so anyway. I refuse to kill anyone. Do what you will."

I felt defeated and yet free. She might smite me down, or something like that, but at least I would leave this world not a killer. I gripped the sides of the chair, feared how much it would hurt.

"Okay," Barbara responded with a nod. "You won't kill him."

That rendered me speechless. I released my death grip and tried a small smile. "Thank you?"

"You may leave now," she said, her black eyes flat.

I darted from the room, pleased, but wary. The smarter part of me understood I missed something important. I had to have.

There was no way the demon would allow me to defy her like that.

CHAPTER SIX

An invitation the next day from Jackson almost distracted me from my terrified waiting-for-the-other-shoe-to-drop feeling. Almost. He had texted with a late invite to dinner. Although he apologized for the last minute text, I understood the unpredictability of a movie shoot.

I stood now before the full-length mirror hanging on the back of my closet door, evaluating my outfit choice. The weather was mild for December and I thought I could get away with wearing a long-sleeve shirt dress over leggings without a jacket. I kept my hair in its serviceable ponytail and skipped makeup.

He seemed to like me for me, so I wasn't going to mess with that. A quick check of my watch told me he would arrive soon.

Sure enough, the doorbell chimed, and I crossed the stone floor from the bedroom through the living room. My breath caught in my throat when I opened the front door. Jackson looked yummy. My gaze traveled the length of him, from his fitted navy blue button-down shirt to his dark jeans and cowboy boots. His permanent five o'clock shadow begged to be touched. He smiled at my clear appreciation, skin crinkling around his eyes.

"You look beautiful," he greeted me.

"Thanks, so do you."

He held his arm out, and I allowed him to lead me to his car, actually a Ford F150 truck. I must have made a noise.

"Yeah, the truck's big," he said. "I like to go camping, plus it's good for lugging camera equipment around." He opened the door and helped me into the cab.

I was rarely in bigger vehicles; I felt incredibly high up. The feeling triggered a giggle. Jackson glanced at me inquisitively. I shook my head.

"Just marveling at the view from up here."

We drove the short bit on South Town Center Drive and turned onto West Charleston Avenue, heading for Red Rock Casino. It was a great complex off-Strip, including a movie theater and bowling alley.

But, we were headed to 8 Noodle Bar, an Asian fusion restaurant, for dinner. Busy for a weeknight, Jackson maneuvered his behemoth toward the back of a parking lot, near a parking lot light. The dark mountains rose in the distance beyond the casino.

Jackson hurried around the front of the truck to open my door and help me down. Our eyes locked and a thrill raced through me.

"Are you hungry?"

My jaw dropped at his double entendre. I failed to respond around the cotton balls in my mouth.

He chuckled. "I meant for food."

"Of course."

"At least right now," he teased.

I threaded my arm through his. Before we took two steps, he tensed. I stole a glance at him, wondering what had changed. His eyes had a glassy, far-away look. He slammed to a halt, causing me to stumble. He remained silent. With small movements, he assessed our surroundings.

Anxiety fluttered in my chest. "Jackson? What's wrong?"

He didn't respond. I looked around, trying to identify the source of his concern. Nothing jumped out. Parked cars. A few people approaching the casino in the distance. Everything seemed normal.

You know how they say, in times of stress, things move fast yet slow. Turned out that was accurate.

I glanced up at the parking lot light illuminating us.

A loud pop broke the silence.

Jackson threw me to the ground, his body shielding mine.

A dome of glowing light shimmered like a force field around us.

Glass shards from the light fixture bounced off the air above us. The lighting unit itself followed. I uttered a choked scream and flung my hands over my head, but the unit bounced harmlessly off the shimmering light and crashed to the ground beside where we huddled.

My brain struggled to process what happened. That falling light could have killed us, probably should have. How did we not get hit? What was that weird shimmering light surrounding us?

Jackson shot to his feet, pulling me with him. He seemed satisfied by whatever he saw when he stared into the darkness before hurrying to the truck. He yanked open my door.

"Get in," he ordered, before running around to his side of the truck.

The tires squealed when he backed up. We roared through the lot. Once on Charleston, I risked speaking. "What happened back there?" The silence stretched and I wondered if he would answer.

"Someone tried to hurt us."

"That wasn't just an accident?"

He glanced at me, worry etched across his face. "No."

CHAPTER SEVEN

"How do you know?" I asked.

Jackson turned the truck onto South Town Center Drive. "I felt an energy change."

"What do you mean?"

"Someone caused that light to fall."

Acid pooled in my belly. Someone tried to kill us? Barbara's flat smile and obsidian eyes flashed in my mind. "Who would do that?" I asked instead.

"Someone with telekinesis."

"Telekinesis? You mean, someone moved the light with their mind?"

"Yes."

"A witch?" I squeaked the question, unsure how he'd respond.

He glanced at me again, expression unreadable. "Maybe."

"Did you keep the light from hitting us?"

He entered the code to open my small community's security gate. "Yes," he answered. We watched the security arm rise.

"Are you a witch?" Even though the overall supernatural underworld had been outed a few months ago, most supernatural beings still preferred not to announce their presence to the world.

He kept his head straight, looking ahead and not at me. "Yes."

"You have telekinesis, too?"

He startled at that and then nodded understanding at what I was asking. "No. I have protection magic."

"You created a personal shield for us?"

We pulled into my driveway and he killed the engine. He turned to face me. "Something like that," he said with a brief smile. "We need to get into the house and off the street."

We exited the vehicle and hastened up the walkway to enter my single-story stucco home. Once I locked the door behind us, my racing heart rate calmed to closer to normal.

"Would you like something to drink?"

Jackson released a breath I hadn't realized he was holding. "Yeah. That would be great."

I indicated he could sit on the chocolate-brown loveseat in my small living room and stepped into the kitchen opposite. "Wine okay? I have both white and red."

"Red would be great."

I poured us each a glass of Merlot. I could hear Jackson moving around. He was at the bay window overlooking the street when I returned to the living room. I paused, shaken at the sight of him standing off to the side, peering through the blinds, guessing from the movies he was trying to make himself a smaller target. A lump formed in my throat. This was all my fault.

"Here's the wine," I announced and set the glasses down on the coffee table in front of the loveseat. Jackson glanced at me before returning to stare out the window. His body tensed when I approached him, which confused me. I hesitantly touched his shoulder. "Hey. Come sit down."

He didn't respond, so I reached to take his hand in mine. "Let's talk about what happened." He nodded and I led him to the loveseat.

We both grabbed our wine like it was water in a desert and took large gulps. Jackson met my eyes. "What do you think happened?"

The demon tried to kill you? "I'm not sure," I hedged. "What do *you* think happened? How did you know that light was going to fall?"

"Part of my ability comes with an increased sensitivity to the use of magic around me. Right after we started walking, I picked up an energy source."

"What kind of energy source?"

"I wasn't sure at first. That's why I stopped walking. I needed to focus on identifying where the mounting energy was coming from. I didn't know if it was intended for harm initially, but then I knew it was being directed toward us."

"How?"

He gave me a lop-sided smile. "That's the million dollar question, I suppose. I can feel it and just sort of know where it'll be sent." He shrugged. "That's all I got."

"So then you used your… protection magic?"

"Once I knew it was coming, yes."

"That's when you erected the force field. Or shield? What would you call it?"

He chuckled. "Either of those works. I imagined a barrier between us and the magic, and then it was there."

"Protecting us from both the magic itself and the resulting damaged light falling?" I broke eye contact with him as I pondered. My gut feeling that Barbara hadn't just accepted my refusal to kill Jackson must have been correct. Who was this new person? A replacement killer?

"What are you thinking?"

I resumed eye contact, striving to keep my face a blank. This would be the perfect time to explain my defunct-witch status. But how to begin?

"You don't seem very surprised." Although said in a neutral tone, I felt the question poking around the words.

"I saw Elizabeth Addison's expose on *Entertainment Daily*," I offered by way of explanation and it worked.

Jackson laughed. "Yeah, I thought that reporter did a number on us with her morning show. But, I was wrong."

"You were?"

He shrugged. "Despite her big exposé and continuing coverage, nothing's really changed for any of us, day to day."

"Mm-hmm." Barbara had predicted we'd be brought to light, and she also wasn't surprised it hadn't become a big deal. None of which I could say to Jackson.

Jackson tilted his head. "What?"

"Just wondering why someone would want to hurt one or both of us."

His expression hardened. "I intend to find out." He placed a hand on my knee. "It'll be okay. Normally I'd say since I'm a witch, I was the target."

No kidding. "Are you going to be okay?"

"I'll talk to the head of the Witches Council about what happened."

"There's a real Witches Council?" Even though I was a nonfunctioning witch, I knew about the Witches Council. But I couldn't acknowledge it without telling him about me – and about Barbara and her order. Not until I understood what was happening.

Jackson squeezed my knee. "That reporter doesn't know the half of what goes on in this town."

"No doubt. Wait a minute," I interrupted myself. "You said 'normally' you'd believe you were the target?"

"You could be the target," he admitted.

"What? Why?" My questioning tone only partly feigned.

"I could tell my magic was drawn to protect you from the first moment I saw you. There's usually a reason."

"Oh." An ugly thought reared its head and my hands formed fists. Disappointment bubbled at the idea that he wasn't interested in me, that I'd misread his protection magic as romantic intentions.

"You're going to be fine," he assured me, misinterpreting.

I uncurled my fingers. "I'm sure I will," I murmured. "You probably need to go. So you can start investigating." I rose and he stood awkwardly beside me.

His eyes showed confusion. "Probably. Rain check?"

I half-smiled. "Absolutely. Call me?"

"I will."

I strode past him toward the front door. We stood in the open doorway for a moment. "Okay," he said. "I'll let you know what I find out."

I nodded, feeling like a bobblehead, but not trusting myself to speak.

Jackson leaned in to hug me, careful not to get too close as my arms limply went around him. Confusion practically radiated off him. I couldn't blame him but I couldn't banish that ugly thought.

I closed the door, listened to the truck's engine roar to life and then fade as he moved further and further away.

A single tear slid down my cheek and I returned to the loveseat, picked my wine glass back up. I downed the rest in one large swallow and considered what I had learned. The ugly thought had told me the truth. Now I understood Jackson's interest. He had never been interested in me for me. It was his magic telling him I needed protection.

I remembered our brief encounters. He sure seemed to be into me. Could I have misread his intent all along? I was so confused. Well, just like I told Jackson, investigation was the next step.

I headed to the kitchen for more wine fortification. I'd need it if I was going to challenge the demon. Again.

CHAPTER EIGHT

The déjà vu was strong today. I sat before Barbara Knollman in her office, once again gripping the sides of the leather chair like my life depended on it. Light streamed through the window behind her, the warmth not penetrating the chill on my skin.

Barbara stared at me, dark eyes revealing nothing. Her hair was pulled back in its typical severe bun and her hands rested on her desk. Waiting.

I swallowed past the lump in my throat. It was now or never. "Did you hire someone else to kill Jackson?"

Barbara blinked then slowly smiled. The predator visible beneath the calm exterior. "To kill Jackson?"

Her question-as-answer confused me. "Yes?"

"Are you sure it was a single target?"

Barbara's not so cryptic response floored me. "You were trying to kill us both?"

Barbara held both hands up. "I did nothing to you; I wasn't there," she denied. "Be careful what accusations you throw around without proof, Ms. Landon."

"You hired a replacement killer?!" My mind buzzed. She tried to kill us. In retrospect, I wasn't truly surprised. She already wanted Jackson dead; she merely added me for refusing to complete the job.

Barbara shrugged. "I did nothing to you."

"Are you saying it was just a coincidence?"

"Choices have consequences."

That was the closest I was likely to get to an admission that the demon tried to kill me. "Now what?" I voiced the biggest question rumbling around in my mind.

Barbara remained quiet, her eyes focused over my shoulder. Thinking. "We may be coming to the end of our relationship."

"You're releasing me from my pact?"

A cruel smile played on her lips. "That isn't what I said."

"Oh."

Her gaze drilled a hole through me. "We may be coming to the end of our relationship," she repeated.

"Am I going to hell?" I whispered.

Barbara shocked me by belly laughing. "Not yet."

Thank goodness! "What does this mean?" I asked.

"You ask so many questions you already know the answer to." She flicked her hand toward the door. "Leave."

I did.

*****

Knowing that Barbara had put a price on my head, the truth slammed home. This was much bigger than I could handle alone. I would need reinforcements. One name came to mind.

I tried to come up with an alternative option during the drive back to my house. I parked my car in the driveway and rested my forehead on the steering wheel. Nothing. Nobody else I knew had any experience dealing with the supernatural, and Barbara specifically. I sighed.

Once inside, I sat at the high-top kitchen table, running my hands along the smooth dark wood surface. Delaying. I knew that. Placing this next call would be harder in some ways even than challenging the demon. What if she refused to help?

I placed my cellphone on the table in front of me, spinning it, straightening it up, fidgeting. I sighed again. Just get it over with. Unlike with Barbara, the worst she could do was say no.

Before I could talk myself out of it, I snatched the phone up and made the call.

"Catherine Rodham speaking."

I found myself unable to respond to the voice of the talent agent on the other end.

"Hello? Is someone there?"

"Catherine," I croaked out.

Crickets on her end.

"Catherine?"

"Robin, is that you?" Disgust curled around each syllable.

"I need your help."

Crickets again. Oh, good grief, this was like sticks under my fingernails.

"Please." I closed my eyes.

A small sigh and then she offered a ray of hope. "How can I help?"

CHAPTER NINE

Despite her reluctance, Catherine was true to her word. She sat with her Paranormal Talent Agency friends in a private booth at the back of *Soprannaturale*. A were-panther from Italy owned the hole-in-the-wall paranormal café; hence the name, Italian for supernatural. It was on a dead-end street off Main Street, such that non-supernatural beings were unlikely to stumble upon it. Although, ever since the paranormal underworld had been thrown into the spotlight, hordes of Vegas tourists had made it their missions to find supernatural hotspots. But, so far, the luck of the café had held steady and none had found it.

I could count on one hand the number of times I'd gone. Being a demon's minion meant I was not exactly welcome. A few patrons glared at me when I stepped into the café out of the cool evening. Vampires had pushed two tables together; their fangs descended halfway and four sets of eyes stared at me like I was now on the menu. I swore I heard growls from where two werewolves with amber eyes sat at a table farther inside. When I saw two older witches whisper a possible incantation in my direction, it confirmed my undesirability.

But I guessed it was true about having connected friends. Nobody approached me or challenged me. Even the owner, the hunky were-panther, Antonio DiMaio, simply observed me dispassionately, chocolate brown eyes hooded. I passed the scattered Formica-covered two-top tables, avoiding eye contact and focusing on the guild-framed canvases depicting lovely pastoral scenes from Italy.

I stood awkwardly at the table, staring at the booth's forest green vinyl upholstery instead of faces, trying not to wince at the hostility emanating from the women already seated. Well, to be fair, only one woman radiated open hostility.

"Hi, Evie," I greeted the vampire. Maybe I could defuse her irritation. Her blue eyes narrowed to slits and she shook her head, blond curls bouncing. Turned in the 1920s, Evie Jones was now an actress who kept that signature style.

"Please, sit, Robin," Mia Fynn said kindly. The nixie's green hair was pulled into a ponytail like my own, and her emerald eyes reflected openness with a dash of wariness. I nodded and slid in next to Catherine, ignoring the way she tensed at the movement. Who was I kidding? I knew they wouldn't make this easy.

I sighed. "Thank you, Catherine," I directed my opening remarks at the empath. "And thank you, Mia and Evie. For agreeing to meet with me." My gaze dropped to my hands fidgeting in my lap. Tears threatened to overflow.

"Why are we here?" Evie demanded.

"Now, Evie, give her a chance," Mia soothed, her musical nixie voice washing over the table, calming us all with her magic.

"You said you needed my help?" Catherine prompted.

"Yes." Best to jump right in. "You know me as Barbara Knollman's minion. The demon's minion. And that's true. I made a deal with the demon in the past." How much to tell them? My mouth chose not to form the words, 'I am a witch'. "I've mostly been her gopher, as you have pointed out before. For the first time, though, she asked something of me that I refused to do."

"I didn't think there was anything off limits for a minion," Evie said.

My cheeks reddened. "It's never come up before."

Evie shrugged. "You reap what you sow."

"I know. And I would understand if you didn't want to help me."

"Gee, I'm glad you're so understanding," Evie said.

"Evie!" Catherine said.

"What? Why are we sitting here like we don't have history with this minion." Evie sat forward, pointed a finger at me. "You've always been a lackey. Why would we want to help you with a problem you're having with your demon?"

"Since you're here, I assumed—" I stopped and looked around the table. Two sets of hooded eyes and one vampire set still narrowed in suspicion.

"What does she want you to do?" Catherine asked. We hadn't discussed the specifics when I called her; she'd preferred to wait and include the ladies in the conversation.

"She wants me to kill someone."

Catherine and Mia gasped. "Why am I not surprised?" Evie said.

"Who does she want you to kill?" Mia asked.

"Jackson McKee." At their blank expressions, I explained, "He's a cameraman on *Forbidden Island*."

"Did she tell you why she wants him dead?" Catherine asked.

I shook my head. "She didn't, except that it would help her achieve her 'goal'. And, before you ask, she wouldn't tell me her goal."

Catherine tapped her fingers on the table top. "Anything else?"

I bit my lower lip. What I was about to say was Jackson's secret to disclose. But he would surely understand I was trying to save his life. "He's a witch."

The ladies didn't even appear shocked.

"He must be some kind of threat to her," Evie guessed.

"I don't think so. His magic is protection magic."

"How do you know that?" Catherine asked.

An image of a lighting fixture falling toward my head flashed in my mind and ribbons of anxiety snaked through me. "Barbara tried to kill us. Jackson used his magic to prevent it."

Again, the gasps of surprise, Evie included this time. "Because you refused to kill him?" she asked.

Was that respect I saw in her eyes? Would wonders never cease? I nodded.

"And she got someone else to do the job?" Evie asked, her disgust now aimed at the demon.

I nodded again.

"How can we help?" Mia asked.

"I'm not sure. I'd like to find and stop this replacement killer." I looked around for water, realized none had been ordered. "I think it's unrealistic to also stop Barbara, but," I exhaled in a rush, "I'd like to at least break the pact before she sends me to hell."

Catherine gently placed her hand on my arm. "We'll do whatever we can." She looked at the other two. "Right, ladies?"

"Absolutely," Mia responded.

Evie quirked an eyebrow, then sighed. "Yeah, I'm in, too."

Relief surged through me. "Thank you all so much." Tears threatened again. "I don't know what to say."

Catherine frowned. "Why isn't Jackson here? Since he's part of the supernatural world and he's the target."

"I'm trying to protect him," I hedged my response. "The less he knows, the better."

"That's it?" Catherine pressed. I had no doubt her magical lie detector was pinging at the incompleteness of my answer.

"I'd just rather he stays away from this as much as possible," I demurred.

Catherine stared at me for a beat. I could practically see her mind file my non-answer for future consideration. "Let's brainstorm. What should be our first step?"

"I would think we need to convince Barbara to cancel the second killer," Evie offered with a slight lift of her right shoulder.

"That's not a bad idea," Mia agreed.

"Thoughts on how?" Catherine asked.

My heart filled with hope as I watched these three women figuring out how to save my life. I could see a faint light at the end of that tunnel everyone talked about.

Soon we had a plan.

The first step? Heading back into the lion's den – or rather, the demon's office. Again.

CHAPTER TEN

I sat in the all-too-familiar leather chair in Barbara's office. The day that I wouldn't have to sit here could not come soon enough. She looked up from her desk. "We need to stop meeting like this."

Was that a joke? Thrown for a moment, I didn't respond.

The demon rolled her eyes. "What can I do for you, Ms. Landon?"

Lying to the non-supernatural was easy; my years in foster care had honed that ability. Supernatural folks, well, I never knew what magical abilities they possessed. "I've changed my mind." I tensed, waiting for her response.

A single eyebrow raised. "About what?"

"Handling that problem we discussed."

My skin crawled as her gaze bore into me. "To what exactly are you referring?"

"I learned my lesson and will do your bidding as agreed." My chin dropped a fraction, like the obedient minion I desperately needed to convince her I still was. "I will kill Jackson McKee." I flinched from an imagined attack response and Barbara smirked. This was going swimmingly. Ugh.

"Will you now?"

"Yes."

"Wonderful."

I breathed a small sigh of relief.

"I truly hope you succeed first."

Wait. What? "First?"

"When we initially discussed this problem, I gave you a week to solve it. When you then expressed concern a day later about being able to do so, I contracted out with a different problem-solver. Another two days have passed. That leaves three remaining," she added, like I was a child who couldn't do basic math. She shrugged. "Whoever gets the job done first."

Thoughts swirled in my mind. She watched me. She was waiting to see if I would beg. After five years, I recognized the futility of that. I controlled my rising panic. The first part of the plan had gone down in flames. On to the next…

"I understand," I responded. "Toward that, I decided to go with unconventional resources."

Barbara sat back in her chair, hands folded in front of her.

"I approached Catherine Rodham of the Paranormal Talent Agency—"

Another eye roll. Barbara was in rare form today. "I know who she is."

I stared straight into her obsidian eyes. Please don't turn red. "I've told them I'm acting against you, to secure their assistance with… solving the problem." This was such a huge risk. The women and I had decided I should stay with one of them or Jackson at all times until this resolved, to remain safe. Being upfront in this way, while baldly lying, had been my idea.

She bristled then smoothed out her features. "Interesting."

That was it? "Thank you?"

"I know they hate me," she said. "No doubt they were only too happy to sign on to get back at me. I trust you have a plan that benefits from their assistance." She held up a hand to stop me from responding. "That was a rhetorical statement. I don't actually care." Her stare glued me to my chair. "We'll see within three days. Won't we?" Barbara stood.

My eyes, of their own volition, furtively checked to learn if today was the day I'd finally glimpse the demon's tail. It wasn't. I bit down hard on the side of my cheek to keep a crazed giggle from escaping, as I didn't have a death wish.

Honest.

*****

"Do you want the good news first, or the bad news?" I asked, without preamble. I hadn't even left the parking lot of the city council building before placing the call to Catherine.

"Good news, I guess."

"Barbara bought my story of you guys helping me as a way to stick it to her."

Catherine snort laughed. "Of course, she did. She knows we don't like or trust her. Hit me with the bad news."

I ran my free hand around my steering wheel to delay.

"Robin? Are you still there? It's not that bad, is it?"

"The first part of the plan was a complete bust."

She gasped. "You're not saying what I think you're saying?"

I nodded though she couldn't see me. "Yep. Barbara isn't calling off the second killer."

Silence on the line. I waited it out. "Okay. That's a blow," Catherine began. "But, let's look at it as extra motivation."

My eyebrows shot upward. "Extra motivation? Staying alive was already my motivation." I gave a shaky chuckle. "Though now it's being threatened from multiple sources. So, I guess you're right."

"I'll let Evie and Mia know what happened. With the replacement killer still in play, it's even more important to learn what Jackson got from the Witches Council. Has he met with them yet?"

At Catherine's use of his name, my heart lurched. "I don't know. I haven't spoken with him since we hammered out our plan."

"That needs to be next on the list."

"I'll call him as soon as I hang up the phone."

"Is that all?"

"What do you mean?"

A nearly imperceptible sigh from Catherine. "Your responses are reading as incomplete," she admitted.

I cursed under my breath. "You and your magical lie detector – I can't get anything past you," I half-joked.

She waited.

"I'm hesitant to call him. But, I will."

"Why are you hesitant?"

"I thought there might be something between us. Romantically. It was obviously only his protection magic."

"While I haven't seen you two together, I have experience in this realm. Just take it one day at a time and try not to read too much into it."

"I don't know," I said slowly.

"Look at it this way. The whole thing will be over in three days. And if neither of you is dead by then," she added in a sing-song voice, "you can see if there might be something there."

I smiled. "You're right. I have to get over myself."

"That's not quite what I meant," Catherine said with a laugh.

"No, but that's the truth. I need to focus on everybody staying alive and breaking my pact with Barbara. Jackson is a critical part of that."

"That's my girl."

Catherine's comment left us speechless. I didn't have mind reading abilities, but I guessed she was as shocked as I was.

Were we becoming… friends?

"Meet at *Soprannaturale* when the sun sets?" She returned to business.

"I'll be there. And I'll let you know what I learn from Jackson." I disconnected and scrolled for Jackson's number. My mouth went dry listening to the ringing of the call.

"Hey, Robin," he answered.

Hearing my name said with his gruff voice sent tingles down my spine.

Oh my.

"Hey, Jackson." I coughed. "I was calling to see what you learned from the Witches Council about the being who attacked us."

"I haven't learned anything—"

The news crushed me. I had put so much hope into their collective knowledge.

"—because I haven't gone yet."

The words filtered through my brain. "I'm sorry, I might have missed something. You haven't gone yet?"

His warm laugh rolled over me. "No, I haven't. Would you like to come with me? I was about to head over. They're meeting this afternoon."

A confused variety of thoughts swirled. How well would I be able to balance not knowing if our attraction was real with keeping my secrets from him and finding a hired killer?

"Robin?"

Ah, screw it. Catherine was right. I needed to focus. Everything would sort itself out. "Text me the address and I'll meet you there."

"Wonderful. I'm really looking forward to seeing you."

"Me too. I'll see you soon." The call ended and an address appeared. My brow furrowed.

That location on Industrial Road was a business district; was that where the Witches Council met? On the plus side, it was only a short drive.

My heart hammered in my chest. I wanted the information on the hired killer. But I also had my private reason, the one I chose to hide from Jackson.

Would the witches be able to help me break my pact with Barbara?

And would they be able to help me with the secret I was keeping from even the ladies?

Help me unbind my powers?

And I'd be lying if I didn't admit I looked forward to seeing Jackson again, too.

54

CHAPTER ELEVEN

The thought that I had only three more days to solve this mess swirled in my mind. I zipped my Jetta into a parking spot in front of a wide, squat metal-gray building. Definitely in the industrial part of town, thus the street name, I supposed. A quick glance around confirmed I beat Jackson here. That gave me time to consider my approach. I could roll with whatever he had planned for the Witches Council. But I'd also need to find somebody I could speak to on the down low about my personal issue. I smiled at myself in the rearview mirror. The down low? Like I was in a mystery novel or something.

Motion drew my attention. My breath caught in my throat. Jackson wore a dark brown pullover with jeans, muscles straining the material as he strode from my right, toward the front door. A man with purpose, but unhurried by anxiety. He must have sensed someone watching him;

he turned his head and our eyes met through the windshield. A wide smile lit his face and desire pooled low in my belly.

I exited my car, wondering about this reaction. It was his protection magic, right?

"Hey, Robin. Have you been waiting long?"

"Nah, a few minutes. Thanks for inviting me."

"You were there, too. Seems only fitting for you to be here." He held the door open for me to enter before him. Despite my immediate physical reaction to him, since deciding to let things progress as they would, I felt less anxiety talking to Jackson.

We entered the utilitarian foyer inches apart, a soft chime announcing our presence. With its linoleum flooring and hard plastic chairs, you'd never guess the Witches Council met here. I wondered how much time the members spent in this building.

A door at the back of the room opened and a woman approached. "Jackson, how great to see you. It's been a minute." A pang of jealousy hit me as they embraced. Good grief, the man can't have friends?

"Jessica, this is Robin. She was there when the incident occurred. Robin, this is Jessica. She's the newest liaison on the Council."

Late-twenties like me, Jessica had curly flames of red hair and bright brown eyes. She clasped my hand, her eyes searching mine. My smile faltered for a moment.

"It's nice to meet you, Robin."

"You as well, Jessica." I recovered from whatever that was and we followed Jessica through to the back.

"We're still waiting on Evan, but everyone else is here and ready," she called over her shoulder. We walked down a short hallway, stopping at a closed door on the left. Jessica knocked twice softly and then opened it to grant us entry.

This room belied what I had just seen. Antique wall sconces held electric lights that reflected off silvery wallpaper. Soft gray carpeting meant our steps remained silent. We crossed the mid-size room to a row of upscale folding chairs (was that even a thing?) facing a half-circle table with five chairs behind it. Three of these fancier chairs were occupied.

Jessica indicated we should sit in the folding chairs and she took a seat behind the table, next to two women and a man tapping away on their cellphones. "We'll get started as soon as Evan arrives."

My shoulders tightened with my heightened anxiety. Gaining information about the replacement killer was the top priority. But this was also the final part of the plan created with the Paranormal Talent Agency women: find someone here who could help me break the pact with Barbara and unbind my powers.

"So sorry I'm late," a male voice broke the silence. A tall, heavyset man nodded at us as he crossed to sit in the remaining open seat behind the table. "Have we done introductions?" he asked, glancing around. "I'm Evan. Welcome."

Jessica chuckled. "I guess we're jumping right in. Now you've met Evan. This is Matt" – she indicated an older bald gentleman – "Theresa" – a middle-aged blond with garish red lipstick – "and Marcie" – a young blond woman who barely looked out of her teens, but surely was older. "Welcome to the Witches Council."

"Thank you for seeing us," Jackson began. "I only wish it was under better circumstances." He brought them up to speed with what happened in the parking lot, including our uncertainty over who was the target, given that his protection magic seemed focused on me.

I tried not to squirm in my seat; this was the perfect opening to explain that we both were targets, and why, but I couldn't make my mouth form the words. I had to admit I didn't want Jackson to know I was a demon's minion. A sigh escaped and Jackson glanced questioningly at me. I smiled weakly in return before deliberately turning to look at the council members. Four of the five watched Jackson, but Jessica stared back at me. A flush crept up my neck. Did she know something? Sense something? Man, a room full of witches was a tough crowd!

Jackson had finished his recitation and taken his seat.

"Thank you for sharing with us," the middle-aged blond, Theresa, said. "We know that someone has begun using black magic in the city." A smudge of red lipstick on her front tooth drew my eye. I stared as she continued, distracted by the mark. "Unfortunately, we have been unable to pinpoint more specifically than that. Whoever is using it, is only using it in short bursts, and is able to throw up a mask almost immediately after." Theresa frowned.

The Council continued to discuss options, but I tuned them out when I realized they didn't have a clue what to do. Tracking the magic wasn't working because of the masking. And the witch wasn't using the magic often enough to try a stronger spell. After all, it had only been two days.

I felt eyes burning a hole in the side of my head and shifted to find Jessica staring at me again. No animosity in her expression, just curiosity. I had hoped to speak with someone at the Council without Jackson finding out. Based on her interest in me, Jessica became my first choice.

The meeting ended with a pledge to continue attempting to track the dark magic user, along with Jackson's promise to keep them informed. A frisson of guilt snaked through me. I shook it off. Telling them about me wouldn't help them track the dark magic user any better.

With the end of the meeting, Theresa, Evan, and Marcie said their goodbyes, but Matt approached Jackson. I started to join them, then noticed Jessica on the other side of the room. Now was my chance to talk with her alone.

"You wanted to speak with me." She spoke first. A statement, not a question. Interesting.

"Yes," I agreed with her non-question.

Jessica waited and when I did not continue, she did. "You're a witch."

"How did you know?"

"I can sense your magic."

Shock coursed through me. "What?"

"What kind of magic do you have?"

"You can sense my magic even though it's bound?" I answered a question with a question.

Her eyebrows furrowed in confusion. "Your magic is bound?"

"Yes."

She shook her head and peered closer at me. "It's muted, yes," she muttered. "Are you sure it's bound?"

"After my parents died—" Guilt flared and I stomped it down. "—I struggled with my magic. And, then—" Bile rose in my throat and I reversed direction. "—after another incident in college, I dropped out—"

Jessica shaking her head again stopped my rambling. "I don't know," she said, with a frown.

"I need your help," I said. "Five years ago, I signed a pact with Barbara Knollman to be her minion. I'd like to break the pact and unbind my powers."

Jessica frowned at the latter half of my request but responded to the former. "Let me do some research into breaking pacts with a low-level demon like her and I'll get back to you."

"Thank you so much," I responded, the tension radiating through my shoulders dropping a notch. Someone familiar with the demon was on the case! It was only a matter of time.

"What are you ladies talking about so intently?" Jackson's voice reached us before he did and our mouths snapped shut.

I gave a small shake of my head at Jessica, praying she would understand what I meant. "Just talking about magic," I answered.

Jackson glanced between us. "I can come back if you're not finished yet," he offered, uncertain.

"Nope, we're finished," I assured him and turned to Jessica. "It was great meeting you."

She leaned in for a goodbye hug, her mouth an inch from my ear. "Be careful," she whispered.

CHAPTER TWELVE

I bit back my disappointment that the Witches Council hadn't been more helpful and focused on the group around me. We were at *Soprannaturale*, this time Jackson included. He had just finished filling in the ladies on what we learned. What little we had learned.

"Too bad they didn't know more," Catherine spoke first, giving voice to my own thoughts.

"At least we confirmed what we suspected – that there's somebody in town up to no good," Jackson countered. "If only we had a better idea of their goal." He frowned and three pairs of eyes bored into me. Oops. I guess they were expecting me to tell him why he was a target.

I sighed and Jackson looked at me. "Um." The waitress chose that moment to check on us. I accepted the reprieve and thought about how to explain that I withheld information from him.

The waitress walked away and all eyes returned to me.

"Did you learn something, Robin?"

Jackson's innocent question broke the dam and burning tears filled my eyes. "You were right about being the target. And you were right about me being the target," I said.

"I don't understand."

I haltingly explained Barbara wanting him dead for an unknown reason, my refusal to do so, and how she added me to the hit list. Jackson interrupted my spiel.

"Why would she ask you to kill me?"

The ladies exchanged glances before pointedly looking at me. I sidestepped. "I've been her gopher for five years. She's never asked something like that of me. I have no idea why she did now." I waited to see if the women would contradict me, or out me. Thankfully they didn't.

Jackson, however, still looked lost even with my explanation. No surprise there. It made little sense without the important fact of my minion status. I just couldn't bring myself to say that to him.

"Of course, now she believes I **am** going to kill you," I quipped.

Jackson's jaw dropped with my statement, so I took the edge off with a crooked grin.

"Misdirection, Jackson. I promise."

He laughed uneasily.

"We had hoped that if I told her I was back in line, that she would call off the replacement killer."

Understanding dawned in Jackson's eyes. "That makes more sense. Did it work?"

"No. She turned it into a game for her amusement," I finished bitterly. "Whoever kills you first – and the replacement killer still has me in his or her sights as well."

"That is unfortunate," he agreed. "At least that explains one thing."

"What?" Mia asked.

"Why my magic is drawn to protect Robin. It somehow sensed we were both targets that night. That's good. She'll have to stay with me for the next couple of days until this is over," Jackson insisted.

Warmth flooded me. I had no objection to staying by his side. "That sounds fine."

Catherine smothered a chuckle and I ignored the twinkle in her eye.

"What do we do now?" Evie bluntly asked. "If the Witches Council has no ideas…"

My disappointment surged again. Not only because of the reminder of their lack of knowledge of the black magic user, but because I didn't get to finish my conversation with Jessica afterward. The witch's confusion about my magic status perplexed me.

Was it possible that because I'd hidden it for years and then had it bound for years that it was distorted? That terrified me. What if my magic malfunctioned once we stopped Barbara and unbound it? I bounced my leg as I considered the alternatives. On the other hand, maybe the magic couldn't be read correctly while bound and it'd be fine after? Man, I hoped so. I'd have to be patient until Jessica did her research into breaking the pact with Barbara.

"Earth to Robin." Catherine waved a hand in front of my face and I blinked.

"Sorry, I was thinking."

"That much was obvious," Evie laughed.

"What's our next step?" I looked around the table after asking the question.

"I'm working on set tomorrow and I want Robin glued to my side."

I bit my lower lip at Jackson's statement and Mia grinned. I might be a great liar generally, but I sure wasn't hiding my… affection… for Jackson very well.

"That's a good idea from more than a protection standpoint," Catherine concurred. "Since both of you are targets, this gives the replacement killer something to target. When the killer makes his or her move, hopefully we'll get more information on their identity. And, more importantly, how to stop them."

Blood drained from my face. Awesome, let's make us targets. Or to be more accurate, we were officially bait.

CHAPTER THIRTEEN

"I really don't think it's necessary to stay at your house," I argued with Jackson. He had followed me back to my home and we were standing in the kitchen.

"I thought you agreed you'd stay with me."

Oh, but I wanted to! "During the day, when we're out and about," I said instead, continuing to argue, but with little insistence.

"I'd stay here," he offered, "but we'd have to go get my equipment from my house for the shoot tomorrow. Plus, Buster would have to stay here too."

"Buster?"

"Didn't I mention him? He's my pittie mix."

"No, you didn't. I love dogs!"

"See," he said with an arched eyebrow, "it's just more logical to stay at my place. Wouldn't you feel bad if we left poor Buster on his own?"

I rolled my eyes. He had to know logic wasn't the issue. The thought of staying at Jackson's home… what would be the sleeping arrangements?

As though reading my mind, he wolfishly smiled. "I have a guest bedroom, if that's the concern."

I flushed and rocked back on my heels. "Um. Cool," I stammered. "That's good."

Jackson brushed his knuckles against my jawline, sending waves of pleasure through me. "If anything happened to you overnight, I'd never forgive myself."

The desire in his eyes brought my confusion to the surface. This couldn't be his protection magic. Could it?

"Pack for tonight and tomorrow. Please."

I melted a little at his tone, hearing the genuine worry underneath. "Okay," I relented. "Let me throw stuff in a bag and we can get going."

"Excellent! This'll be fun. Like a sleepover."

I choked on a laugh. "A sleepover?"

"Got you to laugh, didn't it?"

We smiled goofily at each other. My smile dropped. "Thanks."

"For what?"

"For just being there. For being you."

"I'm glad I could be. For you."

I couldn't believe we'd only met two days ago. I squeezed his upper arm, distracted for a moment by the rock-hard muscle underneath. Focus! "Give me a sec."

I dashed into the bedroom and flung open my closet door. I pulled out two long-sleeve t-shirts, another pair of jeans, and some undergarments. Sexy or plain? The question flashed in my mind. I shook my head and selected cotton undies. This wasn't a romantic getaway. He was protecting me from a demon who wanted us dead. I needed to remember that. My hand grabbed an extra set of lacy underthings. You know, just in case. I rolled my eyes at myself.

After grabbing toiletries from the bathroom, I stood again before Jackson. "Ready," I announced needlessly.

He reached to slide the overnight bag off my arm. "I've got this."

"Such a gentleman, thank you," I murmured.

He winked in reply.

I checked out his delicious backside for a moment before locking up my house and turning to follow him.

He stowed my bag behind the front passenger seat and fired up the truck. I saw his continual scanning for danger as he backed out of the driveway and began the short drive to his home.

"When did you realize you were a witch? Or should I be quiet so you can concentrate? You know, on sensing the danger."

Jackson chuckled. "Now that I'm on alert, I can sense energy changes just fine while we chat." He fiddled with the heater, and I wondered if he didn't want to talk about his paranormal history. "My parents knew I was a witch before I did."

"Wow, really? How?"

"My father is a witch, and the abilities pass on the father's side in my family, so he knew what to watch for. There are signs."

Would things have been different if I'd had that? I refused to start down that path, so I refocused on Jackson. "What kind of signs?"

"Mostly he watched for energy changes around me. Just like I can sense energy changes that signal the presence of magic, so can my Dad. He trained me to control my magic once it manifested at puberty."

"That's so cool." And I genuinely felt that way, though the roiling in my stomach confirmed some mixed feelings. "Where are your parents now?"

"They are traveling the world and very happy."

I could hear the smile in his voice as I stared out the windshield. How I wished I could have had that. Neither of my parents had been witches; they didn't know to watch for what had been happening to me.

"Everything okay?" Jackson asked.

"Why wouldn't it be?"

"Something seems off."

"Do you sense energy changes like before? Is this killer nearby?" We were passing the flashing sign announcing the sprawling Red Rock Casino complex headed toward the overpass for the 215 West Beltway. There were a fair number of cars, and lots of people in the buildings. Could he sense something from that distance? Or was he sensing my bound magic?

My peripheral vision caught his slight frown. "Not exactly."

"Not exactly?"

"It's not an exact science," he explained, and I heard the smile again in his voice, breaking the tension.

"My parents died just after my sixteenth birthday," I blurted out.

"Oh, Robin, I'm so sorry. That must have been tough," Jackson responded, reaching over to place his hand on my knee.

"It was. They died in a car accident. I was in foster care until I turned eighteen and aged out of the system." I glanced at Jackson. Relief flooded me when I saw sadness and not pity in his eyes. I hated people pitying me.

"When I talk about my happy life with my parents, that hurts," he surmised, surprising me.

"That sounds horrible when I hear it out loud, but yeah," I admitted.

"It's not horrible," he disagreed. "You're just being honest."

I shrugged. "Hmm." I feigned nonchalance, but my emotions churned. Jackson was attractive, thoughtful, sweet... perfect. I sighed.

"What's the sigh for?"

"You are entirely too perceptive and frank," I answered with a laugh, sidestepping the question.

Jackson echoed my laughter and turned the truck off of West Charleston Blvd onto a side street. I missed the sign, so didn't know quite where we were, but even in the dark, I could see this was one of the newer communities of cookie-cutter homes.

"I know they all look the same," Jackson said while maneuvering around a bend.

"You need to stop doing that."

"Doing what?"

"Reading my mind."

He grinned. "I don't have to read your mind. Many people have commented on the sameness of the beige stucco houses so close together." He parked in the driveway of a two-story version of precisely that. "And, yes, I can touch my wall and my neighbor's with just my arms outstretched."

I laughed.

"But that misses why people live out here," he continued.

"Why?"

"Easy access to Red Rock Canyon."

We opened our doors and exited the truck. "I could see how that would be a plus," I conceded. I pulled my bag from behind the seat and slammed the door closed.

Jackson slid my bag back off my shoulder like before. "I got that," he said and headed toward his door.

No point in arguing, so I followed him, noting the typical desert landscaping. "Nice cactus," I commented. He looked over his shoulder and I pointed to the massive cactus in the middle of his tiny yard. "It's taller than me."

"Indeed, it is. Beautiful flowers bloom on there, sometimes."

I turned my back to Jackson while he unlocked his door. All the houses around his were dark. Was everybody out or already asleep?

"Welcome to my humble abode," Jackson warmly welcomed me. The sound of claws on tile reached me and a muscular black dog flew across the room to greet me and his master. I crouched to accept the slobbery kisses. Jackson flipped the overhead lights on as I stood. While I took in the space, he rubbed the exposed belly of Buster, who had flopped over in front of him. I grinned before checking out the open floor plan that allowed me to see his living room, dining area, and kitchen all in one swoop. Pretty standard furniture. One feature stood out.

"Those posters are amazing."

"They are my favorite possessions; well, besides my camera equipment."

I walked the perimeter of his first floor, stopping to consider each framed movie poster. Many of them were even signed! I stopped in front of one and chuckled.

Jackson stood beside me. His warmth heated that side of my body.

"Not the best movie ever made," he agreed with my silent appraisal, "but *Sleepwalkers* is a classic bad movie by a master writer."

"Stephen King has contributed some of the worst films to celluloid, no doubt." I peered closer at the poster. "But, that's not his signature."

"Nope. Funny story. I was buying that poster at the San Diego Comic Con years ago—" He gave me the side-eye. "—yes, I go to Comic Cons."

I held up my hands with a laugh. "No judgment here. I love conventions," I enthused. "So, you were buying the poster—" I prompted.

"I was buying the poster and this guy standing next to me says, hey, I was on that set."

"No way!"

"Way!" We smiled at each other. "I asked him all about it and it turned out he was one of the camera guys. Of course, I asked him to sign the poster."

"Of course."

We continued to circle the room, ending up in the kitchen, which was nicely updated with stainless steel appliances and charcoal quartz countertops. Posh and manly. "Would you like a drink?"

"Water would be great. Since you bought this house to be close to Red Rock Canyon, how often do you hike?"

"Nearly every day I'm not working," he answered, his back to me while he poured a glass of water from a Brita pitcher. "Buster loves it." Hearing his name, the pup jumped from the couch and joined us in the kitchen area.

"He's adorable."

"And doesn't he know it." He leaned down to scratch Buster's head.

"Was he a rescue?"

"Not quite."

I raised an eyebrow.

"He's my familiar." Jackson took a sip of water, making eye contact over the top of the glass. "Do you know what that is?"

"I do. They're a witch's companion animal."

"Yep. He showed up when I hit puberty. And he'll be with me for as long as I'm a witch."

"I thought they were always cats," I joked, to cover the sudden tightness in my chest.

"Nope, not always cats."

"I had a cat as a child," I blurted impulsively. "Patches ran away after my parents' accident."

"I'm sorry, Robin." He reached for my hand.

My gaze dropped to his hand on mine. If a witch loses her familiar when she's no longer a witch… I pulled my hand free to grasp my glass, and raised my head.

"I've always wanted to adopt another one. The timing never seemed right." College student on campus.

Homeless. Demon's minion. Yeah, the timing had never been right. I snorted.

"What's that about?"

I shook my head. "Nothing. But one day I plan to adopt a cat."

"We'll have to do a playdate once you adopt," Jackson joked.

I quirked an eyebrow. "We will?"

"We'll want to make sure our animals get along, right?"

"Um. Yes?"

Jackson laughed his low and sexy laugh. "I'm just teasing you, Robin. You turn a delightful shade of red when you're embarrassed."

A flush crept up my neck. "Gee, thanks."

Jackson came around the island and engulfed me in a bear hug.

I held my breath a moment before relaxing into his embrace. He smelled nice, clean. I rested my head on his chest.

"Everything will be okay."

"You promise?" My voice trembled with the question.

"If I have anything to say about it, I will do everything in my power to protect you."

Protect me. Yeah. I disengaged from the hug and stared up at him. "We should go to bed."

My flush deepened when he waggled his eyebrows at me. I pushed against his solid wall of a chest.

"You know what I mean," I protested.

Jackson leaned in and whispered in my ear. "Yes, I do."

I closed my eyes briefly at the wave of anticipation before taking a step back. "You have work in the morning," I reminded him.

"Follow me," he responded with another chuckle, grabbing my overnight bag off the couch. We walked up a flight of carpeted stairs and down a short tiled hallway.

"This is the guest bedroom." A queen-size bed and a single chest of drawers, all in a deep cherry wood, filled the space.

"It looks lovely, thanks."

"There's an attached bathroom, and I'll be just down the hall if you need anything."

I swallowed. "Um, okay."

Jackson twirled a strand of my hair in his fingers. "Don't hesitate to ask."

I folded my hand over his. "I won't."

Pleasure thrummed through me until he pulled back. "I won't let anyone hurt you."

Right. The protection magic. "Goodnight, Jackson."

He stepped out of the room, pausing in the doorway. "Goodnight, Robin. I'll wake you up at 8, okay?"

"Sounds good."

He closed the door soundlessly behind him. Carpet muffled his steps as he walked to his bedroom down the hall. I swallowed again.

I unpacked my few belongings and got cleaned up in the bathroom. Snuggling under the down comforter, perfect for Vegas in December, I sighed.

Was Jackson sending mixed signals or was I misreading? Protection magic was very confusing.

CHAPTER FOURTEEN

Jackson's guest bedroom mattress begged me to stay in it, so I snuggled further under the covers. I thought I heard movement downstairs and sighed. It must be time to get up. The sound drew closer and I smiled when I recognized claws on tile. Soon, an 80-pound dog jumped onto the bed and gave me morning kisses.

"Hey, Buster, good morning to you, too." I scratched him behind his ear and was rewarded with a thumping leg against the bed. "You like that, don't you, big guy?" Buster's head rose and he sniffed the air. A second later, I too smelled the scent of bacon wafting up the stairs. Mmm, was Jackson making breakfast?

I looked down at my pajamas, debating whether to change. Friends don't have to get cleaned up for breakfast, I decided, and headed downstairs toward the delicious smells.

"Good morning, sunshine," Jackson greeted me with a smile.

A hand went to my hair; how bad was my bed head this morning?

He chuckled. "You look fine. Like you just woke up. Did Buster wake you?"

"Yes, but it's not a bad way to start the day."

"Hungry?"

"Very." I approached him, standing in front of the stove. "That looks yummy."

He flipped the omelet with a spatula in one hand and the bacon with a second spatula in the other.

"Impressive."

"I got skills."

"Indeed." My heart sped up at the double entendre in our exchange.

"How did you sleep?"

"Like the dead," I responded before wincing. Maybe not the best analogy when people were trying to kill you.

Jackson belly-laughed. "Perfect." He pointed toward an overhead cupboard to my right. "If you want to grab a couple of plates—" He pointed to a drawer below. "—and silverware, breakfast will be ready in a few minutes."

"How did you time this so perfectly?" I asked, marveling at the coordination.

He grinned. "I didn't. I planned to wake you up if Buster or the smell didn't," he admitted and I laughed.

"That would have worked, too."

After serving up the food, we sat at his dining room table to eat, Buster splayed on the floor, watching hopefully for a piece of bacon to drop.

"This is beautiful," I expressed, running my fingers over the light-ash distressed wood.

"Thank you," he murmured, though I didn't miss how his eyes watched my hand move along the top of the table.

I snatched my hand back and his lips quivered like he was biting back a smile. "What's the plan for today?"

"We were going to be filming in the Bellagio atrium," he started.

"The botanical gardens, where they decorate for the season?" I interrupted. "I love seeing what they've done with the flowers!"

"Unfortunately," he continued, with another smile at my enthusiasm, "production made a last-minute change and now we're shooting at a house in North Las Vegas. I've got the address on my phone."

"Too bad." We ate in silence for a few moments. "I'm looking forward to watching you work."

"I would think with your experience in the industry, it'd be boring by now," he teased.

I flushed and lifted a single shoulder. "It's not." Besides, my traitorous mind added, I planned to enjoy the scenery.

Jackson eyed my empty plate. "I'll clear the table if you want to get ready. We need to leave in fifteen minutes."

"Aye, aye, sir," I responded with a salute. His laughter followed me back up the stairs.

*****

I was right. I was enjoying the view. We'd arrived at the house for filming and after making sure I had everything I needed – sweetly protective, was my Jackson – he got to work. The morning passed in a blur of filming. We were approaching our late afternoon lunch time when I saw Jackson freeze. The hair on the back of my neck rose and I scanned the rooms I could see. The living room was empty, save for the owner's sage green couch and ottoman. Production staff milled around the white dining room table covered end to end with scripts, backpacks, and coffee containers. Lights were being set in the large, country-style kitchen, presumably because that was where the next scene would be shot. Nothing appeared out of the ordinary.

Jackson set his camera equipment on the floor and stood ramrod straight. His gaze found me and I saw the stark fear in his eyes.

"Get out now!" Jackson startled everyone with his unexpected yell. Silence fell over the room. He was already moving toward me. "Get out now!" he repeated, grabbing my arm and pulling me toward the front door. I heard movement behind me, along with shouts and confused questions.

Jackson flung the door open and lifted me through the frame. A crush of bodies followed us. An awful cracking filled the air. I turned to identify the noise. Jackson tackled me to the ground. I landed on the dirt with a thump, thanking the homeowners for not putting in desert rock landscaping. The cracking built until reaching a crescendo. The roof collapsed into itself, dust rising as it fell. My fingers tingled and energy raced along my arms. My eyes cut to the front door, where another person darted out, rubbing his face. A wild glance around the front yard showed nine people outside the building. My eyes settled on Jackson, still clutching me, his body sheltering me from the imploding home, an unreadable expression now on his face.

"Do you feel that?" he asked.

"Feel what?" I sank into his body, heart rate slowing, breathing evening out, and that weird tingling subsiding. He shook his head and held me closer. "Is that everybody?" I asked breathlessly.

The silence that followed was absolute. Nobody spoke. No birds chirped. No cars drove past.

"Are you okay?" Jackson asked, his hands skimming over me, checking for injuries. Normally I would have enjoyed this closeness, but horror held me.

"I'm fine. Did everybody make it out?" I repeated.

Jackson jumped to his feet. His face paled as he made the same count I did. He ran toward the devastated home.

"Jackson!" I yelled after him, terrified the building wasn't safe. I continued to stare after he vanished from sight. Time stood still while I waited. Voices filtered through my haze as the cast and crew checked in with each other. I thought I heard someone calling 9-1-1. My eyes remained fixed on the door.

Jackson appeared. He carried a woman in his arms. At first, I thought she wasn't moving. Then her torso shook with a cough. Thank goodness! Jackson gave me a wan smile when he met my gaze and I clutched my arms tight. I sent positive thoughts into the universe that she'd be okay.

Time resumed normal speed for me. I stood, shaking from the adrenaline dump. The police arrived. An ambulance arrived and took the woman in Jackson's arms away. EMTs checked everybody over. I received only a cursory glance, which was fine. I was fine.

But what had happened?

CHAPTER FIFTEEN

Jackson and I sat in his truck. A blanket wrapped around me kept my shivering to a minimum. But I wasn't shivering from the cold.

"What happened?" I asked, fearing I already knew the answer.

"Someone tried to kill us."

I took a deep, shaky breath. "That's what I thought. What happened?" I asked again.

"Whoever's using the black magic caved in the roof."

I nodded, unable to speak now that my fears had been confirmed.

Jackson's face hardened. "And this time, he or she nearly killed someone. Almost killed Jane."

"This is my fault," I whispered.

Jackson clasped my hands in his. "No, Robin, it's not. It's whoever is using this magic."

I shook my head, unwilling to accept his absolution. "Yes, it is. If I hadn't been working for Barbara, none of this would have happened."

Jackson thumbed a single tear off my cheek. "Yes, it would have. Barbara is out to kill me. You were just supposed to be the one to do it," Jackson reminded me.

"That's true, I suppose," I agreed with a watery smile. "But it was my decision to draw out the hired killer," I reminded him.

"No," he contradicted. "It was a group decision. This is not your fault," he repeated.

"Agree to disagree?"

"No. But, I'll agree to table the discussion for another time," he offered with a half-smile.

I closed my eyes briefly, offered a tired smile of my own in return. "You saved me again."

"Yes. And I will every time."

"We need this to end."

"It will. In two days, right?"

I nodded. The demon's one-week demand would end in two days. This would be over, one way or the other. How many people might die before then? I mentally slapped myself. I couldn't think like that, couldn't allow the possibility of more blood on my hands. A solution would be found. We just needed to be proactive.

"We need to meet with the ladies, talk about next steps." I forced out the next words. "Our choice to be bait almost got someone killed." I held up a hand to stop him from disagreeing. "I can't be responsible for that again. We need to take control."

"Okay. Plan a meeting for tonight." Jackson pulled me into his arms and breathed into my hair. "I promise nothing will happen to you."

I nodded against his shoulder. "Your protection magic won't let it."

A moment passed before he responded. "That's right. It won't."

And I made my own promise. To myself. Nobody would die. And, even if I was wrong that Jackson's interest in me was more than his protection magic, maybe I could convince him that our attraction was real.

CHAPTER SIXTEEN

I couldn't believe only two hours had passed since the roof caved in on set. This time we met in a more private location, Mia's house in The Lakes. A quick ten-minute drive up West Desert Inn Road had brought me to her waterfront home.

Now, I sat on Mia's turquoise couch (I guess as a mermaid – sorry, nixie – she really loved the water!) and surveyed the gathered group. Besides me, Mia, Jackson, Catherine, and Evie, Mia's boyfriend, homicide detective Jacob Dawson, was also present. That threw me for a moment. Did Jackson's co-worker Jane die? Dread increased as I waited for someone to speak.

"Is Jane okay?" I blurted out, unable to stand waiting any longer.

Jacob understood my question. "Yes, she is. She woke up on the way to the hospital and they're keeping her overnight for observation, but they expect her to make a full recovery."

I breathed a sigh of relief. Jackson reached over to squeeze my hand. Catherine caught the movement and smiled knowingly. A blush bloomed across my face. Sheesh.

"And before you ask," Jacob continued. "I'm here because of my involvement in the last major entertainment related attacks."

Mia laughed, the sound like tinkling bells. Everyone turned to her.

Jacob rolled his eyes.

"Tell them your new nickname, Jacob," she demanded playfully.

"I'd rather not."

"Please, tell us," Catherine insisted.

Jacob shook his head. "Detective Hollywood," he mumbled.

Evie belly laughed. "That's fantastic!"

Tension in the room dropped with this ice breaker and after teasing Jacob for a few more moments, we got down to business.

"Thank you all again for your help," Jackson began. "Robin and I know it wasn't easy for you to help her, given your history with Barbara."

"We don't want anyone using black magic in Vegas," Mia said. "This is much bigger than Barbara and Robin."

"True," Jackson agreed. "Let's start with what we know, to bring Jacob up to speed."

"Robin's demon boss ordered her to kill you," Evie jumped in with a wink at me.

"Evie," Catherine admonished the vampire. "Robin said no."

Evie shrugged, but a twinkle remained in her eye. Was she teasing me?

"A new killer was hired," Catherine continued, "with Robin added to the hit list. We had Robin pretend to be back on board."

I picked up the story. "This unfortunately backfired, and if the killer sticks to Barbara's original timetable, he or she has two days left to kill the two of us."

Catherine looked at us, worry etched on her face. "We have that same amount of time, therefore, to find and stop this killer."

And find a way to break my pact with Barbara and unbind my powers, I silently added. Catherine's expression told me she was having the same additional thought.

"And this killer has now tried to kill you both twice?" Jacob asked.

Jackson and I nodded.

"And you've been able to sense the magic being used by this person?"

"Yes," Jackson answered Jacob's follow-up question.

"But nobody has any idea who the new killer is?"

"I checked in with the Family," Evie answered the detective's question. "They said the hired killer isn't known to them."

We considered this declaration. The vampire Family in Las Vegas sometimes used Cleaners who would take out (okay, kill) humans, vampires, or other beings that were a threat to the Family. Taking the Family's response at face value, that meant our replacement killer was unlikely to be a vampire.

"And I checked in with Alex," Catherine added. "He said he's not aware of any nonhuman supernatural being in town who's been hired for a contract killing, nor have his contacts heard any rumblings." If her half-incubus boyfriend, who had an in with most of the supernatural underworld, said the hired killer wasn't a nonhuman supernatural being, that was probably accurate.

"What does that leave us?" I asked.

"A human witch, as I suspected," Jackson answered with a scowl.

"Using you guys as bait turned out to be too dangerous," Mia said. "Does anybody have any ideas about what we can do next? Jacob?"

"Using the media to draw out the last killer worked," he answered. Mia blanched. He took her hand, and she smiled at the offered comfort. From what I understood, it had hit her hard earlier this year, when she killed a djinn in self-defense to protect Jacob.

"How can we do something like that with Liz this time?" Catherine asked.

Elizabeth Addison, co-host of the popular morning show, *Entertainment Daily*, had directly challenged the djinn on her show to lure her out. It had worked and the killing was stopped. Of course, her expose outing the supernatural underworld shortly followed. As far as I knew, nobody liked her anymore.

"Is she still doing that ridiculous *Mythical Being of the Week* segment on the show?" Catherine rolled her eyes.

"Unfortunately, yes. I believe it's the highest rated story every time," Mia answered with a crooked smile.

"I never should have confirmed our existence for her," Evie groused and my eyebrows raised.

"Evie gave Liz an exclusive on the paranormal underworld in exchange for her vouching for Mia when Jacob thought she was in cahoots with the djinn," Catherine explained. "None of this is your fault, Evie."

"I know that," she retorted. "It still just galls me."

"Would Elizabeth even help us?" I asked.

Mia shrugged. "Liz would if there was something in it for her."

Ah, another shining example of the self-interested media. Who was I kidding? A demon's minion judging a reporter? That was pretty cheeky.

"I have an idea," I spoke slowly, the pieces falling into place in my head. When I finished presenting the stages of my plan to the others, slow nods surrounded me. A few suggested tweaks and we were ready. Time to implement Stage One (and yes, I capitalized it; it was our grand plan, after all!).

CHAPTER SEVENTEEN

Jackson and I arrived back at his place well after nightfall. Darkness shrouded his neighbors' homes. He parked the car and we hurried inside. Buster nosed Jackson's hand, whimpering.

"It's okay. We have a plan," Jackson assured his familiar.

The dog chuffed and sat on his haunches, waiting to see what we would do. The first step in our plan was all Jackson. He would create his force field around the house.

"Ready to see the magic happen?"

I clapped like an excited schoolgirl. "You know it."

He walked to one corner of the home. "This is essentially true north," he began. "I'll bring forth my magic—"

"How?" I interrupted. Buster chuffed again, and I swore he was laughing at my question.

Jackson shrugged. "It's not an exact science. I concentrate on the feeling of magic in my core and focus it on this corner. I'll do the same in the other directions."

"Directions?"

"Compass directions. The closest spots in the house to true north, west, east, and south."

I nodded. I vaguely remembered about the importance of the Earth's compass when I first started researching Wicca after my parents' deaths. Jackson didn't buy my feigned understanding.

"In Earth magic, we call to the power of nature."

"Even when it's within you?"

"Yep. Witches draw their strength from Mother Earth, no matter what their specific brand of magic is."

"Okay, that makes sense."

Jackson closed his eyes and reached a hand toward the corner. I waited for him to start a spell or something. He opened his eyes. "Done."

"Wait. That's it? What about a spell? Or incantation?" Even as I asked the questions, I remembered my brief use of magic years ago; I certainly hadn't used any spells. Jackson confirmed what I just concluded.

"It's internal, mostly. Group magic uses spells, but otherwise, it's often inside the witch."

Buster and I followed Jackson as he moved to each of the directional spots and repeated the same silent magic.

"How will it stay active?"

"Since I won't be able to maintain my focus on it to keep it at full strength, it's like a thin layer of force field. Like icing on a cake."

"Very cool."

"All finished. This will somewhat hide us from tracking magic."

"Somewhat?"

"If someone's motivated enough—"

"You mean, like someone who wants us dead?" I quipped.

Jackson chuckled. "Yes, I suppose." His smile dropped. "If someone's motivated enough, they could find us. But, if the killer doesn't know to search deeper, he or she probably won't be able to."

"Probably?" I squeaked.

"The force field would also protect against initial magic attacks. Any attack on my magic would wake me up, and then allow me to focus on the force field to reinforce it."

"That sounds better."

"Bottom line, it's unlikely anyone would bother to attack us here, even if they found us," he reassured me.

"That's good." A big yawn threatened to crack my face in half.

"Looks like it's time for bed."

At the final word, my face flushed and his eyes dilated. I yawned again and the moment was broken. Exhaustion had caught up with me. With a little wave, I scurried from the living room. Buster yelped a goodnight. And was that rumbly noise Jackson laughing? Pssht. Goofball. I changed into my pajamas and fell into a deep sleep the instant my head hit the pillow in Jackson's guest room.

CHAPTER EIGHTEEN

Stage One had the potential to be boring. Luckily it wasn't. Our part of the plan for day six of the Killer Countdown, as I had taken to calling it (joking kept the anxiety at bay… right?), was to stay out of sight. The plan called for us not to be targets until exactly the right moment. That meant we hid out in Jackson's place for the day, beneath his protection force field.

But others were more active.

I knew Mia and Elizabeth Addison had worked together to stop a murderous djinn earlier in the year and thought they had had a falling out. Turned out I was right. Also turned out that Mia was right. As soon as she offered Liz exclusivity in reporting our full story when it concluded, Liz was on board.

Thus, that morning, Jackson and I sat with Buster on the couch waiting for Liz to set our plan into motion.

"Good morning in the Valley!" Liz Addison welcomed viewers to her show, *Entertainment Daily*, her wide, toothy smile in place. "Some of you may have seen the *Forbidden Island* movie production filming scenes around town. If you've ever wanted to be on a movie set," she enticed viewers, "now's your chance. Producers have informed us that they are looking for background talent – that's extras to you and me – for a big scene tonight."

At first, we worried this would be too risky. What would happen if a bunch of people showed up to a fake set? After all, this was a lure. We didn't want anybody showing up. But then we realized, it was easily handled…

"If that's you," Liz pointed a perfectly manicured hand at the camera, "then head to our website, click on the link, and email the production your interest. They'll send the location to the first people to reply. Spots are limited," she warned viewers. What nobody watching (except us, of course) knew was that when they clicked on the link, they'd be sadly informed that all the spots for the evening's filming were filled. Too bad, so sad. But exactly according to our plan. Liz turned to face another camera, her short, curly brown hair gently swinging. "Interested in animal welfare," she began, and Jackson pressed the mute button.

"And there it is. Our invitation to the replacement killer to come and get us," Jackson said quietly.

At the word killer, my heart rate jumped erratically. "Do you think it'll work?"

"It was your plan," he reminded me. "Don't you think it will work?"

I did. The replacement killer knew Jackson and I were together, and that Jackson was working the movie. We hoped that after frustrating the replacement killer all day by hiding out, he or she would jump at the chance to nail us on set.

"One potential flaw in setting up the plan is if the replacement killer doesn't hear about filming tonight," I voiced my concern.

"Didn't Mia say Liz promised to blast the background actor invitation all over social media once the show wrapped?"

"She did." My bouncing leg slowed.

"Wouldn't that then practically guarantee the replacement killer would hear about the filming tonight?"

"Yes, it would." I took a deep breath. "I'm also still concerned about the killer knowing where we'll be."

"Weren't you also the one that said when the replacement killer knows there's filming but not the location, he or she would just wait for us to leave? And then follow us?"

I tilted my head back, contemplating the ceiling. "Yes. I said those things too."

"Then aren't we okay?"

"Yes, we are." I met his gaze. "Thank you. I needed that."

"You're welcome." Jackson took a sip of his coffee. "Tonight's the final night before Barbara's deadline, and possibly the last chance for the replacement killer to strike. He or she will wait for us to leave and follow us to set. It'll work."

I nodded. "Yes." It had to.

*****

When *Entertainment Daily* concluded, Liz was true to her word. Jackson and I popped on our laptops to confirm that word of the filming was all over social media. Now the waiting would begin. We didn't plan to arrive on set until just after the sun set around 5 p.m. That left about six hours to kill, I mean, to wait.

"What do you want to do while we wait?"

Jackson asked the question innocently, but man did my body respond not-so-innocently. "Play a board game?" I responded.

He gave me a knowing smile but didn't comment. "Let me show you what I have."

I'd like to see what you have, my traitorous mind whispered. I ignored it and followed him to a hutch in the dining area filled with board games. That successfully distracted me.

"These are all the games I have. Are any of these speaking to you?"

"How about *Ticket to Ride Europe*?" I'd never played the game, but it looked interesting.

"Great choice," Jackson enthused. "It's a strategy game where the person who builds the most railway wins." He pulled the game out of the hutch and we set up on the kitchen table, Buster in his primary location at our feet.

And thus, the day went by… playing games, chit chatting, watching the noon news. Butterflies took flight in my stomach as the declining sun through the window blinds informed me it was almost time. By that point, we were back sitting on the couch, watching one of those judge shows on television.

"How are you feeling?" Jackson asked, taking one of my hands in his.

I squeezed his fingers. "Nervous," I admitted.

"I'd be worried if you weren't."

"Are you?"

"Nervous? Yes. I would hate if something happened to you." He rubbed my fingers, the sensations sending warmth through my body.

"Same here," I said thickly.

"You would hate if something happened to you?" he asked.

A glance in his direction showed him smirking. "Yes, I would," I responded with a wink. "But I'd also hate if something happened to you."

"It won't."

"You promise?"

"I do."

Feeling more secure, but still acutely aware of that swarm of butterflies in my belly, I stood. "It's time."

CHAPTER NINETEEN

In order to have a fairly isolated set, we chose an abandoned house in Boulder City, about an hour from Jackson's house, just outside metro Las Vegas. This was our attempt to keep damage to a minimum, in case everything went sideways. We listened to the local classic rock station, 97.1 The Point, as we trekked across the city. The music wasn't quite the distraction I'd hoped for, but it kept my leg bouncing to a minimum.

We pulled into the driveway of a sprawling one-story home right on the edge of the desert. This definitely fit the bill for isolated! A handful of cars were already parked in the driveway and along the street.

Given the distance we had to drive, I assumed that meant we were the last to arrive. That was okay; it meant everybody would be more likely to be ready when the replacement killer struck. We couldn't block off the street, secluded though it was, and so Jacob positioned police at the homes on each end. We expected everything to go down fast. I doubted they'd have much of a chance to do anything. But they could act as an early warning system if any cars drove down the street.

Since we didn't know when the replacement killer would strike, we needed to pretend to film. Even so, my jaw dropped when Jackson pulled open the large wooden front door.

It looked like a genuine film set. Evie and Ryan, two of the actors in our group, stood in an empty living room holding sheets of paper. I idly wondered if they brought past scripts with them or if those were blank pages.

A standard three-point lighting set-up surrounded the actors. Someone had positioned the key light, or primary light, behind Evie and Ryan. I smothered a laugh; the dramatic lighting that position provided seemed fitting for this evening's activities. A fill light, to illuminate unwanted shadows, was positioned next to the camera, a nicer-than-expected Canon EOS C300 Mark II (though still only half the cost of a $20,000 RED 8K camera… but I digressed). And, finally, the backlight, an ARRI 150, I thought, was positioned behind and above the actors.

Catherine stood behind the camera, fiddling with it. Did she know anything about them or was she completely pretending?

I shook my head. It was so real – and yet so fake.

Mia and her homicide detective boyfriend, Jacob, stood off to the side of the tableau, pretending to refer to a clipboard of paper.

Alex, Catherine's half-incubus boyfriend, stood on the other side of the room. He was the only one that drew attention; he seemed to be standing guard, which he was.

"Hey, everyone. Are we ready to shoot this thing?" Jackson asked jovially.

A chorus of hellos returned the greeting. I saw worry reflected in several sets of eyes. We would have to pretend to film until Jackson sensed the energy change that heralded the replacement killer's arrival. And then we would have a small window to launch our offensive defense. I didn't know if that was a thing, but it fit what I felt we were doing. We set everything up but we would only respond when the replacement killer launched a volley, so to speak.

*****

Three hours later, we'd run out of fake filming to do and boredom had set in. I hoped this wouldn't be a bust. Then what would we do? The deadline was tomorrow. Who knew what Barbara would do if Jackson wasn't dead? I was on the fence over whether or not she'd care if I was dead.

Jacob pulled his phone from his pocket in response to a text notification. "Another car pulled onto the street," he informed us in a low voice. This was the third car in three hours. The first time we had gone on high alert. And nothing happened. The second time we had gone on high alert. And nothing happened. This time I felt the tension rise, but nobody moved. A fence surrounded the perimeter of the property and we'd locked all the doors to the house. We hoped this would corral our killer to the front, and keep him or her on the street.

Jacob continued to watch his phone. "The car parked one house over."

Alex rolled onto the balls of his feet. He clenched and unclenched his hands.

Minutes passed with no update.

"Car door is opening," Jacob murmured.

Evie and Ryan set their script pages on the floor. Evie faced the front door and Ryan faced the window to their side.

"Someone in a hooded cape has exited the car."

"How cliché," I muttered with an eye roll. Catherine half-snorted in response.

Everyone stood at alert.

"The individual has stopped in front of the house. Unable to tell if male or female. They remain in the street."

Jackson held his hands out in front of him like he was calling for an *amen* from the congregation.

We waited with bated breath.

"It's time!" Jackson flung the front door open.

CHAPTER TWENTY

"You don't have to do this," Jackson implored the figure standing in the street. We formed a loose group behind Jackson at the front door. Watching. Waiting.

"Yes, I do," the figure responded. I felt the startled reactions around me. The voice was decidedly feminine. A female replacement killer. Why was I not surprised? Guess Barbara was into equal opportunity.

"No, you don't," Jackson disagreed. Tension rolled off of him, but his voice remained calm.

"I signed a contract. If I don't fulfill it, I don't get paid." The female witch raised her hands. "I intend to finish the job."

At those words, Jackson raced outside, the rest of us following behind. He stopped about twenty feet from the killer. Even in the dark, at this distance, I could see the woman's features. She appeared mid-twenties, her eyes weirdly lit. Oh, wait, they just reflected the light pouring from the open door of our fake set.

Jackson raised his arms in front of him to match hers. This was looking like a high noon duel. You know, if they happened at night between two witches. I shook my head at the crazy thought. Those anxious butterflies from before seemed caught in a maelstrom in my stomach.

"I've never not finished a contract," the female witch continued. "The two of you will end up dead before the sun rises." She dropped her hands for a moment. "And any of you who get in my way," she added.

"Her energy is building," Jackson yelled as the female witch raised her hands above her head. "Mia! You're up."

Mia stepped in front of Jackson, her green hair flowing down her back and lifting slightly in the breeze. "None of this is necessary, is it? Everyone can walk away tonight, unharmed." Her melodious magical voice washed over all of us.

She was right. There was no reason for any of this unpleasantness. The female witch lowered her arms. I breathed a sigh of relief that everything would be okay.

Mia faced us, breaking the spell. "Evie!"

I had a moment to remember that Mia had warned us that we would be bewitched along with the replacement killer.

And she couldn't do it for long because it could interfere with the rest of the plan.

The female witch immediately raised her hands. Several large boulders from the yard around us rose with them. Sweat beaded on my forehead.

Evie stepped forward. The female witch's arms ceased moving. The boulders hung suspended in the air. Evie did it! I wouldn't have believed it if I hadn't seen it for myself. The vampire stopped time. She excluded our small bubble of people of course. "Jacob, you're up."

Jacob took several steps toward the female witch. I hugged myself in delight. It was going to work! Jacob would get the cuffs on the female witch while she stood frozen in time. When he was still five feet away, the witch's hands trembled.

"She's breaking free! I can't hold all of this much longer! Time's going to restart!" Evie shouted. "Jacob, grab her quickly! Jackson, the force field!"

Each of Evie's shouts rocked me. No, no, no. This couldn't happen. The plan would work.

I reached out both hands, uncertain how I could help keep the plan from failing. My fingers began to tingle and energy raced along my skin. I shook my arms as though the pins and needles feeling was caused by them falling asleep. I didn't know what was happening, but something was building and itching for release.

A vague memory from my teenage years surfaced, and I knew.

I remembered what happened with my parents.

"Jacob, get back! I can handle this." I felt the eyes of the others on me. Time fully restarted and the female witch prepared to hurl the boulders at our group.

Energy crackled off of me, around me. My fingers lit up with blue electricity. The wind howled, almost like a cyclone. Distracted, the witch dropped the boulders and stared. I met her eyes and smiled grimly.

A lightning bolt sizzled out of the sky, striking the female witch. She crumpled to the ground. A scent of ozone permeated the air.

Jacob raced forward to check the unmoving witch's pulse. He looked back at the group and shook his head.

I dropped my hands in shock. The witch was dead. The immediate danger had passed. We would still need to handle Barbara. But a bigger question loomed. I knew it and as the eyes of the group fell upon me again, they knew it.

What had just happened? My magic was back. How was that possible?

A tentative hand touched my shoulder from behind. I sensed it was Jackson before he spoke. "Are you okay?" That one question held volumes of unasked questions. I turned to face him, to face the others.

"I think so," I whispered.

My phone trilled an incoming call. Out of habit, I answered. "Hi, Jessica," I greeted her, nary a tremor in my voice.

"What happened?" She echoed my earlier internal question. "We sensed a huge display of magic outside of town."

"It's over," I told her, a bone-deep weariness settling over me. "The replacement killer is dead."

"Come to the Council. Now," Jessica demanded.

I glanced around at Catherine, Evie, Ryan, Mia, Jacob, Alex, and Jackson. Looking for permission? I didn't even know. My mind swirled.

"Go. We'll take care of everything here," Catherine assured me, having heard Jessica's directive. Jacob nodded. If local law enforcement said it was okay... I guessed it was.

"Come with me?" I asked Jackson.

"Of course."

He propped me up, and I shuffled beside him to his truck. He helped me into the front passenger seat. A wave of exhaustion washed over me; maybe a quick cat nap during the drive would be okay.

CHAPTER TWENTY-ONE

Warm breath in my ear woke me from my restless sleep. "We're here, Robin. Time to talk to Jessica and the Witches Council."

At the phrase, I bolted upright in the seat and trained wide eyes on Jackson. "I hope they have some answers."

"I'm sure they will," he responded while lifting me out of the truck and setting me gently on the ground. His face held an inscrutable expression.

There were lots of questions there, I knew. He supported me as we walked up the short sidewalk to the squat industrial building housing the Council chamber. Soon we stood before the five council members seated behind the half-circle table. I had trouble meeting their gazes. Instead, my eyes wandered over the silvery wallpaper reflecting the light from the antique wall sconces. I stood rigidly in front of my chair.

"You are a witch," Theresa began. A statement, not a question. She had replaced her red lipstick with bright purple today.

"Yes."

"Please tell us what happened in Boulder City," Matt, the older gentleman requested.

With only a few verbal stumbles, I relayed what had happened earlier that evening with the replacement killer. A few eyebrows rose when I revealed the witch was female, but otherwise, the Council remained silent until I finished.

"How were you able to summon the lightning bolt?" Marcie, the young woman who still struck me as barely out of her teens, but surely was older, asked the question. I heard genuine curiosity and wondered if Jessica had told the Council about my bound magic.

I glanced at Jackson. Now was a moment of truth. He knew I had hidden my witch status from him. Time to lay all my cards on the table, as they said. "I discovered I had abilities after puberty. I'm not sure what to call them, but I discovered I could—" I hesitated, uncertain how to describe my skills. "—control the weather? I guess that's the best way to explain it."

"Elemental powers, then?" Evan, the tall, heavyset witch asked.

"I suppose so. But my parents didn't understand what was happening any more than I did." My voice choked with the mention of my parents.

"They weren't witches?" Marcie appeared surprised.

"Not as far as I know." I swallowed. "I think they were afraid of me." Tears filled my eyes. "They should have been."

"What happened, Robin?" Jessica asked.

"When I was sixteen, we were driving to yet another appointment with a psychiatrist. Over the three years prior, they had taken me to doctor after doctor, who tried medication after medication." I winced at the bitterness in my voice.

"We were arguing. I remember being so angry at them. I couldn't understand why they couldn't understand how cool this was. I could control the weather. What teenager wouldn't want something like out of a comic book movie?" I smiled sadly.

"But everything came apart that day. We were yelling, and suddenly I felt my arms tingling from my shoulders to the tips of my fingers. I hadn't experienced it so strongly and didn't at first realize what was happening." I dropped my gaze to my fidgeting fingers.

"A bolt of lightning struck the car and we drove off the highway into a light pole. My parents died instantly," I finished in a rush of words. I heard pens on papers in the stillness following my admission.

I risked a glance at Jackson. My heart froze at his expressionless face. I returned my gaze to the Council. "I buried my magic deep after that, while I was in foster care.

After aging out of the program at eighteen, I attempted college." I stopped, unable to catch my breath.

"What happened during college?" Evan asked.

"My magic went on the fritz," I answered. "Lightning bolts, hurricane force winds. I lost control. So, I dropped out and lived on the street where I couldn't hurt anyone."

"How did you wind up in Vegas?" Marcie asked.

"I just drifted here," I said with a shrug. "But one day I had had enough. After four years on the street, I couldn't do it anymore and I begged the universe to help me." I rolled onto the balls of my feet. My final big reveal to Jackson. How his mind must be reeling. "Barbara Knollman answered my call."

The Council members stirred in their seats at my admission. Of course, they knew she was a demon. Everyone in the paranormal world knew that.

"I signed a pact with the demon to be her minion if she would help me. She created the circumstances for me to start my talent agency and bound my magic. Everything was stable, if not actually good, until she ordered me to kill Jackson McKee. And I refused."

Matt was frowning, bald head tilted up toward the ceiling. He refocused on me. "How did you release your magic?"

"I don't know. I was hoping you could answer that."

"I can," Jessica interjected. All eyes swiveled to her. "The demon never bound your magic, Robin."

My jaw dropped. "Yes, she did."

"No, she didn't."

"Then why couldn't I feel it anymore."

"You denied it for so long it became trapped within you."

"I did?"

"If I had to guess," Jessica continued, "I'd say guilt over your parents' deaths and the instability in college drove you to burying your powers."

A tear fell. "I bound my own powers?"

"In a manner of speaking, yes."

Evan shifted his bulk to sit forward in his seat. Kind eyes peered at me. "And then you could access it when your friends were in danger." The other Council members nodded.

"I could?"

"Yes, Robin, you could," Jessica answered.

Jackson spoke. "How does she break the pact with the demon?"

CHAPTER TWENTY-TWO

Jackson settled his hand on my shoulder following his question. I took comfort in the touch while we waited for the Council to reply. I wasn't sure if Jessica had informed the other members about our conversation… had that only been two days ago? Time flies when you're having fun. Not.

"That's a good question, Jackson," Jessica responded. "I did some research after Robin and I spoke last time." Jackson's hand on my shoulder tensed for a moment. "Given Barbara's status as a low-level demon, and the fact that she never bound Robin's magic, breaking the pact is surprisingly straightforward."

"It is?" That shocked me. Had I lived this long under Barbara's thumb, getting weaker and feeling miserable, for no reason?

"It is. But, don't beat yourself up over that," Jessica said.

I nodded, unable to speak. If she was right, this would be over soon.

Evan and Matt came around from behind the half-circle table. "Jackson, help us move the chairs out of the way?" Evan asked.

"We need room for the ritual circle," Matt explained.

Jackson, Matt, and Evan moved the folding chairs to the edges of the room, clearing a large space. Theresa placed and lit four candles across from each other, as if at the edges of an unseen circle. Seeing my look, she chuckled.

"It's hard to draw a circle on the carpet. We learned that it's not always necessary." She shrugged and turned to confer with Jessica.

"We'll use the feminine strength of the Goddess for this ritual. So, men, we do not need you for this one. Could you stand behind the council table?" Jackson, Matt, and Evan obliged. "Marcie, please stand at due North. Theresa, due South. I'll go to East. And, Robin, you'll be West."

I waited until the other three had taken up their positions, since I wasn't sure which direction west would be, before assuming my own position.

"Is everybody ready?" Jessica asked.

We assented.

"At all times, remember our purpose in conducting this ritual. To break the pact between Robin and Barbara. First, we will call the corners. This will cleanse our space and help us open communication with the Goddess," Jessica said. She closed her brown eyes, took a deep breath.

I thought I would find the whole thing silly, but I found myself captivated by the process. It was as though something missing in my life for years was awakening.

"I call to the North, the element of Earth," Marcie began, her voice low and melodious.

"I call to the East, the element of Air," Jessica continued.

"I call to the South, the element of Fire," Theresa said.

I opened my mouth and nothing emerged. I swallowed past the lump in my throat, remembered my intention in calling the corners, and lifted my chin a fraction. "I call to the West, the element of Water."

Jessica nodded at me. "Robin, declare your intention. Use your name and be specific."

With a strong, clear voice, I spoke into the circle. "I, Robin Landon, desire to break my pact with Barbara Knollman." My hands fluttered. "Do we need her demon name?" I asked Jessica softly, but with audible panic in my voice. She shook her head.

Jessica pulled a vial of liquid from an unseen pocket of her loose green t-shirt dress. She opened the vial and sprinkled some into the center of the circle.

"I use this salt water for purification," she stated, clearly directing this explanation at me. She closed her eyes. I swore her red hair was glowing.

"We call upon the Goddess to hear Robin's plea, to break the pact with the demon, Barbara Knollman. We call upon Mother Earth to intervene to prevent the bond from reforming."

Wait. That could happen? My shoulders tensed and I gnawed at my lower lip.

"Farewell and blessed be," Jessica stated with a note of finality.

"Blessed be," the other ladies repeated. I think I caught on in time for at least the last two syllables. I assumed that would be sufficient.

The women lowered their heads in a moment of silence. I copied their mannerisms, and in my own moment of seriousness, sent my pure request into the world.

"Thank you, ladies," Jessica said with a bright smile around the circle.

Theresa walked the circle, blowing out and retrieving the candles. The men came forward to return the folding chairs to their prior positions.

It all seemed very anti-climactic. "And that'll work? To make the pact, I had to sign the bond in blood." I shuddered at the memory.

Jessica grinned. "Trust me, it worked."

My phone trilled an incoming call. Barbara. Blood drained from my face. "Hello?" I answered with a trembling voice.

"Hello, Robin. You've been busy."

I closed my eyes for a moment, gathering strength. "Yes, I have."

"I'd like to see you," she requested in a conversational tone.

"Why?"

"Old times' sake?"

I swore I heard a smile in her voice. Did she know something we didn't? "Sure. How about tomorrow morning?" I offered nonchalantly, but my pulse hammered in my head.

"See you then." She disconnected the call.

I turned to Jackson, the hand holding my cell phone shaking. He closed his strong fingers around mine.

"She can't hurt you," he said.

"You can't know that," I argued. "She'll kill me for breaking the pact. How did she even know I broke the pact?" I heard the hysterical note in my rising voice.

"She would have sensed an energy change," Jessica offered from across the room.

I nodded as I considered that. I made eye contact with Jackson. "Now what?"

"We need to talk," he said.

CHAPTER TWENTY-THREE

Hurt shown in Jackson's eyes. The others had moved out of earshot to provide us privacy. He stood with his arms dangling at his sides. He seemed to be deciding how to open the conversation.

"So, you're a witch?"

"Yes."

"Interesting."

"Uh-huh."

"That might have been good information to have earlier." His voice had an edge to it.

"Probably."

"Could I get more than a one-word response, please?"

The exasperation in his voice was unsurprising and justified. "I missed my opportunity to tell you initially," I said. "Then it seemed too big a thing to mention until after all the issues were taken care of."

"That sounds like an excuse," he said in a tired voice.

"That's because it is," I admitted with a bark of unhappy laughter. "I didn't want to be judged for my poor choices."

"In signing a pact with a demon?"

"Um, yeah."

His eyes met mine and he gave a small shake of his head. "You didn't trust me."

"That's not exactly it," I floundered in my reply. "I didn't trust anybody and…" I swallowed. "I wanted you to like me." Good grief that sounded pathetic.

A real smile flitted across his face. "I did like you. I do like you," he amended. He reached out a hand to caress my neck. "I liked you from the beginning."

"Well, sure, your protection magic drew you to me." My heart hammered in my chest.

"That's true," he responded.

That's it? You've got nothing else? Frustration zinged through me. "At least now you don't have to protect me anymore," I said with feigned nonchalance.

"Mm-hmm," he agreed.

I picked at a cuticle then dropped my arms to my sides, mirroring him. "I should have been honest with you about it all," I blurted out.

"I could understand why you wouldn't want to go into details, but you kept some pretty big secrets from me. For no reason."

The confusion in his voice physically hurt. "I did."

"You were a witch. Believed your magic was bound. By a demon. With whom you signed a blood pact. Did I leave anything out?"

"I hurt people with my magic," I mumbled, as pain seared through me.

"Maybe."

"What do you mean, maybe? I killed my parents," I said in a hollow voice.

He collected his thoughts for a moment. "Your parents didn't understand what you were. Are. You therefore never received guidance for how to control your magic. Many things are set in stone; you don't know that your parents' fate wasn't already sealed," he said.

"That's a cop out, and you know it," I protested.

Jackson shrugged. "Maybe. Maybe not." He gave me a crooked smile. "Either way, you've paid penance. It's time to move forward."

With you? I wanted to ask the question, but I didn't. I simply nodded.

"I guess we'll be in touch?" His expression mixed hopeful longing with something shuttered that I couldn't read.

Ugh. More mixed signals. "I guess so."

With that apparently settled in his mind, Jackson turned and strode from the room. Jessica approached and took me by the elbow. She leaned in, almost conspiratorially. "Give him time."

"Why is that always what people recommend?"

She laughed. "Because people need time to process information that shocks their system."

I supposed she was right. Besides, I had a demon to meet with in – I checked my watch – eight hours. If I wanted to get some sleep so I could be bright-eyed and bushy-tailed in the morning, I needed to head for home. Oh, wait, Jackson drove me here.

"Would you mind giving me a lift home?"

"Not at all."

I wanted to be ready for my final scene with the demon. Hopefully, it wouldn't also be my curtain call.

*****

"Quit fidgeting," Barbara ordered. Her hands rested on the desk in front of her, talons clicking while she spoke.

I stilled my bouncing leg and twisting fingers, unaware I'd been doing either. "Sorry."

"You're apologizing?"

"You're right," I agreed. "Sorry." I rolled my eyes at myself.

Barbara stood from her desk and walked to the window overlooking Main Street. I stared at her sleek bun and red power suit. "You recovered your magic."

"I did." I allowed a bit of pride to seep into my voice. That was a mistake.

"You broke the pact," she said in a voice that froze the blood in my veins.

"We did."

She turned at that. "We?"

Quick internal debate on whether to disclose… "The Witches Council."

She nodded and retook her seat. "I didn't think you had the ability to break it on your own."

"I could have done that?"

She smiled her predatory smile, all sharp teeth and thinned lips. "Obviously not."

My face reddened at the insult to my magic. "Hey, I thought you bound my magic," I objected.

"You did think that. That was convenient for me, for you to think that," she said.

"Sneaky."

"I'm a demon."

"How did you know we broke the pact?"

She stared at me like I'd been dropped on my head too many times as a child. "I sensed the energy change between us."

Just like Jessica had guessed. "What happens now?" I asked and glanced down at the floor. Could she still suck me down to hell? Could she ever have done that?

Barbara sighed. "It's fine. As I predicted at our previous meeting, we've come to the end of our relationship."

I gulped.

"I'm. Not. Going. To. Kill. You," she said, enunciating each syllable.

"Thank Goddess," slipped out before I could stop the words.

Barbara rolled her eyes. "Little girl, you are no longer a concern of mine. Our pact is broken. The contract for the killing is null and void. I won't be pursuing that angle anymore. I've got some thinking to do on my next steps." She abruptly stopped, an expression of surprise on her face. Probably shocked she told me even that much.

Feeling emboldened by her uncertainty – and her declaration that she wasn't going to kill me – I stood tall and stared directly into her obsidian eyes. "I can't say this has been a positive experience. But it has been a learning one. Thank you for that, I suppose." I turned my back on her and took two steps toward the door.

"Are you sure you want to turn your back on me?" she asked in a silky voice and I froze. She laughed and I started moving again. "Good luck, little witch."

Her mocking laughter followed me out of the office and down the hall. At least it was over. I had plans that night to celebrate with my new friends. Should I invite Jackson? I knew I'd ponder the question all day.

CHAPTER TWENTY-FOUR

"*Ciao*, Robin," Antonio's rich Italian voice greeted me when I entered the café that night. He air kissed my cheeks and then grasped my hands. His brown eyes met mine. "Welcome back to your family. For leaving the demon."

"Thank you, I haven't felt this good in years."

"*Prego, prego.* Please, join your friends. Anything you want tonight is on the house."

"*Grazi.*" Warmth suffused me as I walked through *Soprannaturale.* Nobody avoided my gaze, glared at me behind hooded lids, or frowned when they saw me. I hastened my steps at the sight of Catherine, Alex, Evie, Ryan, Mia, and Jacob sitting around the back booth. I wasn't surprised Liz wasn't there. Those fences hadn't been mended yet, I guessed.

My heart stuttered at the lack of Jackson. I never did call to invite him, though.

"Robin!" Catherine pushed the others over to make room for me.

"I can pull up a chair," I said uncertainly. Seven around the booth seemed tight.

"Not at all," Mia responded. "Have a seat."

I slid in beside Catherine. Ryan handed me a menu. I perused it while the group's chatter resumed.

"What do you think she'll do next?" Evie asked.

"I don't know," Catherine answered. "From the moment I arrived in town, she's acted like we have a connection and I'm somehow important to her goals." She shrugged. "But, since I helped thwart her this time, I imagine she feels differently now." Laughter erupted at the sentiment.

"What do you think, Robin?" Evie asked. I set the menu down. "You worked with her for years. Did she ever give any hint of her end game?"

I shook my head. "No, she didn't. Catherine's right, though. She became Barbara's focus from the moment she arrived; and then by extension, everyone connected with the Paranormal Talent Agency."

"So strange," Alex said.

"I know. She dropped cryptic hints all the time," I said, "but never anything substantial. But I don't care anymore," I declared. "She's out of my life."

"Here, here," the group chanted, everyone lifting their water in unison.

"To Robin living her full life again," Mia toasted.

"To Robin," they repeated.

"Yeah, I have to say," Evie chimed in. "You looked washed out before. You look so much better now."

"Evie!" Mia chastised her.

"No, it's okay," I assured them. "I understand. I didn't realize it was happening at the time, but being tethered to the demon was sucking out my life force." That statement piqued Alex's interest. "Not quite the way an incubus does, Alex," I explained. "Just a slow steady drain. Fatigue. Lack of joy. But I didn't really notice, believe it or not. I thought I was sad because I'd decided to work with a demon."

"Choices have consequences," Evie quipped.

I nodded. "I know. I just never made the connection. I became paranoid. Didn't want to be around anyone. Didn't want anybody in my life. It became all about Barbara. Until I met—" I bit off Jackson's name. "—all of you. Thanks."

"You're welcome," Catherine responded. "It's great to see how your eyes sparkle and your skin glows now."

"I feel like I've rediscovered who I am, even apart from simply not being a demon's minion."

Catherine tilted her head. Dang, I'd bet her magical abilities identified that as an incomplete truth. But I didn't want to talk about Jackson. Tonight's dinner was focused on celebrating our victories.

I lifted my water again. "To reaching Day 7 of Barbara's Killer Countdown with nobody being killed."

"To reaching Day 7," they repeated, spilling water with their vigorous bumping of glasses.

"To Robin getting her magic back," Catherine toasted.

"To Robin breaking the contract with the demon," Mia added.

"And to you guys. Without your help—" I set my glass down, swallowed past the lump in my throat, ignored the burning tears in my eyes. "Without your help, none of this would have been possible. I can never thank you enough."

Catherine hugged me tightly. "Don't give up on him," she whispered. She didn't explain her comment. Of course, I knew who she meant.

Jackson.

I pulled out my phone and texted him.

Sorry for the last minute invite. Wanna swing by the café on Main Street to celebrate with us?

I placed the cellphone on the vinyl beside me. "What's next for you guys?" I asked the group. I half-listened to their answers, waiting for the vibration of Jackson's reply.

There!

"Excuse me," I told them before picking up the phone. They exchanged knowing glances. My super-secret spy skills were clearly subpar.

Working another hour or so. After?

How about my place?

It's a date.

It was a date?

CHAPTER TWENTY-FIVE

An hour later I didn't move when the doorbell rang. I knew it was Jackson, since I invited him, but I didn't know what I was going to say. So, of course, I went with awkward.

"You're here."

"Like an unexpected sequel." He leaned toward me, hands braced on either side of the doorway. "May I come in?"

I pretended to consider his request. "Sequels are usually disappointing."

He gripped his chest in mock pain. "What about *The Godfather Part II*?"

"Ooh, a classic." We grinned at each other. I moved from the doorway. "In that case, come on in. Besides, I invited you, didn't I?"

Jackson gave an exaggerated bow and stepped through my doorway. I giggled at the theatrics. A meow stopped me from closing the door. I peered past Jackson into the dark and my eyes widened when a flash of fur ran by me into the house.

"Hey!" I turned to follow the animal, but it hadn't gone far, sitting only a few feet inside the door.

"Did you adopt a cat?" Jackson asked.

"No," I answered, but my eyes were glued to the cat sitting before me, whiskers twitching. "Patches," I whispered. "It can't be."

"Patches? Wasn't that your cat who—"

"Ran off almost ten years ago," I said. "How is this possible?"

My mind flooded with images from my life, from the moment of the accident to this moment right now. I watched the cat; she almost seemed to be nodding. Could she be seeing these images too?

"She's your familiar," Jackson said into my ear.

"My what? Oh, my."

"Meow," the cat said again.

I crouched down and the cat padded over. We head-butted, unshed tears blurring my vision. "Are you my familiar?"

"Meow."

New images flooded my mind, and they seemed to be coming from… the cat. I watched the last ten years of her life flash by like a movie in my mind. When it finished, I rose and faced Jackson.

"And?"

I chuckled. "After the accident and I disavowed my abilities, she was… temporarily reassigned, I guess. To another teenaged witch who needed a familiar." I bit my lower lip and met Jackson's eyes. "This other witch was fated to die," I said. "And then Patches came back to me when I'd rediscovered my abilities."

"Wow."

"That's an understatement," I agreed. "Welcome home, Patches." At her name, my little black, white, and orange furball strolled to the couch, stretched out her front legs, and then jumped up. She settled herself in and began bathing. With a shake of my head, I turned back to Jackson.

"I'm going to need a minute to adjust to that." I stepped toward the kitchen. "Do you want something to drink?"

"Sure, I'll take a glass of red wine. Whatever you have is fine."

"Long day of filming?" I asked from the kitchen.

"Not too bad."

I handed him a wineglass and sat beside him on the loveseat. Patches' quiet purring created background noise. Jackson and I simultaneously sipped our wine. Was he nervous, too?

"How have you been?"

"Since yesterday?" I asked with a grin.

"Your life is full of adventure."

My smile slipped. "Yeah, a little too much."

Jackson set his wineglass on the coffee table. "I sense this is a more serious meeting than I thought from your text."

I traced the edge of my wineglass with my finger before setting it down next to his. "I like you. I liked you from the first moment I saw you." I held up a hand to stop him from interrupting. "It started out as attraction—" I flushed at his wolfish grin. "—but then you stepped up, supporting me, helping me reclaim my life. Plus, you're smart, funny…" I shook my head and his grin faded. "But I don't know if it's real."

He gave me his inscrutable look that I'd already come to recognize as his deep-thinking face. "Why would you doubt if it's real?"

I waved my hand dismissively. "I thought there was something there… until you explained about your protection magic drawing you to me. I'm telling you this because I'm trying to start my reclaimed life on the right foot. With total honesty. I don't want you to feel obligated to—" He put his finger up to my lips.

In shock, I stopped talking. Was he shushing me? Was I making him that uncomfortable? Although, the gleam in his eye confused me. This whole honesty thing was a challenge!

Jackson took my hands in his, rubbing his thumbs along the pads of my palms. "Robin. You're correct that my protection magic drew me to you. But it was never just about protection. I was attracted to you from the first moment I saw you, too."

"Even with the demon energy diminishing me?" I couldn't help but ask.

He chuckled. "I'll admit, I wondered if you had recently been ill, the first time I saw you. Even still, there was a spark."

"My magic?"

He lifted a single shoulder in a shrug. "Maybe. I don't know. That spark drew me in. And yes, my magic told me you needed protecting. Then…" He paused and leaned in closer, his breath warm against my cheek. "These past few days I saw the real you, hidden beneath the demon influence and self-doubt."

"In only a few days?"

"Didn't you just say you felt the same way after a few days?"

"Your logic is infallible," I agreed, voice husky and breathy.

"Thank you. I am drawn to you in every way that a man can be to a woman. Protection magic or not."

"Me too," I whispered. I felt the now-familiar tingle as magic raced along my arms to my fingers. Tiny sparks showered us as we embraced and I ran my hand over his buzz cut hair. Jackson pulled back and the sparks extinguished. His eyes were wide.

"Where are you getting the energy? Is a storm coming?"

"Oh yes, there is," I purred and leaned into him again. His lips met mine, gentle pressure sending non-magical energy through my body. His arms tightened around me and we enjoyed the moment. We separated with a sigh.

"I discovered I could pull energy from just a simple household outlet," I informed him with a Cheshire-cat grin. He laughed low and sexy and we embraced again, enjoying our happily-for-right-now that just might become our happily-ever-after.

EPILOGUE

"Robin Landon, fancy meeting you here." The iron voice brought me to a dead stop, and I turned to find myself staring into Barbara's unblinking obsidian eyes.

"Hi, Barbara," I stammered out. "Not too surprising, since we're both members of the Chamber."

She lifted an eyebrow at my tone. "I see you've also found your backbone."

I reflexively stood up straighter and Barbara chuckled. "Yes, I have," I said in a low, but clear voice. I might have found my backbone since breaking the pact; I still didn't want to make unnecessary waves by drawing attention.

"I'm glad," Barbara said.

"You are?"

She shrugged. "I don't hold a grudge."

I belly laughed and then clapped hands over my mouth. "Maybe not, but you ordered Jackson's death. You ordered my death!" Her eyes bored into my skull at my exhalation and I waited to be pulled down to Hell, before remembering she said all was forgiven. Maybe she didn't hold grudges? Demons were confusing when they didn't stay heartless and deadly.

"That might have been a mistake," she said.

"What?" I surely misheard that.

"That might have been a mistake, ordering your deaths," she repeated and expanded.

"You're a demon. A killer," I insisted.

"I've never actually killed anyone," Barbara said archly. "Directly or indirectly."

"Now why do I find that hard to believe?"

"Because you don't like me." Her smile revealed rows of tiny, sharp teeth. "Because you were my minion for years."

"That's true." I hesitated. Oh, why not? "What will you do now?"

Barbara's eyebrows rose in surprise. "Why do you care?"

I shrugged. "Natural curiosity, I suppose."

She opened and closed her mouth. "I don't know," she admitted. "Everything had been going according to plan, as I saw in my premonitions. But, this series of events was unseen. And I don't know what that means." She bit her lower lip, a strangely human action that threw me for a moment.

"I hope you figure it out. Maybe you don't have to let your—" I coughed. "—demon status determine your actions."

Barbara chuckled. "You mean, I can choose to be good."

Despite her sarcastic response, I thought I heard an undercurrent of genuine uncertainty. "Yes. You can choose a different path." Did demons have free will like that? I had no idea.

Barbara's eyes flashed red for a moment and the blood chilled in my veins. Had I gone too far? They returned to their normal obsidian, and I breathed a sigh of relief into the uncomfortable silence.

"Maybe I will." Barbara sighed. "Maybe I will."

Turn the page to read the continuing story of Barbara Knollman, repentant demon, in Episode Five of the Paranormal Talent Agency!

Episode Five

Jumping the Shark

CHAPTER ONE

Humanity drove me bananas; how hard was it to do what a demon wanted? I glanced at the humans surrounding me. They seemed so excited to support my bid for Mayor, after my years representing them on the city council. Of course, they didn't know I was a demon.

Tonight was a big night for all of us – the final debate before the primary elections in only one week. I was hanging out with my campaign volunteers to show my thanks for their support, but the metal folding chairs in campaign headquarters were uncomfortable. Who ordered these wretched things?

"Barbara, we'll be getting on the bus in about an hour. Need to leave in thirty minutes."

The voice interrupted my pointless wandering thoughts and I focused on the young woman standing before me, brown eyes wide behind bright red glasses. "Thank you,

Lynn." I stood and stretched my arms to the side. Taking the form of a middle-aged human somehow brought aches and pains with it. Not cool. "I'll be in my office. Please come get me when it's time."

"Yes, ma'am." Lynn Fox, my campaign manager, walked away and I watched her confer with two volunteers. I smiled at the volunteers I passed on my way to my office, and closed the door firmly behind me. And sighed. I understood why they wanted the candidates to arrive together; it made for a better visual. On the other hand, that meant extra travel time to meet the bus.

Unlike in campaigns past, this debate had importance. There were four challengers for the position. I normally wouldn't care, except that, for the supernatural, the head of the city council is also usually the ruler of the underworld. I'd been the unofficial head of the city council because the current mayor was a human, and an idiot. But he was stepping down. I couldn't risk a supernatural taking his place who might not want to recognize the existing power structure. I wasn't planning on giving up my status as Ruler of the Supernatural Underworld.

One of the challengers was a popular local actor, Jeffrey Jenkins. He'd been getting a lot of press lately. That made me nervous, though I still expected to be victorious. It was my destiny. I sighed again. I needed to do well in the debate tonight to solidify my position. Polls showed the two of us running neck and neck, with a fellow supernatural a close third. He was an interesting one, Mark Mammon. Though I hadn't met him yet.

A mist swirled before me and I braced myself. The mist existed only in my mind, and signaled an impending premonition. I closed my eyes and waited. My mind's eye showed me the bus for the debate tonight. Hmm. As future me walked toward the bus, movement became tortured. I trudged forward, fighting against the feeling of walking through molasses, knowing I needed to get on that bus. It became too difficult. Future me stopped fighting and froze, a weight lifted. I watched the bus doors close and the bus drive away. Part of me felt like I should call after it; I couldn't not get on the bus. I needed to be at the debate. But, future me felt relieved.

Present me snapped her eyes open in the office. The premonition was over. Now to figure out what it meant. I tapped my fingers on the plastic folding table before me. This could be tricky.

Everything had fallen apart in the past three months. After literally hundreds of years of accurate premonitions, things had become wonky. Only a few months ago, even my minion had been able to break her pact with me. I narrowed my eyes at the thought of Robin Landon's cheekiness. My premonitions hadn't breathed a word of that betrayal. More importantly, I'd had a premonition that a witch, Jackson McKee – Robin's new boyfriend (hard eye roll at that thought) – was involved in a loss of my power, but I'd been unsuccessful in eliminating him. As I admitted to Robin in our last encounter, my precognition was on the fritz. What other explanation could there be for these outcomes?

Thus, my current dilemma. My premonition suggested I shouldn't get on the bus. Could that be the wrong interpretation? Or maybe the premonition was wrong entirely. I ground my teeth together. A soft knock on the door drew my attention. Lynn poked her head in.

"It's time, Ms. Knollman."

I frowned and did not stand.

"Sorry. Barbara." When I still didn't respond, Lynn matched my frown. "Is everything okay?"

"Yes. I won't be taking the debate bus," I declared, decision made.

Her mouth dropped open for a moment before she recovered. "I'll inform the coordinator." She closed the door. At least she knew better than to question me.

Now to see what happened.

CHAPTER TWO

A ding signaled an incoming text message. 702 area code, but not a number I knew. I lifted a single eyebrow at the message on the phone's screen.

Hi Barbara. This is Mark. You didn't get on the bus.

Curious. *No.*

Turn on the news.

"Lynn, turn the television to Channel 5," I instructed my campaign manager. We were in a limo heading to the debate, which was set to start in twenty minutes. The television clicked on and Lynn scrolled. Elizabeth Addison's sorrowful face filled the small screen on the back of the car seat.

"I'm at the scene of a horrific accident," the newscaster said. "About fifteen minutes ago, the bus carrying the mayoral candidates to their final debate crashed. Details remain hazy, but it appears there were no survivors."

Lynn gasped.

I listened for the approximate location of the crash, muted the broadcast, and lowered the divider between us and the driver.

"There's been an accident involving the debate bus. Please head toward DI and Las Vegas Boulevard. Get as close to the accident as you can."

"Yes, ma'am."

I raised the divider and unmuted the broadcast. Elizabeth stood a block from the accident. Flashing lights illuminated much of what was behind her. A bus lay on its side, front crumpled like a soda can.

You weren't on the bus either.

I wondered what Mark's response to my text would be. I listened to Elizabeth's continued coverage while I waited.

The brunette broadcaster put a hand to her ear, probably trying to isolate a voice coming through her earpiece. "I've just been informed that the Sheriff has arrived on scene." Elizabeth nodded at the camera and then turned to sprint toward the accident. The image returned to an anchor in-studio and I muted the broadcast again. I'd wait until they had more information. My mind was spinning with what I'd already learned.

A bus crashed that I was supposed to be on. A bus crash that my premonition saved me from.

Why?

Mark Mammon also wasn't on the bus.

The camera returned to Elizabeth standing next to the tall, gray-haired Sheriff. His city had seen some rough stuff since he won election. He looked at least a decade older than he had when he'd taken office. Such were the perils of power.

I unmuted the broadcast.

"What can you tell us?"

"The last body has been pulled from the wreckage. At this time, I can confirm three of the five candidates—"

"Which candidates?" Elizabeth interrupted, but given Mark's text, I knew.

"—along with three staff members," the Sheriff continued without acknowledging her question, "and the bus driver, have been killed."

"What happened?"

"The cause of the accident is unknown, though witnesses report the bus did not seem to slow as it crested Desert Inn toward the Las Vegas Boulevard traffic light."

"Does the department believe this was a terrorist attack?"

"We have no reason to believe that at this time," the Sheriff concluded, smiled tightly at viewers, and turned to hurry away from the reporter.

I doubted it was a terrorist attack either. I also doubted it was just an accident.

My limo had nearly arrived at the intersection of the accident when Mark responded.

And then there were two.

I chuckled at the audacity. I guessed that confirmed what Elizabeth had reported. He and I were the only candidates remaining. Seemed only fitting, since we were the two paranormal beings. Both demons, in fact. I thinned my lips in thought. This begged two very important questions.

It seemed unlikely, but did Mark not know I was a demon?

And, I had my premonition warning me away from the bus; how did Mark know not to board the bus?

CHAPTER THREE

The slowing of the limo and the sound of the divider lowering pulled me from my thoughts. I made eye contact with the driver in the rearview mirror.

"Ma'am, we've arrived."

He didn't have to specify where. The lights from emergency vehicles pierced the limo's window tint, and controlled chaos ruled the scene.

"Good luck," Lynn offered.

I paused in opening my door. Sarcastic or sincere? Maybe I could play nice for a bit until I figured out what was going on. I smiled wide at her. "Thank you." I exited the vehicle and took in the scene before me.

Controlled chaos was definitely an accurate description. I counted five ambulances. No, wait, six. Three firetrucks and five police vehicles scattered around the debate bus, indeed lying on its side, front end crumpled. I spotted

Elizabeth and her cameraman, still shooting live coverage, and headed in her direction.

Elizabeth's eyes lit up when she saw me. She recognized a scoop when she saw it. "Councilwoman, why weren't you on the bus?" Her shouted question reached me.

I did not respond. Yelling across the space between us wasn't dignified. And I was the head of the city council after all.

She wisely did not repeat her question and simply watched me approach.

"Good evening, Ms. Addison. I'm happy to answer any questions that you have."

"Why weren't you on the bus?"

"A last-minute change of plans resulted in my choosing to drive myself to the debate."

"Well, technically, you have a limo."

A pulse throbbed in my neck. "Yes, you are correct. What I meant to say was that my campaign arranged private transportation when it was decided I wouldn't be taking the bus."

"And what were these last-minute plans that kept you from the bus?"

Like a dog with a bone. "Confidential campaign activities."

"That's convenient."

"Are you insinuating that I had anything to do with this crash, Ms. Addison?"

She winced at my sharp tone and her cheeks flushed. She knew I called her bluff. "Of course not. I'm only asking what my viewers will be wondering. How did you know not to get on the bus?"

I paused as if collecting my thoughts. I wasn't about to mention I had a premonition, but I needed to nip this in the bud. "I had no advance knowledge that anything was going to happen to the bus. Of course, I didn't. There was no nefarious reason I wasn't on board. I am as shocked and devastated as the rest of Las Vegas at this senseless accident and loss of life."

"Maybe not quite as devastated, though, right?"

I remained silent, hyper-aware of the camera likely zoomed in on my face, waiting for any micro-reaction.

"After all, now there are only two candidates for your position," she finished triumphantly.

I allowed a half-smile to surface. "Ms. Addison, I have every confidence that I will win this election. Neither myself, nor Mark Mammon, who also was not on the bus tonight, wanted the race to be reduced through such means."

I saw the internal calculations play out across Elizabeth's face. The Sheriff hadn't told her who the other surviving candidate was. Like me, she was considering what Mark might know or not know about the bus crash.

"My thoughts and prayers go out to the victims of tonight's crash, as well as their friends and family. Thank you." With that, I walked away. Elizabeth shouted something, her words lost on the wind that picked that moment to blow harsher. I hurried to the limo. The door tried to slip from my grasp but I was able to hold it open long enough to slip inside.

"Are you okay?"

The broadcast continued on the screen behind her and I assumed she watched my interview. It could have been better. It could have been worse. I shrugged. "I'm fine." I lowered the partition. "Please bring me to my office."

"Yes, ma'am."

I raised the partition and faced Lynn. "I'll head to work for a bit, in case there's anything requiring my immediate attention. We should assume for now that the next week will involve minimal continued campaigning."

Lynn nodded and whipped out her cellphone. I turned my attention inward as her fingers flew across the device, probably alerting anybody who needed to know that I would be laying low for the time being. I was savvy enough to understand I didn't want it to appear I was taking advantage of the tragedy. Although, Mark was correct.

Only two candidates remained.

CHAPTER FOUR

I drummed my fingernails on my solid wood monstrosity of a desk. In between providing soundbites to other members of the media concerning the tragedy, I reviewed the papers scattered across the surface of the desk. Once the final candidates had filed their paperwork, I'd hired a private investigator to dig up everything they could on the other four. The actor had been the biggest obvious threat. The two nobodies were exactly that. I set aside their dossiers and opened the one remaining.

Mark Mammon. I'd hired a supernatural private investigator because I'd assumed at least one of the other candidates would be supernatural. I'd been right. The investigator had struggled to follow the leads on Mr. Mammon. I wasn't surprised once the preliminary information came in; he was a demon like me and we weren't exactly known for wanting to share that.

Mark was older than my 500 years, but the trail of personas ran cold at about 750 years. He could be 1000 years old, for all I knew. That was worrisome because he may or may not be stronger as a result. I placed his picture on top of the pile.

Devilishly handsome man. I chuckled at my wit. Thick black hair, depthless black eyes that pulled at you. High cheekbones and a strong chin rounded out his striking features. Could be Greek or Roman, with that profile.

I laughed aloud when I considered his name. The name Mark meant God of War. And Mammon was a higher-level demon who evoked greed and deceit. So, a greedy demon starting war. Someone like that might crash a debate bus. Someone like that most certainly could want to rule the supernatural underworld.

Here I pursed my lips in thought. Although a large region, Las Vegas wasn't the biggest region to rule. Why was Mark here, trying to snatch my rule from me? Wouldn't he want to go after New York City, or one of the bigger regions in Europe maybe? I gnashed my teeth in frustration. What was his end game?

My cellphone rang. I frowned at it for a moment before answering. "Barbara Knollman speaking."

"Ms. Knollman, this is Detective Jacob Dawson, with the Las Vegas Police Department."

I rolled my eyes; I was well aware of the owner of the gruff voice. Although just a human, he was involved with

Mia Fynn, a fellow supernatural allied with the Paranormal Talent Agency. "What can I do for you, Detective?"

"I'd like to schedule a time to speak with you regarding the bus crash that occurred earlier tonight."

No preamble. He probably saw my interview with Elizabeth. I wasn't keen on being interviewed by him, but perhaps I could gain my own knowledge. While I knew I had nothing to do with the accident, it was very likely someone, maybe Mark, was involved. Perhaps I could pull some of that information from the detective.

"Ma'am? Are you there?"

"Sorry, I was reviewing my schedule in my head." The lie rolled easily off my tongue. "How about tomorrow at 9? Would you like me to come to the station?" I offered only to appear agreeable. He and I both knew I wouldn't be coming down to the station.

"That's not necessary, ma'am. I'll come to you. Thank you."

"You're most welcome, Detective. I'll see you in the morning." I ended the call and leaned back in the overstuffed dark leather chair. Now this was a comfortable chair. Why couldn't I have gotten one like this for at least my campaign headquarters office?

I turned my attention back to the dossier for Mark Mammon, although there was little left to review. The list of names he'd used, going back 750 years. Interestingly, he almost always used a variant of Mark — such as Marc,

Markus, Marcus – and a surname with a deeper meaning. Maybe my demon competitor possessed unknown depths?

I laughed and my eyes burned. If anyone had been in the room, they would have seen the unearthly red glow emanating from them. I didn't actually care whether or not Mark had depth. I needed to find out if he caused the bus crash and if he'd really been so insolent as to have tried to kill me.

CHAPTER FIVE

My dark house beckoned. I maneuvered the Cadillac Escalade – black of course – onto the driveway of my two-story abode. I lived in the Las Vegas Country Club Estates, not because I cared about being on a golf course, but because of the implied prestige and the wheeling-and-dealing I'd done on the course before. Appearances were important. Thus, I lived in a 4000 square foot McMansion. Normally this didn't bother me; it was a necessary evil. Tonight, something niggled.

Was it because of my faulty precognitions? Maybe that had me more off-kilter than I thought.

The coldness and impersonality of the muted grays and gleaming metal interior of my house bothered me tonight too. I hurried through the entryway from the garage, ignoring the soaring 30-foot ceilings and open floorplan, eager to get to my bedroom. My heels click-clacked on the marble floors, quieting when I started up the carpeted stairway.

I peeled off my red power-suit, more of an 80s look, I supposed, but still striking.

What should be my next steps? I always had a plan. And Plans B, C, and D, to be honest. I was always prepared and ready with a backup. That was how I attained and maintained my position for so many years.

I'd never had a problem with my precognition before. That niggling sensation returned. Could it be that my precognition wasn't on the fritz? Could it be I'd been misinterpreting? I stood frozen in my walk-in closet as the enormity of that question hit. No, that couldn't be it.

Mist swirled before me and I sat on the carpet to accept the incoming premonition. A person appeared in the haze. A man, I thought. The vision moved closer; yes, it was the back of a man. Dark hair. Black or brown, I wasn't sure. The image stilled and emotions threatened to overwhelm me. Love, hate, power, and betrayal.

"Show me his face," I demanded of the premonition. "Give me more to go on," I insisted. Premonitions didn't work like that and the image stubbornly refused to move. It continued to show the back of this unknown man with dark hair.

Then my premonition did move, though my excitement was short-lived. Instead of showing me something useful about the man, the image shifted to show a female I knew.

Her bright blue eyes flashed in a pale face surrounded by waves of blue hair. The importance of her struck like a physical assault. The image faded and I lay back on the carpet. I stared at the ceiling and considered what I'd received.

I hadn't been given enough to guess the identity of the man in the vision. The second image gave more information. Olivia Williams.

This wasn't the first time this supernatural being had appeared in one of my premonitions. I had dealt with the Paranormal Talent Agency last year when Evie's idiot vampire sire surfaced in Vegas, as a Family Cleaner, no less. He'd been hired to clean Olivia, but luckily, he'd screwed up. She'd already gone underground in New Mexico, if I remembered correctly. My premonition then had been very clear – she needed to remain alive. She was important.

And, now here she was again. Though I wasn't any closer to figuring out her importance. I groaned and returned to the first, more perplexing, image.

A man. With brown or black hair. Eliciting love, hate, power, and betrayal. Irritation spiked through me and I clenched my fists.

With a groan, I relaxed my fists, sat up, and contemplated further.

Who did I know with dark hair? An image of Mark Mammon popped up, smirk in place. Hmm. Hate would not be unexpected connected to him. Power, certainly, as a competitor. Even possibly betrayal, if he was the one who killed the other candidates.

But love? That made no sense that I could understand.

I'd let the premonition percolate a bit and wait to see what information I could glean from the detective tomorrow.

CHAPTER SIX

Jacob Dawson sat opposite me in my office, blue eyes indecipherable. He held a small notebook in one hand and a disposable pen in the other. Ready to take down the pearls of wisdom I'd soon be offering. I bit back a chortle. He leaned forward, maroon button-down dress shirt straining against his shoulders.

"Please, Detective, ask your questions. I have nothing to hide," I volunteered, and his eyebrows rose in surprise.

"Thank you, Councilwoman—"

"Please, call me Barbara," I interrupted, a smile splitting my face. He shuddered and I remembered that my teeth weren't aging well in this body; apparently, they were small and sharp-looking. I brought it down a notch, smiling without showing teeth. Jacob relaxed.

"Barbara," he complied. "Thank you for agreeing to answer my questions."

"Of course, anything to help the investigation."

"Let's start with your decision not to take the bus to the debate."

"That was a last-minute decision," I began, the explanation already sounding rehearsed. The drawback to having repeated the story so many times to members of the press the previous night. He scribbled, mouth pulled down in a frown, while I unspooled the story of needing extra time at campaign headquarters before the debate. I rather magnanimously had not wanted to delay the entire show by holding up the bus until I was ready.

"Do you know why Mark Mammon didn't take the bus either?"

"I do not."

"Have you spoken with Mr. Mammon since the accident?"

"I have not."

"Let me rephrase. Have you been in contact with Mr. Mammon at all since the accident?"

Now it was my turn with the eyebrow raise. "You've already spoken with Mr. Mammon."

"This morning," Jacob confirmed.

"I apologize for the inaccuracy. While it is true I did not speak with him, we exchanged several texts."

"May I see those texts?"

I hesitated for only a moment, but Jacob didn't miss the hesitation. His expression hardened. He expected me to lie.

I smoothed out my own expression. "Of course." My cellphone sat on the desk before me. I unlocked the screen, clicked on the text icon, and slid the phone toward the detective. "The exchange is at the top."

Jacob scrolled through the minimal texts, seeming satisfied. While the texts were terse, and somewhat odd perhaps, there was nothing there suggesting my involvement. Or Mark's, I realized.

"Are you at liberty to tell me what happened?" I asked.

"Normally I wouldn't, but I understand you have sources."

I smirked. He knew I could pick up the phone the instant he turned in any kind of a report and have the full information. I only asked to save myself the hassle.

"The accident was no accident," he said slowly, watching for my reaction.

"What makes you believe that?"

"There was no evidence the driver tried to brake."

"He could have fallen asleep," I offered an alternative explanation.

"He could have. Except a last text came from one of the occupants, stating concern about the driver."

"Anything specific?"

"Nope."

"Wouldn't that suggest the driver did it on purpose?"

"It would."

"Any background on the driver to suggest a motive?"

"Nope."

"The press suggested it might be a terrorist attack."

Jacob frowned. "The press would do well not to speculate at the drop of a hat."

I laughed, knowing there was no love lost between Elizabeth Addison and his girlfriend, Mia. "So probably not terrorism?"

"There's no evidence to suggest that."

"Then why would he do it?"

"We're still investigating, ma'am," Jacob said.

"Could he have done it on behalf of someone else?"

"That's my prevailing theory," he admitted. "Someone who *did* have a reason to kill the candidates."

I chewed on my lower lip. "Any suspects?"

Jacob gave me a blank look and I blanched.

"I'm a suspect."

"I can neither confirm nor deny—"

"And, I presume Mr. Mammon is a suspect."

"I can neither—"

I held up a hand to stop him. "I know, you can neither confirm nor deny my presumption." I tapped my fingernails on the desk. Jacob's eyes cut to them and he watched the fire-engine-red nails tap, tap, tap. My fingernails stilled and he met my gaze.

"I know you don't like me," I began. Jacob had a good poker face. "I also know you know I am… paranormal." Still no reaction. "Understand that I expect you to do your job." He narrowed his eyes at my tone. "I expect you to find out who the actual killer is; prove it isn't me."

Jacob chuckled. "Ma'am, with all due respect, you only got half of that right. I will do my job and find the killer. If you aren't the killer," he gave a fierce smile, "then you have nothing to worry about."

I nodded. "That sounds fair."

His eyes narrowed in disbelief.

"I can be fair. Sometimes a reputation is just a reputation," I reminded him.

"That's true."

"Have I answered all of your questions?"

"Yes, ma'am. I'll be in touch if any follow up is necessary." He stood and I did not.

I inclined my head in response and he stepped from the room. Once he closed my office door, I rose from the desk and stood at the window, overlooking Main Street.

I was clearly a prime suspect. Was that because I hadn't been on the bus? I supposed that was a big factor, given that Mark Mammon was also a suspect.

But, I figured I was more of a suspect than Mark. Not because I had more of a reason to want to eliminate the competition; if that were the sole factor, Mark would have that honor.

No, I knew I was the prime suspect based on my history with Detective Dawson and the Paranormal Talent Agency. So previously I mis-stepped and hired a contract killer to eliminate a witch. I hadn't been successful. Couldn't a demon catch a break?

CHAPTER SEVEN

"Well, this is a surprise," I told the lanky man standing in my doorway. He didn't buy my forced casual tone. Liam Collins, angel and my ex-boyfriend from many, many years ago, somehow was at my house in Las Vegas. Would wonders never cease.

Liam squinted his Caribbean blue eyes and tilted his head. "You look… different."

"Old."

"Mature."

"Old," I insisted, but with a laugh.

"Why?"

I shrugged. "I arrived in Vegas twenty years ago at 25; I needed to age accordingly."

Liam nodded, eyes twinkling. "You still look good."

"For an old lady."

"For an any-age woman."

My cheeks flushed. Dang, that man could still get me, even after hundreds of years. He ran a hand through his curly brown hair, still a touch too long and unruly, and gave me a crooked smile.

"May I come in?"

I stepped aside to allow him access, enjoying the view from behind as much as from the front. But this was a no-win rabbit hole for me. I made my choice a long time ago. Liam paused just inside the door, waiting for me to lead the way. He followed me to the black leather couches in the living room. I didn't miss the frown flit across his face. Guess he didn't like the décor.

"To what do I owe the honor of your visit? I had a long day at work and I'm tired."

Liam allowed a bittersweet smile before getting down to business. "I would like to request your assistance."

"So formal."

"It seems appropriate, now."

"Because I'm the head of the supernatural underworld for the Vegas region?"

"Something like that."

"What can I assist you with?"

"Mark Mammon ordered the hit on the mayoral candidates."

I raised a single eyebrow. "That's a bold accusation." Not that I disagreed.

"You were supposed to be on that bus."

Anger surged through me at this apparent confirmation. "Was I?"

Liam laughed, the loud sound echoing through my cavernous space. "You're kidding, right? The Barbara I knew would never have doubted it."

A small sigh escaped. "You're right. I knew. To hear it confirmed…"

Liam reached out to touch a lock of my brown hair, recently set free from my typical bun I wore for work. "I'm glad you weren't on the bus."

I jerked back and he dropped his hand. "Thank you. Though you know it wouldn't have hurt me."

"Still."

An uncomfortable warmth spread through me. "Does Mark know I'm a demon?" I changed the subject.

"We don't know."

"He would know a bus crash couldn't kill me," I continued, more to myself. "Anyway, what can I do for you?"

"I'd like to request your help in us proving his guilt, so he can be held accountable."

"Us?"

He smirked. "You know them. A group connected with… I believe its nickname is the Paranormal Talent Agency."

My eyes rolled in reflex at the phrase and Liam chuckled.

"I guess you do know them."

"How do *you* know them?"

"I was told to reach out to Mia, and she introduced me to Catherine."

Catherine Rodham, head of the Paranormal Talent Agency in Las Vegas. Mia Fynn, film producer and 200-year-old nixie. And, Jacob, Mia's boyfriend, had already interviewed me. I wondered when Evie Jones, the snarky vampire actress, would pop up too. Were we getting the whole band back together? I snorted. "What's the plan?" The image of the dark-haired man from my vision surfaced. Could it have been Liam, not Mark?

Liam tilted his head again. "What just went through your mind?"

I hesitated. Oh heck, why not? He already knew about my precognitive powers. "I had a premonition about a dark-haired man involving power and betrayal." And love, my mind reminded me. I smacked that thought down.

Liam nodded. "That could definitely be Mark. He's certainly power-hungry and wouldn't hesitate to betray you."

"He already tried to kill me," I responded drily.

"Too true."

"Here's the thing. If I'm being completely honest—" His eyebrows rose a fraction and I flushed. "—my involvement in the past has not gone well with the Agency."

"I heard they cost you a minion."

"Nice, Liam, very nice." He chuckled and I grinned. This felt so easy, like before— My grin dropped. "My plan had been to stay out of it. The vision was quite indistinct." And I don't want to make a mistake, my mind added. I grimaced.

"That doesn't sound like the Barbara I know, either. You want to stay on the sidelines, licking your wounds?" The taunt was gentle, but still I bristled. His reverse psychology was totally going to work.

"Fine, I'll help."

"Fantastic," he replied with a broad smile.

"Did you win the bet?"

"Bet?"

"I know you. Since gambling with river rocks as a boy, you always liked wagering."

He winked.

"Did you win the bet with, I'm guessing Catherine, on whether or not I'd agree to help?"

His smile widened. "Maybe."

I laughed, and suddenly was very aware of the heat between us. Just like old times; 100 years together left an impression. Our smiles fell at the same time and his blue eyes gazed into my black ones. He broke the contact first, rising to his feet and heading toward the front door.

"I'll let the crew know and we'll make plans to meet," he called over his shoulder.

I stood slower and followed him to the door, where he paused and faced me.

"I'm sorry for the circumstances, Barbara, but I'm glad to see you."

I nodded stiffly. "Thank you."

Liam's smile wavered at my failure to echo his sentiment. "I'll get your number from Catherine and let you know when we're meeting tomorrow. Is there any time that doesn't work for you?"

I shook my head. Mute.

He took my hand in his, warmth suffusing me. "Until tomorrow." He released my hand and closed the door.

I walked back to the couch and collapsed on the supple surface. Working with the Paranormal Talent Agency crew could be a good thing. It would keep me in the loop. And they might even have some good ideas, I grudgingly admitted.

My involvement had nothing to do with Liam, with the way he looked at me, how my body responded when he touched my hair, my hand. Nope, not at all.

Then why was I counting down the hours until I saw him again?

CHAPTER EIGHT

Production staff called out uncomfortable greetings as I strode past them. I managed not to roll my eyes. Sycophants. None of them liked me, they just feared me. Like I'd care if they didn't say hello. Okay, maybe I'd care. Luckily, my unhelpful thoughts short-circuited when I spotted the group with whom I was meeting.

Liam had texted the address this morning – an independent film location in Sun City. A simple three-bedroom, one-story home in the 55+ community within Summerlin. Since most of the group was in the entertainment world, and my image involved keeping my finger on the pulse of that industry, nobody would question my presence. Even if they weren't thrilled by it.

Chatter ceased the moment I stood in the doorway of a back bedroom. An eight-foot, white, plastic folding table sat in the middle of the space. A group of actors and crew, a mix of human and supernatural, occupied the metal folding chairs surrounding the table.

Liam jumped to his feet and hurried to me. "Barbara, welcome. We're glad you're here."

"Not all of us," a voice muttered and Evie Jones smirked when our eyes met. The 1920s blond vampire actress was easily the snarkiest of the bunch.

"Evie, that's enough," Catherine Rodham, head of the Paranormal Talent Agency, chastised her, but with a smile in her blue eyes.

Liam led me to an empty chair between him and Catherine. I lowered into the uncomfortable seat and gazed around the table. In addition to Liam, Catherine, and Evie, four others were present. Including Robin, my ex-minion (also a witch and owner of another talent agency) and her new boyfriend, Jackson, the witch who I tried unsuccessfully to have killed a few months ago. Guess they were willing to let bygones be bygones. I honed in on one of the humans present.

"Jacob, I didn't know you involved civilians in your cases."

"Ma'am, even you must admit they've demonstrated their helpfulness before," he responded, his eyes meeting his girlfriend's. Mia blushed.

"Touché. What's the plan?" I wanted to get down to business so I could leave. The tension radiating off the group around me was suffocating. I imagined Catherine was struggling with the emotions too, given her empath abilities; although I wasn't sure she understood the extent of them yet any more than I did.

"I've caught everyone up. Our goal is to stop Mark Mammon," Liam began, blue eyes sparking, "before anyone else gets hurt." Everyone murmured their agreement. "Thoughts on how to do that?"

"Can't we just hire someone to kill him?" I asked, as a joke. Nobody laughed. Tough crowd. "I'm kidding," I assured them.

"It's a bit too soon for that," Robin bit off.

Maybe we weren't letting bygones be bygones. I stayed quiet.

"We need to, at a minimum, incapacitate him," Liam said, "but, like it or not, we may need to eliminate him."

"That doesn't seem necessary," Catherine objected.

"I hate to agree with the demon," Evie chimed in, "except that she and Liam are probably right. Mark's a demon—" Her eyes cut to mine. "—and we know how difficult they can be."

"Hey, I've never actually killed anyone," I protested.

"Not for lack of trying," Jackson tossed off.

"I'm sorry that I tried to kill you," I told him formally. "It seemed the most expedient at the time. I was mistaken." I thought I was mistaken, anyway; I failed, certainly.

"Thank you," he accepted hesitantly. "I guess."

"Evie and Liam are right," Mia said, and several people gasped. I supposed she was usually peacemaker. I knew her kind could use their voices to calm beings down; and bewitch people, but I doubted that was the reason for the gasps.

"You can't mean that," Catherine argued.

Mia ran her hand through her green hair and shrugged. "He's a demon bent on removing threat and consolidating power." She deliberately avoided eye contact with me. This wasn't awkward at all. Not one bit. She continued. "Unlike some—" She threw me a bone. "—I don't think he'd be amenable to backing off."

"We don't know that," Catherine said.

"Besides, folks, planning to kill someone is a crime," Jacob the homicide detective reminded the table. "Let's be clear on this. Our goal is to stop him, not kill him. If he dies in the process, that's different."

"Since Mark texted Barbara before the crash, it would make sense that she would be our liaison to him, so to speak," Evie said. Nods of agreement met her statement.

"We need to get him to admit to causing the crash," Jacob added.

"Or hiring someone to do it," Robin amended, with a side glance at me.

I sighed.

"Will you want her to wear a wire?" Liam asked. Did I hear an undertone of concern?

Jacob shook his head. "Given how you supernatural folks are—" Mia gave him a playful smack on the arm and he smiled. "It's probably better if at least some of us are present, including me. That way, she just needs to get him to admit he did it. Then I can arrest him."

"Sounds so simple when you put it that way," Evie said drily and I laughed. Heads swiveled toward me.

"He's a demon. We don't know his power. It could be passive or active," I reminded them.

Jacob frowned. "What's the likelihood it's active?"

I shrugged. "If he caused the accident himself, then I'd say it's pretty active. If he hired someone, he probably has a passive power. I don't know."

"That's not very helpful, Barbara," Evie taunted.

"Watch the glowing, ma'am," Jacob warned and I realized my eyes were burning red.

"Regardless of his power type, our goal is to get him to admit he caused or ordered the accident. If his power type turns out to be active, you guys can do your thing," I waved my hand dismissively.

"Our *thing* saved Jackson and thwarted your plans," Robin spat out.

"Thwarted?" I snorted. I took an emotional step back. "Look, I get that none of you like me." Except maybe Liam. I hoped. "I appreciate your willingness to help me." And I was a bit surprised to discover that was true. It had been a long time since I felt connected to anyone, even superficially. "We have five days until the election. Five days to stop him. Since I'm in his crosshairs, I'll be our liaison, bait, whatever you want to call it."

"This is starting to be a habit with us," Catherine said with a shake of her head.

"Let's plan on two meetings with Mark," Liam said. "The first one, to explore and build rapport, and the second one, to get an admission of guilt and lower the boom."

Nods of agreement again.

"We'll start tonight." He met my gaze. "I'll stay with Barbara for this one."

A flush crept up my neck and I wondered if the others could see it. "That's acceptable," I agreed, and Liam grinned.

"This is quite a vehicle," Liam commented as he hoisted himself into the Escalade. I ignored the veiled barb and started the engine. It purred in response. The drive from Sun City to my gated community took about thirty minutes; thankfully construction on Summerlin Parkway was finally completed. At least for now.

Liam stared out the window into the dark for the entirety of the drive. I tapped my fingers on the leather steering wheel in time to the 1980s music on the radio. Yeah, I liked my 80s rock.

"Keep it simple," Liam finally spoke once we were seated on the couch.

I raised a single eyebrow.

"I know you know what you're doing," he clarified. "But, you know, when you send the text, keep it simple." He smiled, dimples forming on his cheeks, and I laughed.

"Got it, boss." I found Mark's previous text and started typing.

We need to meet.

We do?

Yes. Tonight.

Where?

My house.

Be there in thirty.

"He knows where you live?" Liam's tone betrayed his concern and irritation.

"He's never been here before. It's public record."

"Hmm, okay."

"What do we do while we wait?"

An unreadable look crossed Liam's face before he responded. "Let's review our game plan."

"When Mark arrives, I'm going to ask him his plan. I'm not going to ask him if he killed the candidates."

"Succinct."

"I try."

We shared a smile.

"I've missed this," I blurted out. Liam and I wore matching looks of surprise before he responded with a ghost of a smile.

"If you could go back, would you make the same choice?" Liam stared intently, waiting for my answer.

I hesitated. Go back 400 years? Our flirtation was always fun, but it wasn't my destiny. "Probably," I admitted and he nodded.

"Have you thought about how you'll ask him?" Liam deftly changed the subject.

"So it doesn't sound like a trap?"

"Something like that."

"I'll just play on his expectations."

"Yeah?"

"If he knows I'm a demon, he wouldn't have expected me to die. He has to figure I'll want to know more. He almost certainly expected me to call a meeting like this."

"At your home?" Liam pursed his lips.

"Less threatening that way. More open."

"Maybe."

"Probably." I shrugged. "He and I have been playing this game a long time."

"Indeed."

That unreadable look passed over Liam's face again. The doorbell rang.

"He's here," I said needlessly.

"I'll hide in the bedroom."

I bit my lip at the image. Liam smiled wolfishly before loping out of the room. I crossed to the front door in seconds, took a deep breath, and opened it with authority.

CHAPTER NINE

Mark Mammon was a handsome man, and knew it. He sidled close to me in the open doorway and offered a sly smile.

"May I come in?"

Taken aback, I hesitated in responding.

"You asked me here, remember?" He winked.

I shook my head. "Of course, come in." I stood to the side and he sauntered past. Hand on my hip, I watched with increasing irritation as he made himself right at home on the living room couch. He crossed one slacks-clad leg over the other.

"Are you coming?"

"Mmm-mm," I mumbled and followed his path.

Heat rolled off of him. I inched back further from him on the couch. His knowing smile snapped me out of it. I was a demon, too. Why was I letting him get to me?

"Thank you for meeting with me," I started. "You must be wondering why I invited you here."

Mark's black eyes stayed on my face, unblinking. Two could play that game. I allowed a bit of red to glow around my pupils. His smile slipped a fraction, but there was no exclamation of surprise. That answered the question of whether or not he knew I was a demon.

"On the night of the bus crash, you texted me. Why?"

"Why wouldn't I?" His look of confusion was convincing. If I didn't know better, I'd believe it.

"You expected me to be on the bus," I pushed.

"We were both supposed to be on the bus."

"Why weren't you on the bus?"

"Last minute change of plans."

"That was convenient."

"For you, too."

"Did you know the driver never hit the brakes?"

A slight rise of his eyebrows was the only indicator that my question surprised him. "How do you know that?"

"Sources. You didn't answer my question."

"I didn't."

That stymied me for a moment. "What changed in your plans to keep you off the bus?"

"What changed in yours?"

I thinned my lips in displeasure.

Mark laughed. "I can do this all night." He leaned his elbows on his knees. "Why do you care about the crash?"

"Why should I care if someone tried to kill me?"

He shrugged. "They didn't succeed."

"No. It's almost as if they didn't know I was a demon and couldn't be killed that way."

Mark rolled with my admission. "Or they had some other intent."

I lifted an eyebrow.

"Maybe the goal wasn't to kill all the candidates. You've been around. You know what the reduction in candidates means. It's easier now. It's just between you and me," he said with a grin. "With only two candidates, one of us will have the majority in the primary election in five days, and then there won't be a need for a general election later in the year."

"Technically, the other names remain on the ballot, this close to the election. People can still vote for any of us, even the dead ones."

He frowned and I smiled.

"You've been around so long and you didn't know that?"

He coughed and my smile widened.

"Besides, possibly someone may still try to kill me. Or you," I added, watching for even the most minute of reactions.

"That's true. Anything could happen."

"You wouldn't happen to know more about it, would you?"

Mark coyly smiled. "What more could I know?"

"Nothing, I guess." I bit my lower lip, an action he didn't miss. "How did you do it?" I finally just baldly asked him.

"Hypothetically?"

"If you wish."

"How would I do it?"

"Yes."

"Wouldn't you like to know."

I stood. "I think we're done here." This was one of those times I wished for my enchanted bullets. Immortal demons could be killed; you just needed the right weapon. He infuriated me.

He rose and smoothed imaginary wrinkles from the front of his navy-blue cashmere sweater. "Thank you for the invitation. This has been… educational."

"Indeed." I walked toward the front door, listening to the sound of his footsteps behind me on the marble.

At the doorway, Mark took my hand and kissed it. "Until next time." I snatched it back, ignoring his grin, and flashed red eyes. "Now, now, Barbara. That's not necessary."

I watched him until he got in his car, then I closed the door. I didn't slam it, though I really, really wanted to. When I turned around, Liam was standing next to the couch, that unreadable look on his face.

CHAPTER TEN

"That went well," I spat out, stalking over to stand beside Liam. His face softened. He took my hands in his, startling me.

"It wasn't that bad. We learned more information."

"Like he doesn't know how local elections work?"

Liam laughed and released my hands. We sat on the couch, knees inches apart. "Yeah, we did learn that," he agreed.

I rolled my head in a circle, releasing tension from my neck. "I don't know why I let him infuriate me. I'm a demon who's been in power here for years." That unreadable look passed again on Liam's face. I considered commenting this time, but it vanished almost as fast as it arrived.

"I understand you're… dissatisfied with how that meeting went."

"That's an understatement."

"No doubt. I think, though, we should focus on what else we learned."

"Ah, that angel positivity," I quipped and Liam chuckled.

"You had that once, too," he reminded me.

I sobered. "That was a long time ago. But, you're right. Although he didn't acknowledge it, I think we're safe in assuming our presumption was correct, given his *hypothetical.*"

"An assumption about our presumption? Say that three times fast," he joked.

A giggle escaped before I could demand he take this seriously. "I don't think I can," I said instead. "You know what I mean!"

"I do," he said softly. The energy between us thickened. I wondered if he could see my desire in my black eyes as clearly as I could see his desire in his blue ones. He blinked and glanced away, breaking the moment. Disappointment flooded me.

Back to business. "We confirmed indirectly he's the killer – or at least arranged the killing. He also suggested I'm still on his hit list. Not that he'd be successful," I boasted.

"You're that confident?"

"When you have a built-in warning system…"

"Of course."

No need to mention I wasn't sure if my precognition was on the fritz. I'd stick with being confident; it was my area of strength, after all.

"I trust you're not suggesting we not worry about him."

"Absolutely not. He's a danger. Possibly to me physically. And politically." Liam and I wore matching frowns. I suspected his frown had a different meaning. No reason to speculate on that now.

"Plus, he could hurt other innocents," Liam reminded me.

"Right, right. Our goal remains unchanged," I concluded.

"I'll speak with Catherine, Mia, and the others. Catch them up on tonight's meeting. Our goal is still to get him to confess. I'll speak with them about how best to approach that, since tonight you basically asked him, and he refused to answer."

"I think we've shown the direct approach won't work. We need to sneak up on him, verbally."

"I'll let you know what they say."

"Thanks. And thanks for being here tonight."

"Of course." Liam offered a crooked smile.

Impulsively, I leaned in to give Liam a hug. He tensed and I began to pull away, then his strong arms encircled me. He felt good. This felt good. An angel and a demon wouldn't have a future together – I had made sure of that years ago – but that didn't mean I couldn't enjoy this time.

"I have to go," he whispered into my ear, his breath warm against my skin.

I pulled back and offered him my own crooked smile. "I know."

"I'll let myself out."

I nodded, not trusting myself to speak. Liam rested his hand against my cheek for a moment before standing. He walked toward the front door, his shoes silent against the marble. I continued staring at the door after he was gone, until the swirling mist informed me of an impending premonition.

CHAPTER ELEVEN

I reclined on the couch, hoping this premonition would clarify what I had seen before. A man appeared in the haze. I frowned. It was the same man as before, still only visible from behind. Dark hair. Feelings of love, hate, power, and betrayal. A frustrated growl slipped out. This wasn't helping. I didn't need a repeat of the prior premonition.

As if hearing my unspoken gripe, the vision faded and a new one appeared. I sighed. Olivia Williams again, blue eyes sparkling, a half-smile on her face. Blue hair contained in a French braid. The smile dropped and Olivia stared, seemingly at me, beseeching me.

To do what?

Olivia turned and walked away. After about ten feet, she stopped. My breath caught in my throat. This was different from last time. She glared at me over her shoulder. When I didn't seem to "get it", she shook her head and gestured that I should follow her. My vision of the image zoomed in and she smiled – before blinking out of existence.

The dark-haired man replaced her. I squished my eyes closed tighter, willing the man to turn around so I could see his face. The mist obscured even the texture of his hair. His head dipped back. In pain? In joy? The image vanished and my eyes popped open.

I realized with a start that I was drenched in sweat. This was an unwelcome development. A frown flitted across my face as I considered this new premonition. The dark-haired man, I still assumed, must be Mark or Liam. I bit my lip in concentration. Maybe I could be more certain if I figured out the emphasis on Olivia. Because the premonition definitely emphasized her.

Olivia's apparent irritation; I assumed that was with me. But why? She beckoned me toward her. Again, the question of why reverberated in my brain. She had been important to my visions before, and here she was yet again. If my precognition was back on track, it was even more important for me to correctly figure out its intention with these images.

Olivia beckoned me. That much was clear. And it was related to the dark-haired man. Given those overriding emotions, especially of hate and betrayal, I felt safe in believing the dark-haired man was Mark Mammon.

What would Olivia have to do with Mark? Like a lightning bolt, if that wasn't too cliché, it hit me. Olivia came to my premonition before when she was being targeted by a hitman. She wanted me to reach out to her… for assistance in removing the source of the hate and betrayal? I ruminated on this possibility.

What if?

I organized my thoughts.

What if the premonition was telling me that Olivia could solve the problem with Mark? I didn't fully know her background. My previous premonition featuring her had never clearly stated her importance. I'd just trusted that she was important.

But I'd heard rumors that Olivia had taken care of supernatural beings in the past. Could she be a contract killer like Evie's sire had been?

I sat up and snapped my fingers. That had to be it. The premonition was telling me to hire Olivia to kill Mark.

A voice at the back of my mind reminded me I had never killed anyone before and that maybe now wasn't the time to start. I stomped on that little voice.

If my visions were accurate again, I didn't want to disregard one. Just because it had gone sideways before didn't mean this was the wrong choice.

With another shake of my head, I walked to my home office to fire up my laptop. The last I heard, Olivia was in New Mexico.

I dashed off a quick email to a contact there requesting information.

That voice in my head reminded me of the disastrous last time I tried to hire a contract killer. My fists clenched on the desk. This time would be different.

A ding announced a new email and I scanned it quickly. My contacts were good. I called the number listed.

CHAPTER TWELVE

"Thank you for agreeing to see me on such short notice," I greeted the blue-haired ethereal woman now seated on my couch. I didn't normally like to conduct business in my home, but that seemed to be the way this situation was staying. A nervous energy trilled through me. Something about this woman… being. I wasn't entirely sure what she was. She wasn't human, I could tell that.

"Thank you for sending the private jet for me," Olivia Williams responded, an odd glint in her bright blue eyes. "I've never traveled on one before. It was an interesting experience."

"It seemed the most efficient. I'm glad you enjoyed it." I paused, taking in her flowing white shift, and regal bearing. She looked like an angel, if I was being honest. A knot formed in my stomach. Was I about to make another huge mistake?

No, I had to trust my instincts. How much to tell her? She stared at me impassively, waiting while I wrestled with my inner thoughts. So serene. Screw it.

"In four days, a primary election for the mayor of Las Vegas will be held. A fatal bus crash reduced the field to myself and one other candidate, Mark Mammon." Her eyes narrowed for a moment at the name. "Do you know him?"

"I do."

Distracted from my purpose, I switched directions. "What can you tell me about him?"

"What do you already know?"

"He's a demon older than I am."

Olivia nodded. "Indeed."

"That's all I really know. I could give you the details of the names my investigator ran down, if you'd like. All it does is confirm those basics. He's a demon older than I am," I repeated.

"Mark… Mammon," she stumbled at his last name, "was friends with Caesar."

I gasped. That made him Roman, as I'd suspected. Also, over 2000 years old.

She held up her hand. "That's all I can tell you."

Interesting that she didn't say that was all she knew. I returned to my original goal. "I understand that you take care of problems."

Olivia gave a Cheshire-cat grin. "That's one way to describe what I do."

Her response threw me. "How would you describe what you do?"

"I reward and punish behavior."

Hmm, okay. "That's an interesting description," I said cautiously, mind swirling. Maybe my sources were wrong?

"What is it you would like me to do?"

I seized on her earlier words. "I would like you to punish someone for his behavior."

She nodded. "Mark Mammon, I presume. For what?"

"For killing the other mayoral candidates."

She tilted her head. "You have proof of this?"

I reddened. "It's fairly well acknowledged."

"It is."

I couldn't tell if this was agreement or simply confirming what I had said. I felt flustered. "I'm also worried that he may still try to kill me," I added. "He implied as much to me." She nodded again. "There's only four days until the election…" I continued before trailing off.

"You would need this situation handled before that deadline."

Once again, I couldn't tell if this was agreement or simply confirming she understood what I had said.

"Your eyes are glowing," she said.

The conversational tone calmed me. "Apologies."

She waved off the apology. "The situation will be handled before the deadline."

"Um, great?"

"I'll be in touch." She grinned again and stood from the couch. "I'll see myself out."

When the door closed behind her, I released the breath I hadn't realized I was holding. I had done it. Mark Mammon would be a problem no more. And then I could get back to managing this city and the paranormal underworld.

CHAPTER THIRTEEN

Butterflies fluttered in my belly and I nearly rolled my eyes at myself. Nervous like a teenage girl before a first date. When Liam texted to invite me to lunch, I didn't even try to deny the thrill that went through me. It dimmed a little at the location choice – *Soprannaturale*, a paranormals-only café near my office. To say a demon would not be welcome there would be an understatement. But maybe Liam didn't know that.

"Are you in the right place, ma'am?" The owner, Antonio DiMaio, greeted me formally and with a strained smile. I glanced over his shoulder to find Liam. He lifted a hand when our eyes met and I gestured toward him.

"Yes, I'm meeting someone," I answered, pointing toward Liam.

Antonio shifted to look behind him and his brown eyes took in Liam. The owner stepped to the side. "Welcome."

It was my first time in the café. Standard wannabe Italian-café style, frankly. Still seemed like an odd choice for Liam. A genuine smile formed though as I began the long walk through the café. Until I passed a large occupied table (were those elves?) and spotted the secluded booth Liam had chosen. A confused frown replaced my smile. Liam was not alone. Catherine, Mia, Robin, Jackson, and Jacob were seated around him. And Olivia. What the—

I plastered a fake smile on my face. "This is a surprise."

"Please sit, Councilwoman," Jacob requested.

I complied, sliding in next to Liam. Tension rolled off of him, mitigating any joy I might have felt in sitting so close. "Councilwoman? I see we're back with formalities," I joked.

"It has come to my attention that you allegedly committed criminal solicitation," Jacob responded.

My gaze involuntarily swung to Olivia, whose face remained impassive, assessing. "Is that so?"

"Don't disrespect us by denying it, Barbara." The corners of Liam's mouth turned down and genuine sadness shown in his eyes.

Guilt flared and I tamped it down. "This is an ambush," I accused him.

"That's one way to look at it," he responded.

"How else should I look at it?"

"An intervention," Mia answered for him, her soothing voice rolling over me.

"Stop trying to calm me," I commanded, feeling my eyes burn. Mia nodded but did not deny the implied accusation. The feeling of calm receded. "An intervention?" The word choice hit me. "Are you helping me choose the right path?" I barked a nasty laugh and aimed a mocking grin at Robin, who flushed. She and I had had a similar conversation recently. Something about how I could choose the path of the righteous. Or some such nonsense.

"You always have choices," Jackson added, with a loaded look at Olivia.

I frowned, perplexed by the missed meaning in that glance.

"Why did you hire Olivia to kill Mark?" Liam asked, a tone of desperation in his voice that further baffled me.

I debated whether or not to admit I committed the… what did Jacob call it? Criminal solicitation.

As if hearing my internal debate, Jacob drily commented, "As an officer of the court, I am ceding our interest in this possible case to the underworld to handle as it sees fit."

"So you can tell the truth," Catherine explained.

I stared around the booth at these people, these beings, trying to understand why any of them cared about this. We weren't friends. Were they just looking for a way to trip me up? My gaze ended on Liam and the hurt there unexpectedly stung.

Why would he be surprised? The memory of our final argument flashed through my mind. After 100 years together, I had grown weary of humanity's stupidity and wanted to do things my way. Liam tried to argue that I was going through a rough patch and things would be fine. But, no. I yelled at him that being an angel was too limiting and I'd rather put my self-interest first. His eyes almost comically widened, his mouth dropped open. A blinding light bathed me, warmth that became sharp like needles across my entire body. The last I heard was Liam crying out my name while I screamed. I awoke in darkness like molasses. Then, I blanked again, waking a final time as a demon. It was glorious. Not answering to the angel bureaucracy. Not worrying if my choices hurt anybody else. Even the pain of losing Liam faded over time to a dull ache. I'd thought I'd gotten over him entirely, until he appeared at my door.

In any event, my hiring Olivia simply reinforced the decision I made all that time ago to follow my own path. I lifted a single shoulder in a blasé shrug. "Sure, why not? I hired Olivia. Well, I suppose to be accurate, I thought I hired Olivia. To kill Mark Mammon," I clearly enunciated.

"I thought we agreed to a plan," Liam protested.

I shrugged again. "I decided to go in another direction."

"Why?" His disappointed eyes searched mine, as if he thought he'd find some answer in their black fathomless depths. Hardly.

"Expediency." My clipped tone brooked no argument and nobody tried. I stood. "Thank you for the invitation to discuss this issue," I stated with a nod at the group. "I obviously did not hire Olivia as I thought I had. And now that I'm on your radar," I directed toward Jacob, "I will not attempt to hire anyone else. I appreciate your concern for my handling of the situation, I offer my sincerest apologies for any inconvenience, and I will handle my issues on my own."

With nary a glance at the table – and especially not Liam – I spun in my sensible shoes and strode from the café. I kept my head held high and avoided eye contact.

The café door closed behind me and I walked to my SUV, the cool spring air nipping at the exposed skin on my face. I considered what had happened. A crushing sense of defeat enveloped me.

Either my precognition was still broken, or I massively misunderstood its meaning. Olivia had some importance I just wasn't getting. And I probably blew any chance I had with Liam. I slammed the door to my vehicle shut. The engine roared to life.

What chance with Liam? That ship sailed hundreds of years ago.

My resolve hardened. I may have blown it with Liam. And I might not have any idea who or what Olivia was. But I could still beat Mark in the primary election and secure my seat and position of power in the paranormal underworld. I had gotten sidetracked by Liam's reemergence in my life and the strange underpinnings of my evolving relationships with the Paranormal Talent Agency folks. That was done. I'd do this my way.

CHAPTER FOURTEEN

Bright set lights blinded me and then lowered. I smiled at the brunette sitting across from me. Her own smile's wattage dimmed slightly. Yeah, my teeth. What's a demon to do? You made sacrifices to your human form.

"Are you ready?" Elizabeth Addison, host of the morning show, *Entertainment Daily*, and sometimes anchor for the news, recovered her smile.

"Always."

She flicked a glance toward her producer and then nodded at me. She faced the camera closest to her. "Good evening, Las Vegas. Welcome to the news at 6." She worked her way through the promos for that evening's show, before sobering.

"Last week, a fatal bus crash rocked the upcoming mayoral election, leaving only two candidates for the primaries, Barbara Knollman, a current city councilwoman, and Mark Mammon, the dark horse challenger. Here to answer questions in advance of what has turned into the most-watched regional election on the West Coast, is current councilwoman, Barbara Knollman." She turned to face me. "Welcome, Councilwoman."

"Thank you, as always, for having me. Even under such unusual circumstances."

"Unusual? Interesting choice of words."

"In my decades in politics, I'm not sure I've ever heard of, let alone been involved in, an election where several candidates were killed. I think that qualifies as unusual."

Elizabeth laughed a fake, newscaster laugh, then grew serious. "Let's talk about those deaths. I understand that you were interviewed by the police following the crash."

"That is correct. Both myself and Mr. Mammon were interviewed. As the remaining candidates—"

"Who were supposed to be on the bus," Elizabeth interrupted and added as an aside for viewers.

"Yes, who were supposed to be on the bus," I continued smoothly.

"Why weren't you on the bus?" Elizabeth interrupted again with her question.

My eyebrows rose but I smiled. "I've given you that information, remember, Elizabeth? The night of the accident."

She lifted her hands in a mea culpa, and continued. "You told me that night that you had a change in your schedule. What was that change again?" She tilted her head and didn't quite hide her smirk.

"As I told Metro, that is confidential campaign information that I am not at liberty to disclose."

"And Metro bought that?"

"Excuse me?" I barely maintained my conversational tone.

"You're the candidate," she said pointedly. "What reason could there be that you couldn't choose to disclose?"

"Not everything is intended for public consumption, as much as you wish that wasn't the case," I chided her with a fake grin. Time to get back on track. "It was expected that we would be interviewed. Metro did a stellar job, as always."

Elizabeth cocked an eyebrow. "Have they arrested anybody, though?"

"That's complicated, Elizabeth. We don't want them to rush into a wrongful arrest."

"Do they have any suspects? Did they clear the other candidate?" She pushed with her questions.

I thinned my lips, as if in thought. This was the opening I was waiting for. "I've been cleared."

"What about Mark Mammon?"

"To my knowledge, he has not been cleared."

"Are you saying Mark Mammon is responsible for the other candidates' murders?" Elizabeth asked salaciously.

With wide-eyed innocence, I held up my hands. "Of course not. I would never be so incendiary as to accuse someone of something so heinous—"

"But?"

I shrugged. "But he and I were the only ones not on the bus. And the citizens of the Valley have known me for two decades." I looked away from Elizabeth's hazel eyes and directly into the camera. "Who is Mark Mammon?"

"And there you have it folks," Elizabeth said to the viewers. "Not an accusation at all, a concern. Do you share the Councilwoman's concerns? Let us know on social media." The brunette newscaster provided the handles for the station's social media accounts. When the producer signaled the live feed ended, she turned to me with a wide smile. "That was awesome. I'll bet our numbers will skyrocket."

"Glad I could help. Thank you for squeezing me in tonight."

And now for the fallout. In three, two, one...

CHAPTER FIFTEEN

"Good evening, Liam. Come on in." I stepped to the side to allow him entry. His blue eyes met my black ones and with a slight shake of his head, he did as I invited.

We sat on the couch in silence for several long moments. Liam stared at me, probably uncertain as to what he wanted to say. I put him out of his misery.

"Liam, what can I do for you?" I smiled to take the edge off of the question.

"I'm worried."

"For me?"

"Of course, for you!"

"I've taken care of myself for literally hundreds of years," I reminded my ex-paramour. "I can manage for the three days until the election."

"Do you not understand you don't poke the beast? He already killed the other candidates!"

"I'm a demon, too. He doesn't scare me."

"He should."

"What do you know that I don't?"

"Nothing, I'm just worried for you." Liam clasped my hands in his, setting off tingles throughout my body in response. He rubbed the tops of my hands with his thumbs.

"Mmm, that feels good," slipped out before I could censor myself.

Liam's eyes dilated in response. We savored the moment before reality crashed back in. "This is what we could have had."

I withdrew my hands. "I know." Had I made the right choice? I'd never second guessed myself as much as I had just in the past few days. I hated it.

"That day when you," he swallowed audibly, "declared you didn't want to be an angel anymore..." Pain shone in his eyes. "I loved you. I thought we'd be together forever."

Stab me in the heart, why don't you? I bit my lower lip. "I loved you too." I shrugged. "Sometimes that's not enough. I made the choice that was right for me." My voice sounded much more confident than I actually felt. When I'd woken up as a demon and realized I'd lost Liam with my choice to reject being an angel... well, let's just say the pain hurt worse than even falling to Hell. But the decision was made, and over the years focusing on myself became even easier. And fun, if I'm honest.

"I'll always care for you."

"You will?"

Hurt glinted in his eyes. "Of course, how could you doubt that?"

"I'm sorry. This has been tough." I was horrified when my voice cracked on the last word. Liam reached a hand toward me and when I didn't pull away, he stroked my cheek with his palm. His skin was rough; I wondered what he'd been doing all these years.

"Please be more careful," he begged me.

"I'm not sure it's in my nature," I said with a laugh, breaking the tension.

"I suppose not." Liam stood and smiled down at me. "I should leave." I stood next to him. "Think about what you really want. Okay?"

"Okay," I promised, but I might as well have had my fingers crossed. I'd chosen this path a long time ago; and I was so close to cementing my control of Las Vegas for both the normal and the paranormal. I wasn't giving that up. Though his being here sure was confounding me. We walked to the front door and I opened it for him to leave. "Goodbye, Liam."

"Until later, Barbara," he responded with a grin.

"Until later," I amended, matching his grin.

I closed the door behind him, stood there listening to his engine start and him backing his car down my driveway. I waited a few more moments, awash with uncertainty.

About to turn away, I paused when I heard tires on the driveway. Had Liam come back?

"I must not be the visitor you were expecting," Mia said, her laughter like tinkling bells.

Guess my poker face was slipping. "What can I do for you, Mia?"

"May I come in?"

"Of course." I repeated my earlier actions and in moments, Mia and I sat next to each other on my couch.

"I'm sure you're wondering why I'm here."

"The thought had crossed my mind."

"I saw your interview earlier this evening."

"What did you think?"

"Seemed risky to deliberately antagonize Mark."

Had she and Liam compared notes? Sheesh. "It's only three more days. I wanted him to know that I'm not cowering, waiting for him to strike." My eyes burned and Mia's expression confirmed I was glowing red. I took a calming breath.

"Why didn't you stick to the plan?"

"Are we going to repeat the conversation from the café? Because that didn't really go well."

Mia appeared thoughtful for a moment. "Barbara, we've had a checkered history."

I chuckled. "That's one way of putting it."

She smiled. "But that doesn't have to determine our future."

"What are you saying?"

"I haven't been around quite as long as you have. And you've been mostly benevolent, if not exactly honest and open."

"I'm a demon," I reminded her, flabbergasted by this continuing insistence I be something I wasn't. Just because a long time ago, I had different priorities. Couldn't people keep track of that? I put myself first.

"You could still work with us and prove Mark guilty. It still ultimately benefits you," she said with a sly look.

"Now that's a better way to entice me," I confirmed flippantly.

Mia smiled but disappointment shone in her eyes. "Olivia—" She abruptly stopped.

"Olivia what?"

Mia shook her head. "She can help with handling Mark."

"Is that all?"

Mia glanced down at her fidgeting fingers.

What was she nervous about not telling me? "Does this have something to do with her telling me she punishes and rewards people for their behavior?"

Mia half-smiled. "Something like that. It's her story to tell, not mine."

These cryptic comments and half-conversations would drive me batty. I nodded rather than demand she tell me. It wouldn't do any good.

"We are in the best position to address Mark Mammon," Mia said. "Please reconsider joining us. For real."

"I'll think about it." And I would. Between my wonky premonitions and my misinterpretations of them, this had become more complicated than maybe it needed to be. I wondered what would come next.

CHAPTER SIXTEEN

"Good grief, my place is starting to feel as busy as The Strip," I quipped at the man standing in my doorway the next morning. "What can I do for you, Mark?"

"May I come in?"

"I don't think that's a good idea."

If it was possible, his black eyes darkened. "I saw your interview."

"And?"

"Seems risky to throw me under the bus like that."

"Pun intended?"

He flashed a wicked grin. "Why would you do that?"

"All's fair in love and war."

"We're at war?"

"We're not in love."

"Not yet."

I belly laughed. "Are you trying to seduce me?"

His smile turned enigmatic. "This is a conversation better had away from prying eyes and ears."

I leaned out past him and looked in the direction of my neighbors' homes. "I doubt anybody cares one way or the other." I sighed. "Fine, come on in."

Seated once again on my couch, entertaining a visitor, I waited for him to state his purpose. We stared at each other, and a strong sense of déjà vu rocked me. What was it with all these folks and their meaningful glances? "What do you want?"

"To win the election."

"Why?"

"Why, what?"

"Why do you want to win this election? Why Las Vegas? Why now? You've been around over 2000 years. If you want power, there are larger regions."

A look of consternation flashed across his face. "Someone's done their research."

"Mm-hmm." No reason to tell him Olivia told me that little tidbit.

"I don't want so much power that I draw unwanted attention," he answered.

"That's it?"

"What's your plan?" he asked instead.

I cocked an eyebrow at him. "To win the election."

"Touché." He laughed. "That's all?"

"What else is there?"

"What about seeing me punished for what I did?"

Mia's visit and entreaty to rejoin them flitted through my mind. "You mean my throwing you under the bus, as you so quaintly put it?"

"Yes." His smile dropped.

"I don't care about any of that," I lied.

"Really?"

"I said what I needed to in order to knock you down a few pegs in the polls. With only two days left before the election, I'm giving the citizens something negative about you." I shrugged. "That's all."

Now Mark quirked an eyebrow. "That's all? Why don't I believe that?"

"Because you're not a very trusting demon?"

He chuckled. "Listen, Barbara. I don't know what the group—"

"Group?"

He waved his hand dismissively. "The ones connected to that talent agency." He looked baffled by the idea of an investigative talent agency and I snorted.

"They're more effective than you might think," I mumbled.

"Anyway, I don't know what they've told you. But they lied."

"If you don't know what they've told me, then how do you know they lied?" I thought my question was rather obvious. Still, Mark's face darkened.

"I can imagine what they've said."

"And you're here, why? To correct the misinformation?"

"They probably told you that Olivia could take care of me, right?" His triumphant smirk told me my shock showed on my face. "They did."

I nodded.

"They're lying."

"They are?"

"Did they tell you who – or rather, what – Olivia is?"

Curiosity got the better of me. "No, they didn't, actually. I presume you know?"

"She's an archangel."

My eyes widened and I leaned back against the couch. "Wow."

"You know what this means, right?"

"Of course," I snapped. "She can send beings to Hell." I slyly smiled. "That's what they meant, then. Olivia will send you back to Hell once they can prove you killed those people."

His face tightened. "Or, they'll send you back."

Blood drained from my face. "They wouldn't."

"Are you sure?"

"They're after you."

"This time. What happens when you do something they don't like?" He stayed silent, no doubt watching the emotions play out across my face.

Was this all a trap? Would Olivia send me to Hell after taking care of Mark? As punishment for trying to get my former minion Robin to kill Jackson? Or even for hiring Olivia to kill Mark? Would Liam go along with that?

"You're here to convince me to work with you, so neither of us gets sent to Hell?" I clarified.

"Yes. I have a plan, but it will only work with your help."

"I'm listening."

"You need to mislead the talent agency group for two more days."

"Until after the election."

"Then, regardless of outcome, you and I can run the paranormal underworld together."

"We're supposed to trust each other?"

"We both have everything to lose if we don't."

"Until the election," I corrected. "Once one of us loses, the winner could easily choose to disregard this agreement."

He frowned. I was genuinely surprised that had not occurred to him. His face smoothed out. "We could make a pact."

Now I frowned. I had never made a pact with a fellow demon before, and wasn't entirely sure how they worked. "I'm not comfortable with that."

"Then what do you suggest?"

"We'll just have to trust each other."

"Sure, I can do that," he said easily.

I hoped I wasn't making another mistake, but holding onto my power was my destiny. I gave up so much, suffered in Hell even, for my destiny. And if I had to make a verbal agreement with another demon to hold on to my power, then so be it. Besides, it stung that the Paranormal Talent Agency group lied to me about Olivia. I couldn't trust them; why not throw my hat in the ring with Mark? I nodded my agreement.

"Here's my plan," he stated, and laid out the next couple of days.

CHAPTER SEVENTEEN

"Thank you all for coming," I greeted the group scattered around my living room, seated on the couch, and chairs brought in from the kitchen. Mark had left an hour earlier after I made my flurry of calls and texts. Liam, Catherine, Mia, Jacob, Jackson, and Olivia stared at me. No Evie, of course; daylight didn't mix well with vampires.

"What is this about?" Catherine asked.

"I met with Mark today." I ignored the gasps in response and held up my hands. "It's not what you think." Well, actually, it was undoubtedly exactly what they thought. Time to disabuse them of that. The best lies contained mostly truth. "He showed up here unannounced."

Liam watched me with hooded eyes.

"He asked me to join him against you."

"What did you tell him?" Mia asked.

"I countered by asking why I should join with him. I wanted to get an idea of his game plan."

"How did that go?" Jacob asked.

"He offered for us to team together to mislead you and, whatever the actual outcome of the election, we'd rule the underworld together."

"Interesting," Robin commented. I looked at her for more. She remained silent, only exchanging a glance with Jackson.

I made eye contact with Liam. This next piece was critical. "He told me that Olivia had the power to send him to Hell and that he assumed that was your plan."

"He did?" Liam asked.

"He did. I was surprised to hear that Olivia was an archangel." I took a calming breath before my eyes glowed red, and switched my gaze to the archangel in question.

"We planned on telling you, Barbara," Olivia explained.

"You did?"

"Yes. Honestly, we weren't sure if you were aligned with us or not," Mia answered.

"Well, after I recovered from my shock, I asked Mark how I could trust him."

"He did try to kill you," Jackson pointed out.

"Not really. He knew the crash wouldn't kill me. But, he had no real answer regarding me trusting him."

"How did the conversation end?" Liam asked this, his casual tone seemingly forced.

"I told him I couldn't trust him and that if I were him, I'd leave town before Olivia had the chance to send him to Hell."

Olivia leaned forward in her chair. "What was his response?"

"At first he tried to argue that he was safe because you couldn't prove he had done anything wrong."

"This isn't a court of law," Jacob commented with a shake of his head.

Olivia was nodding. "True, Jacob, but you all know that Mark is right. Without true belief in his guilt, I am unable to do anything."

"What about past wrongdoings?" Catherine asked.

"That gets complicated," Olivia side-stepped. She looked at me to continue.

"I told him that I intended to assist you in bringing him down. Literally," I added with a twisted smile. "He didn't like that and decided being here wasn't worth all this trouble."

"He did?" Catherine asked, her mouth dropping open.

"He did. I think he's planning on approaching New York. Bigger market and all that," I added.

"Just like the entertainment industry," Catherine chimed in with a laugh. "Sorry, occupational hazard."

"What does everybody think?" Jacob asked the group.

Brows furrowed, frowns surfaced, and several sets of shoulders shrugged. They were definitely not sure. Of me.

Of what Mark allegedly said. I caught myself tapping my fingers against my thigh and stilled them. I couldn't appear uncertain. I waited them out. It was important that they came to this conclusion on their own.

Mark and I had agreed we wanted to buy ourselves some time until the election. If they believed he left town, the little group would disband. And once he and I shared the power, we'd be unstoppable.

Power was my destiny; and my visions told me repeatedly that for my future, even if the details weren't clear, I needed to remain in power.

"Okay," Olivia said. "For now, we should operate as if this is true."

I bristled at the implication, though wasn't too irritated, since technically, I was lying and she shouldn't trust me. Oh the tangled webs we weave.

"Will you be leaving town then?" I asked. Olivia gave me an odd look and I hurried to clarify. "To go to New York after Mark?"

"Not just yet," she answered slowly. "I'll wait and see how the election goes."

Disappointment hit me. Mark and I had hoped that once she believed he'd left town, that she'd follow after.

"Is that a problem?"

"Of course not, Olivia. I would just hate for you to waste your time."

"How magnanimous," Robin sniped.

I glared at her. She needed to get over the whole minion thing; she'd willingly signed the pact with me, I didn't force her.

"It makes sense," Jackson commented. "Since his name is still on the ballot. He could have lied to you. Giving you the benefit of the doubt that you're telling the truth."

I nodded; how to spin this? I wasn't going to convince Olivia to leave, so I needed to show I supported the group. "You're absolutely correct. This late in the election cycle, there's no legal way to remove any names from the ballot. Makes complete sense to just wait."

"Thanks for letting us know," Mia said. "And thanks for joining back with us."

A flurry of guilt rose at her genuineness. "I like to pick the winning side." I ignored Robin rolling her eyes at the comment.

Jacob stood. "Thank you, Councilwoman. We'll be in touch." At this clear signal to the others, they stood and, after putting chairs back in the kitchen, headed en masse toward my front door. Liam held back some. I wondered why.

After the others exited, Liam paused at the door. His foot tapped, a sure sign of his nervousness.

"Did you want to stay?"

Liam wordlessly closed the door and walked to my kitchen table. He waited for me to take a seat before joining me.

"I know this is hard for you," he began.

You have no idea, I thought, but didn't say. "Hmm-mm."

"I caught your little joke at the end, about the winning side."

"That wasn't really a joke."

Liam reached for my hands and I let him. "Maybe not. You're still trying to come back."

"I am?"

"Don't you see that." The earnestness in his tone reignited my guilt over lying. "After all this time, you're starting back down the path of good. Don't you remember the beginning?"

"The 1500s were a long time ago," I said, biting my lip.

Liam chuckled. "They were; and a long way away."

"Not anymore," I corrected. "They have nonstop flights from Las Vegas to Ireland daily now." We shared small smiles.

"You gave your life to save others," he continued, voice straining as he tried to convince me of his argument.

I shook my head, yet didn't remove my hands from the warmth and comfort of his. That day in the village, protecting the children from the marauders, was so long ago. I couldn't lie and say I didn't remember the feeling of dying, Liam dying by my side, bleeding from multiple stab wounds. Then the love of the white light that made me an angel. Liam squeezed my hand in the present.

"Yes. You did, and you are. I know it feels foreign. It'll come back to you."

"It will?" I whispered.

"It's like riding a bike."

"Which I've never done."

"Never?"

"I've been busy."

"Consolidating power," he said, unable to disguise the bitterness. His fingers tightened on mine.

"Something like that," I agreed. Turned out the wish for power hurt when you got cast down to Hell. But only briefly.

"Maybe."

"Yes?" I didn't understand his comment.

"Maybe, when this is all over, we could try again."

My heart soared at the statement. Then it fell down to earth. I shook my head again. "Let's not rehash that old argument. I made my choice."

Liam stroked my jawline with his knuckles. "You did, once. Yes. But you don't have to make the same choice again. You're already making different choices than you have in the past," he insisted.

"True." I leaned my head into his fingers, enjoying the feel of his skin on mine. "Maybe," I finally agreed and a wide smile lit up his face. I thought he might kiss me. Instead, he released me and stood.

"Let's wrap this up so we can move forward."

I nodded, not trusting myself to speak, and followed him to the door. When it closed behind him, I leaned my forehead against the cool wood.

What was I doing?

Could Liam and I really turn back time and try again?

Was Mark lying to me about Olivia?

No, the Paranormal Talent Agency folks confirmed she could send both of us back to Hell.

I had to protect myself. Even if it cost me my heart.

I'd stick with the plan. While it was disappointing that Olivia wasn't leaving town, that didn't change anything. Tomorrow morning, Mark would launch the second step.

CHAPTER EIGHTEEN

"Good morning in the Valley," Elizabeth Addison's cheerful voice greeted viewers to her morning show, *Entertainment Daily*. I lounged on my couch, cup of coffee in hand – black, of course. The camera panned to show a man in a sharp charcoal suit sitting in a blue chair across from Elizabeth. The camera panned back to her now-solemn face.

"As many of you know, Mark Mammon is running against Councilwoman Barbara Knollman for the position of Mayor. The councilwoman came on this show and implied certain things about Mr. Mammon. He is here today to set the record straight." She turned to face him and nodded. "Mr. Mammon, what do you want the viewers to know?"

"First, thank you for allowing me this opportunity to clear the air. And, second, thank you for supporting this city with everything you do." Elizabeth preened at the praise and I rolled my eyes. Oh, get on with it, Mark!

Mark stared into the camera lens, which obligingly zoomed in on his handsome face. "Let me start by saying that this is not an attack on the Councilwoman," he began. "She's as much a victim in all of this as I am." He straightened his not-crooked tie and thinned his lips. "This pains me to say. The bus crash that killed the other candidates was intended for me." His eyes glistened as if fighting back tears.

"Without providing details—" He held up his hand to stop Elizabeth from asking any questions. "—in order to preserve the ongoing investigation, I have been targeted. And lives have been lost as a result. Because of this, I debated dropping out of the race entirely. I would hate for something to happen to the Councilwoman in an attempt to get to me.

"But," and his eyes became steel, "I will not hide from those seeking to harm me. I know I would be good for this city. And whether the citizens of Las Vegas vote for me tomorrow or not, I want them to have that choice. So many of their choices have already been taken away."

The camera switched to Elizabeth. I chuckled at her jaw dropped open. She snapped her mouth closed and smiled grimly. "And, there you have it folks. These are sinister times." The camera pulled back; Mark opened his mouth to speak. Elizabeth jumped in with a finger raised.

"Just one more thing, Mr. Mammon. What does all of this have to do with the paranormal underworld?" She smiled sweetly.

He floundered in his response. "I'm not sure I understand the question."

"I know you're newer to Las Vegas, but you may have heard about my series of exposés regarding the supernatural beings that call Vegas home."

He nodded.

"I've heard unsubstantiated whispers that the city council has something to do with the local governance of these beings."

Having figured out where Elizabeth was going, Mark recovered. "I wouldn't know anything about that, Elizabeth," he responded, voice slick as an oil field.

"Are you denying that there's a connection between the supernatural underworld, the acting industry, and the city council?" she pushed, all traces of a smile vanished. The brunette human could certainly be tenacious.

"I do not," he enunciated. "I simply wish for the opportunity to guide my adopted home to the greatest heights possible."

Elizabeth swung her head to face the nearest camera and grinned. "As many questions as answers. Don't forget to tune in on Friday for my latest *Mythical Being of the Week* segment. Have a wonderful day in the Valley," she signed off and a commercial played.

I wasn't sure what impact those last questions would have, but Mark put on a great show. I figured he'd call in about a minute. I set my coffee mug down on the table just as my phone rang. Perfectly predictable.

"Do you know where that human was going with those questions?"

No social niceties, I saw. "I don't. She exposed aspects of the supernatural underworld last year. And as she mentioned, she does that weekly show. That's all I know."

Mark remained silent. I waited him out. "I wasn't expecting those," he finally admitted.

"That was obvious."

"Gee, thanks."

"You covered well though. After."

"Thanks for throwing me a bone."

"I'm not your cheerleader."

"Definitely not." He chuckled. "You know you're in more danger now."

My attention sharpened. "What do you mean?"

"Even if they didn't watch, I'm sure word will get to that acting group quickly."

"And?"

"They'll think you lied to them about me dropping out of the race."

"In point of fact, I did lie to them," I responded with a laugh. "I'm not worried. They'll more likely just think *you* lied to me. Not that I lied to them."

"What if you're wrong?"

"What's the worst they can do?"

"Olivia can send you to Hell."

"For lying?"

"For evidence that you're connected to me, a killer."

"Right." I frowned. "What do you suggest?"

"Strike first."

"Excuse me?"

"Take care of Liam and Olivia."

I was sure I misheard him. "Did you just say I should kill Liam and Olivia?"

He ignored my question. "Certain steps need to be taken to secure our future."

"Don't you think that's a bit of jumping the shark?"

"This isn't a television show, so I wouldn't worry about it." I heard the grin in his voice.

At least he understood my reference, I groused silently. "Still, it seems unnecessarily dramatic," I argued.

"Do what you want, of course. But, if I'm right…" He trailed off to allow me to fill in the blanks.

"Fine, I'll do it."

"I'm on my way."

"Why?"

"Just in case you need me."

"Why would I need you?"

"What if one of them tries something? Don't you want back-up?"

"Fine," I agreed wearily. "Let's get this over with."

The call disconnected and I stewed in my uncertainty. Was this the right choice? I was a demon after all. Isn't this what we did? Frankly, it was amazing I had made it hundreds of years without killing anyone. Of course, that was because of the power of my premonitions. I frowned and dialed Liam's number. In an hour this would all be over.

CHAPTER NINETEEN

I swung my door open and glared at Mark. He sauntered past me like he owned the place. His overconfidence rankled.

"Make yourself at home."

"I will."

I followed him to the living room and we stood next to the couch. His eyes cut to the revolver on the coffee table and he cocked an eyebrow.

"I decided to go old school," I answered his unasked question with a shrug. Inside, my heart was racing. I could still call this off.

He nodded. "That'll work. Enchanted bullets, I assume?"

"I've had them on hand for years. Never thought I'd actually use them," I answered, though the latter seemed directed more at myself.

"I like it. We can concoct a story about them breaking in and you shooting them in self-defense." He looked around the room. "I'll wait in the bedroom, just in case you need me. But it looks like you're good. How soon will they arrive?"

I glanced at my watch. "Liam will arrive in thirty and Olivia about twenty after that." He frowned. "Did you have somewhere else you needed to be?" His frown deepened at my sarcasm.

"I don't like the delay. They could be planning something."

"I doubt it."

Mark searched my face for a moment before shrugging and smiling. "I'll be in the bedroom, then." He waggled his eyebrows at me and I raised one in return.

"Are you flirting?"

"Not at all," he called over his shoulder as he left the room.

I took my seat on the couch and picked up the gun. It felt heavy in my hands. I knew how to shoot, had learned a long time ago. It had been awhile, though. I hoped it would come back to me. Would this also be like riding a bike, to use Liam's phrase? I pointed the gun forward, sighted the other end of the room. They were arriving separately so I wouldn't have to get off two shots in rapid succession. How close would they need to get for me to increase my chance of a kill with the first shots?

My hands trembled and I lowered the gun to my lap. Maybe they were planning something. If they spoke to each other and realized I requested to see them separately, would they know something was up?

I swallowed past a large lump in my throat. Who was I kidding? I wasn't trembling due to nervousness about them. I was trembling because that voice in the back of my head wouldn't stop screaming that this was the wrong path. Why was I trusting Mark? Why did I believe him that the group would be planning to send us both to Hell? Liam wouldn't do that.

Liam.

My heart constricted at the thought of his death. Especially at my hands. I had loved him once. I inwardly groaned. I loved him still. They say you never forget your first love, especially if it began when you were only teenagers. We'd been like star-crossed lovers; except for instead of staying dead after the invaders killed us during the attack on our village, Liam and I had been elevated to angels for giving our lives to protect others. If we still had a chance…

I shook my head. No, I'd stick with the plan. Swirling mist formed in front of me and I frantically tried to stop it in my head. I wasn't successful. I slumped back against the couch and the vision formed.

I almost groaned aloud when I saw the familiar form of the back of the dark-haired man. Except something new.

He put one hand behind his head and rubbed at the base of his neck. Now I did gasp. That was Liam, not Mark. He began to walk away and the image shifted to Olivia again, bright blue eyes flashing – angrily? – at me. She shook her head, then looked over her shoulder at the retreating form of Liam. When she looked at me again, her eyes glistened with unshed tears. The image vanished and I sat up, wide-eyed.

"I've been wrong this entire time." The words came out a whisper. As I continued, they strengthened. "The feeling of betrayal was me betraying Liam for false power. Love is my destiny. He came back into my life to help me see that." Peace settled over me for the first time since this whole mess began and I knew I finally had it right. "What is wrong with me?"

"Did you say something?" Mark asked from the bedroom.

"I know I'm a demon, but could demons have love too?" I continued in a whisper.

Mark's voice, closer now. "What are you mumbling about?" He must have come out of the bedroom. "Liam'll be here any minute."

I made eye contact with the demon now standing fifteen feet away. I set the gun on the coffee table and stood to face him. "I can't do it."

Mark's eyes glowed red.

CHAPTER TWENTY

The doorbell chimed. I couldn't pull my gaze from Mark's glowing red eyes. He smiled cruelly before turning to walk back to the bedroom. "You will follow the plan." I tried to take a step toward him and deliver an angry retort, but found myself unable to do so.

"What are you doing to me?" I managed to ask this before realizing I no longer controlled my actions. I leaned down to pick up the gun.

The door slammed open with a crash. Liam rushed into the living room.

I pointed the gun at Liam and he held his hands up.

"You're choosing this again?"

I opened my mouth, and could not speak. What was wrong with me? It felt like someone was pulling marionette strings and I had become the puppet. I took a step toward Liam.

Disappointment shone in his eyes. "I thought you were choosing a new path."

Tears filled my eyes. I still couldn't speak.

"You don't have to do this."

With every ounce of willpower I had, I ordered my arm to lower. It shook but did not comply. Liam noticed the movement.

"Barbara, there's still a chance for you. For us."

Tears spilled out of my eyes. Still my arm did not lower.

"I've missed you," Liam whispered. "I thought maybe this time…"

I still didn't respond and his expression hardened. "You chose the power of a demon once before."

I cocked the weapon, my arm steady, despite my renewed attempts to lower it. Anxiety zinged through me. What was going on?

"Wasn't losing your angel status enough. Is power really worth all this?" His voice softened, desperation saturating the words. "Do you really want to return to Hell?"

My finger started to pull the trigger. Liam's eyes widened and the fierce love I had for the angel standing before me surged. I released the trigger and opened my mouth.

"He's controlling me. I can't fight him. He's in the bedroom." I swung the gun away from Liam as my finger pulled the trigger. The bullet shattered a window, glass tinkling when it hit the hard floor. The recoil shoved my shoulder back and the sound was loud in the enclosed space. Liam's eyes cut to behind me.

Liam raced past. My arm holding the gun dropped and I turned to see an enraged Mark emerging from the bedroom. His focus on Liam meant he released me from his hold. Liam raised a fist to punch Mark, but froze. Mental manipulation. Mark had an active power after all.

Mark walked up to Liam and leaned in to whisper. "You think you had this all figured out." Mark glared at me, then a smile split his face. "You, on the other hand, are much stronger than I gave you credit for. Maybe I won't kill you when this is all over."

I started to raise the gun and he wagged his finger at me.

"Don't do it. I may change my mind again and kill you after all."

I hesitated. Was I fast enough to raise the gun and shoot him before he could grab my mind again? If I did, would that give Liam enough time to stop him?

I raised the gun and Mark turned the full force of his power on me. I cried out at the mental invasion. It was like an alien presence in my brain.

Liam pounced, grabbing Mark in a bear hug. The distraction broke Mark's hold over me and I trained the gun on the grappling men. I couldn't get a good shot. Liam got several good hits in – and it was weird to see supernatural beings engaging in fisticuffs, I'll be honest – before freezing again. Mark decked him and Liam slumped to the ground. My arm froze halfway up and Mark smiled lazily at me. He knew he had won.

He stalked toward me like a lion approaching a gazelle. His finger reached out to brush my cheek. He shook his head. "It's too bad. We might have worked well together."

Motion at the front door drew my attention. Olivia had arrived.

CHAPTER TWENTY-ONE

Olivia walked in, absorbing the scene before her. She trained her sights on Mark, ignoring me with the gun. As if she knew…

"Release her," she commanded.

Mark's face contorted but he did not comply.

"Is this how you did it?" My question snuck out during his lapse in concentration. When Olivia looked at me, I realized I distracted her. Mark's eyes glowed red as he swung his head back and forth between me and Olivia. He sneered.

"Trying to keep me talking?"

"Don't you want to gloat," I taunted, "about how you've accomplished all of this under our noses?"

I could practically read his internal debate on his face. He shrugged. "Sure, why not? We have a minute." I noticed that although I could now speak and control myself, Olivia's face had taken on a strained look. Was he controlling her now? He was right. I needed to keep him talking while I figured out if I had enough time to stop him.

When I gestured for him to continue, he grinned. "Yes, this is how I did it. You've seen my power."

"Mental manipulation."

"Mind control. Mental manipulation. You can call it whatever you like. It's effective."

"How did you crash the bus?"

His gaze flicked between me and the frozen Olivia again. "Who has the most control in an accident?"

"The driver."

"Exactly."

My mouth gaped open. "You weren't anywhere near the driver. How could you—"

"I have a long reach," he interrupted my question, the answer a clear threat. He sighed with a shake of his head. "Caesar never understood that, either."

My eyes squinted in confusion. "Caesar? Julius Caesar?" Olivia had said they'd known each other.

Mark chortled. "He wouldn't listen to me, either. So, I took care of him."

My eyes widened. "His own men stabbed him to death," I contradicted.

He cocked an eyebrow. "Did they?"

"Understood." I raised the gun slightly and Mark tilted his head.

"You do understand. I killed the others. You're the last candidate left. When you kill them—" He gestured toward the prone Liam and frozen Olivia. "—that takes care of the Olivia problem. You get arrested and I win the election. Don't worry," he added in a conciliatory tone. "I'll allow you to escape. As long as you leave my jurisdiction."

I nodded. "I can do that." I frowned. "I'm confused about one point."

"Yes?"

"This really can't be all about the Las Vegas region. I know that's what you told me before, but…"

Mark eyed me, made some internal decision. "You're very perceptive, Barbara. This was never about Las Vegas."

"Never?"

His eyes burned in Olivia's direction. "It was always about her. The only being left who could send me back to Hell." I gaped and he focused on me. "I needed help. I needed a distraction. Your silly election did the trick."

My silly election? I formulated my plan. I raised the gun the rest of the way, pointed at Olivia. A calm settled over me. It was now or never. My arm swung toward Mark. He snarled and his control enveloped me. My arm dropped.

It was enough.

"That's all I needed to hear," Olivia stated and strode toward him.

The glowing in Mark's eyes increased exponentially. It hurt to look at him, so I turned my face toward Olivia.

She held her arms outstretched toward him. The glowing bathed her in an unnatural red light but she seemed unaffected.

Mark emitted an inhuman growl, drawing my attention. He raised his own hands.

I started to raise my arm again.

"Don't," came Liam's weak voice from the floor. "Don't."

A white light flowed from Olivia's hands and wrapped itself around Mark like a cobra. It darkened, becoming blue, then violet, and finally a pulsing red. The light appeared alive, but it couldn't be.

Mark's skin rippled, the glow from his eyes dimmed. He dropped his hands, futilely pulling at the strands of light surrounding him. His skin disintegrated showing the beast beneath, only for a moment, before he collapsed to the floor and winked out of existence.

I fully faced Olivia. "You did it. You sent him to Hell," I said, awestruck.

She turned her glowing white eyes toward me and my legs became jelly. I looked to Liam, who was now standing, with a sorrowful expression on his face. He couldn't save me. And I wouldn't ask him to. The gun fell to the floor beside me. I closed my eyes.

"Do it," I told the avenging angel. "I deserve it."

I hoped it wouldn't hurt too much.

CHAPTER TWENTY-TWO

Nothing happened. I opened one eye a slit. Olivia's eyes had returned to their startling shade of blue. She was looking at me with compassion.

Compassion?

"You can open your eyes, Barbara."

I did. "You aren't going to send me to Hell?"

"Do you want me to?"

I seriously considered the question. "No, I don't. Why don't you?"

Olivia crossed the room and took my hands in hers. Light tingling ran up my arms. She released my hands with a chuckle. "Sorry about that. Residual energy."

"I allied myself with Mark. More than once."

"True," she agreed. "But you were different. Are different."

"How so?"

"He was only concerned with himself."

"And that's different from me how?" I heard the bitterness in my voice.

"You had second doubts from the beginning."

"Yes. But, look what I almost did," I whispered, my arm sweeping to encompass the room. I made the mistake of meeting Liam's eyes. They were blank. Whatever feelings we might have been rekindling had vanished.

"But, you didn't," Olivia gently reminded me.

I sunk down onto the couch and buried my head in my hands. "Did you know?"

"That I was his target? Yes."

"How?"

"I've been after him for… some time now," she said with a chuckle. "Whenever I'd get close, he'd go underground or the evidence would magically vanish. He's one of the last elder demons."

"There's a hierarchy?" I snort laughed. "Bureaucracy everywhere."

"I was going to get him eventually. When I heard he was on the ballot, the only rational reason I could think of was that he wanted me to know."

"And the only reason he'd want that would be if he had a plan to take care of you," I completed the thought.

"Exactly."

I frowned. "How could he know I would contact you? Am I that predictable?"

"My guess is he had a backup plan in case you didn't. He probably knew you'd protected me last year."

"Not that you needed protection."

She grinned. "You didn't know that. And Mark thought he was strong enough to manipulate you."

"He was," I said in a small voice.

"Not in the end. He couldn't hold you. You didn't shoot me. I was able to get my confession. You helped with that, Barbara."

I raised my head and nodded. "I did."

"And you didn't have to."

"I didn't." My voice sounded stronger. Maybe this would be okay after all.

"You'll be fine, Barbara," Olivia assured me. "I have to go. Paperwork to file."

"I remember angel bureaucracy. I can only imagine it's exponentially worse as an archangel." We shared a smile.

"Liam, I'll be in touch." And with that, she left.

Liam started to follow, without a glance at me.

"Wait."

He turned, that blank expression still lodged on his face. "Yes?"

"Can we talk?"

A grimace of pain indicated the crack in his façade. The act of speaking appeared difficult. "This might be too much. I thought you turned a corner. Now…"

Tears filled my eyes. "It's too late?"

"I can't, I won't, go down that path again with you." With a sorrowful shake of his head, he continued walking toward my front door.

"Goodbye, Barbara."

A heart I didn't think could still love shattered into a million pieces. After all this time, I finally chose the right path. It was too late. I lost my love. Again.

CHAPTER TWENTY-THREE

The next morning dawned far too beautiful for my mood. April in Las Vegas could be so wonderful. It was the day of the election. Such a tortured twisted road to get here. And I no longer really cared.

I trudged through my morning routine, running through the expectations for Candidate Barbara Knollman. A glance at my clock confirmed I still had a few hours before I was expected at campaign headquarters for monitoring the voting returns.

My mind swirled with the choices I'd made over the past months, years, decades even, but most importantly the past week. So many opportunities to choose the right path. I couldn't fully blame it on misunderstanding my premonitions. They were never clear cut; I knew a being's personality filtered the interpretation of them. Had I continually interpreted them to support my desire for power? Apparently so. And what had that gotten me? Well, I was probably about to win the mayor's seat. There was that.

I stepped out of the shower and grabbed a towel. What could be my next steps? Assuming I won – fairly clear-cut, I mused, given I was the only candidate still alive – maybe I could focus on improving the image of supernaturals, now that humanity knew of our existence. This energized me some.

If I couldn't have love, I could use my powers for good. I barked a laugh in my empty kitchen. A demon doing good. Would wonders never cease.

Breakfast consisted of whatever I had on hand, I didn't even pay attention. Soon I was heading to campaign headquarters. Although not expected for another couple of hours, I didn't want to sit home alone in my sterile house, staring at the walls.

I pulled open the door to the building, catching sight of busy-bee volunteers manning phones and chatting with each other. They were excited, though I wasn't sure how known it was that I was the only candidate left.

"Are you okay?" Lynn Fox, my campaign manager greeted me just inside the door, her expression concerned behind her red-rimmed glasses.

"Why do you ask?"

"Elizabeth Addison mentioned on her show this morning that Mammon was killed – and you were present."

"She did, huh?"

Lynn frowned. "Yes. What happened?"

I debated how to answer, before deciding on a half-truth. "He came to my home, threatening me and several members of the entertainment industry. He was… eliminated. Self-defense?" My inflection suggested I wasn't so sure of that and Lynn's eyebrows rose. She recovered quickly.

"I'm glad you're okay," she stated. "The upside of the crazy last week is that you're the only candidate left. You've got it in the bag."

"Unless they pick None of the Above," I quipped.

Lynn bit back a laugh at my joke. "I doubt they'll do that."

I smiled. "No, I don't think they will."

"What would you like to do?" She glanced at her watch. Results wouldn't be coming in for quite a while, so she probably didn't know what to do with me.

"I'd like to chat with the volunteers about how this election has been for them and what they'd like me to focus on when I win."

Lynn couldn't cover her surprise fast enough. If my disinterest in my constituency had been this obvious, how on earth did I keep getting volunteers, let alone winning elections?

"That'd be great, Madam Councilwoman. Follow me." She turned and I followed.

The next hours passed in a blur of getting to know the various volunteers that I had only smiled at and said hello to in the past. It was gratifying to hear from them what they'd enjoyed and what they'd like to see from me. I could also tell they were happy I was asking their opinions. Why hadn't I done this sooner?

"Okay, everybody, it looks like FOX5 is about to call the election," Lynn announced late that evening. We'd pulled the uncomfortable metal folding chairs around the large flat screen television in one corner of the space. Volunteers munched on finger food. Excitement was palpable in the air. This was kind of fun.

The camera framed Elizabeth Addison following a local car commercial. Her brown hair shined under the lights and she wore her anchor expression. I inwardly laughed; sometimes it seemed she was the only newscaster in town!

"Welcome back to our continuing coverage of the primary elections for the mayor and open city council seats. We'll get to the other seats in a moment. Not surprisingly, we are able to call the election for Mayor. As the only remaining candidate alive, we can confidently state that Barbara Knollman has won in a landslide and will be your new Mayor."

Elizabeth continued to talk, but the cheering volunteers around me drowned her out. People patted me on the back and hugged each other. Congratulations floated around the room. Lynn leaned in to me.

"Congratulations, ma'am," she said with a wide smile.

"Speech, speech, speech." The chanting rose in volume. I noticed a couple of cameramen filming us, the reporters standing just off to the side.

I fixed a smile on my face and held my hands up to silence the crowd. They complied. The cameras and reporters moved in closer.

"Thank you all for all of your hard work. It paid off." Cheers rose again from the crowd, and then silenced. "I would not be here tonight if not for the many people working tirelessly behind the scenes on my behalf.

"Thank you, first and foremost, to Lynn Fox, my campaign manager." I turned toward her. "You kept me going and focused on the right things, right up to the end." I was piling the manure a little high, but it was expected. I then proceeded to thank some of the lead volunteers, and the group more generally. After the applause died down, I paused, my smile dipping for a moment. Tension increased in the room.

"For the past months, a new world has been identified here in Las Vegas," I started, my voice quiet, though building steam. "What has been dubbed the paranormal underworld." I ignored the gasps from the audience. I was way off-book.

"I am familiar with this underworld." The gasps were louder. "I plan to ask Elizabeth Addison to have me on her show tomorrow morning, to discuss the rumors and misinformation that has been swirling for these past months. I hope you will all tune in. Thank you." You could hear a pin drop in the absolute silence that followed my statement.

I nodded at the crowd, at Lynn, and strode to the back office, the blood pounding in my head. This was a bold move. I heard my cellphone vibrating on the desk.

I closed the door behind me and answered my phone. "Hi, Liam."

"That was some speech."

"Did you like it?"

"I have mixed feelings. What are you playing at?"

That stung. "I'm not playing. Supernatural creatures are only nominally out of the closet. I aim to change that."

"Why?"

"What do you mean, why?"

"What's in it for you?"

"That's unnecessarily harsh," I snapped, then softened my tone. "I told you. I'm making new choices now. I had a premonition last year—" I stopped. Mist had begun swirling before me.

"Barbara?"

"Liam, I have to go." I ended the call, vaguely aware he was still speaking. I closed my eyes to focus on the image forming.

A dark-haired man, seen from behind, though I knew without question it was Liam. The man turned to face me, his face open yet questioning. He looked to the side and Catherine came into view. I wondered if this was related to me thinking about the prior premonition. Liam nodded at Catherine, who seemed perplexed. She closed her eyes and when she opened them, I gasped.

White light glowed from within Catherine. Liam nodded and seemed to stare at me. He approached, reached out a hand. Even though premonitions didn't come with tactile sensations, I swore I could feel his fingers on my cheek. He smiled, nodded again at Catherine, and turned away. I felt hollow as I watched him walk further and further until I could no longer see him.

Catherine blinked and the white light vanished. Peace surrounded her. That didn't make sense to me, yet I knew it to be true. She also smiled at me, then turned to follow Liam, walking until she too vanished from the premonition.

Where were they going? Why was Liam following Catherine? Was the premonition telling me he would be on her path?

Whatever that was.

I opened my eyes, and gasped when I saw Liam standing there, an uncertain expression on his face. I held onto that peace from the premonition and smiled at him.

"Is everything okay?" he asked, a frown playing on his lips.

"It's good that you came," I answered.

"It is?"

"I know what to do now."

CHAPTER TWENTY-FOUR

Liam stepped fully into the office and closed the door behind him. He hesitated.

"Please have a seat."

He did and we stared at each other for a beat.

"Putting aside your doubts about my motivation, what do you think about supernatural beings being more visible? Being truly considered in the world."

"I'm honestly not sure, given how humanity sometimes reacts to individuals different than themselves." He shrugged. "Remember the clashing that killed us hundreds of years ago. But, this may be the new way of things."

I nodded. "I agree. I believe there could, should, be more for us."

"What do you propose? What do you plan to say on the show tomorrow?"

"Let me back up a bit first."

He nodded.

"Last year, I had a premonition of the importance of Catherine Rodham to my future. Or what I thought was my future. I believe I misread that premonition."

"You do?"

I reddened. "I've been misreading a few of them of late," I admitted and a small smile formed on his face in response. "You realize I was experiencing another premonition when you arrived?"

"I assumed. I wasn't sure why you disconnected the call—"

"Were you worried about me?"

"Maybe." He coughed. "When I walked in, I recognized that blank stare," he hurried to add. The premonitions had started when we'd been given angel status, and Liam had watched me have them for a hundred years.

Oddly, they hadn't stopped when I'd been struck down as a demon after telling Liam in a fit of anger that I was tired of humanity and would rather pursue my own interests as a demon rather than continue as an angel. Maybe a piece of my angelic nature still remained.

I rather liked that thought, but that was a consideration for another day. I stilled my wandering thoughts and focused on his questioning expression.

"The premonition tonight also featured Catherine."

He quirked an eyebrow.

"I'm not entirely sure what it meant." I hesitated.

"But you have an idea?"

"I'm almost certain it is related to bringing the supernatural world fully into the realm of humanity."

"How come?"

I hesitated again. "I'd rather not say. In case I'm wrong again."

We shared a smile.

"There was more," I continued, tapping my nails on the desk. His expression told me he recognized my nervous fidgeting for what it was.

"Yes?"

"You were in the premonition." His eyes dilated, his desire surprising me.

"I was?" he asked.

"Yes." I dropped my gaze, gathering my courage. "My victory tonight was hollow." I raised my head. "I know one piece is what I plan to speak about tomorrow. However, the premonition tonight confirmed something else."

He remained silent.

"I love you." He frowned. Not the reaction I hoped for. "I've always loved you."

"Love was never our problem."

"I agree. My choice of power over love was. Has been." I cleared my throat. "I want to change that."

"How?"

"I know you said that you couldn't walk this path with me again. And, if that remains the case, I won't bother you further. If you're open to it… if it's not too late, I would like to try again. I made the wrong choice before. And I made the wrong choice with Mark. I won't blame it on my premonitions. Those were mine to interpret, and I chose interpretations that fit with my lust for power. But, when the announcement was made that I'd won tonight, I didn't care. My greed for power blinded me to what was real." I stopped.

"How do I know this isn't just a blip?" His words questioned. His open posture said he was listening.

"As a show of good faith, I'll resign my position as Mayor."

"You just won," he reminded me.

"I'd stay on long enough for a smooth transition. You're stalling."

"I am."

"Why?"

"My heart tells me to jump at this chance. My brain tells me I'll be burned again." He half-smiled. "No pun intended."

I belly laughed at the reference to my glowing eyes, startling Liam. "That's why I'm offering to resign. I want you to know that I'm all in this time. Forever."

"On one condition. Tell me why you changed your name to Barbara?"

"That's your condition?" I shrugged. "Having the name of a pagan goddess seemed wrong as a demon."

"I liked Brighid."

"As did I."

"I like Barbara, too," Liam admitted.

"I'm glad, since it'd be awkward to change it back at this point."

"Okay."

"Okay?"

He stood and walked around the chair to stand over me. His hand cupped my chin and I leaned in to the touch. "I'll accept that your name is Barbara, not Brighid, going forward."

"Is that all?" I whispered.

"It's not too late for us. I've been waiting hundreds of years for you to come to your senses."

"Even though I'm a demon?"

"What's a relationship if it doesn't have some challenges?"

I stood and we embraced, his warm arms encircling me. I inhaled his scent, reveling in how good he felt. "I'll let the Council know immediately of my resignation."

Liam held me at arms' length. "You don't need to resign."

I pulled fully away with a shake of my head. "I appreciate that, but I do. I don't want to be tempted down the wrong path again."

"I don't believe you will," he countered.

"You don't?"

"I don't. You haven't talked about helping others since you lost your angel status and became a demon. I believe you've truly turned over a new leaf with your goal of developing human-supernatural relations."

"As do I," came a female voice.

CHAPTER TWENTY-FIVE

Olivia stood five feet from us, in all her blue-haired archangel glory. She smiled benevolently. Somehow I wasn't surprised she could materialize. No wonder she'd never ridden on a private jet before, I thought with an internal chuckle. She walked toward us, so graceful she appeared to be gliding. Heck, maybe she was.

"You do, too?" I asked.

"I do."

"Why?"

"Besides the reasons Liam gave? Because I've been watching your evolution, and you're ready."

"You've been watching me?" I asked, ignoring the rest of her statement.

"Of course. When you chose power over love, I was the one who stripped you of your angel status and relegated you to living as a demon."

My hand flew to my mouth, but nothing emerged. My eyes cut to Liam's similarly surprised expression.

Olivia grinned. "Guess you guys didn't know that."

I shook my head.

"I also was the one who elevated you both," she said.

"That shapeless light Liam and I saw? That was you?"

"Yes, it was."

I met Liam's eyes. That light was the last thing either of us remembered before waking up as angels. Olivia really got around. I wondered idly how long she'd been around.

"This was always going to be your path," she continued.

"Destiny?"

"Something like that?"

"Don't we have free will like the humans?"

"Of course."

She didn't even hesitate stating these completely contradictory statements. I frowned.

"I know it doesn't make sense." The unspoken *to you* made me smile.

"I'll accept it as gospel."

Olivia snort laughed. "Nice."

"I'll be here all night."

"You've reached the point where it is time for a chance. Though—" She clasped her hands together. "—I don't know if I should tell you this."

"Please. At this point, I'd like to know everything I possibly can."

"You might not like it," she warned.

"What could be worse than existing as a demon worried about being sent back to Hell?"

"Ah, yes." She released her hands and played with the sides of her flowing sage dress.

"Is it that bad?"

She searched my face, found what she was looking for. "You always could have chosen a different path."

A sense of confused disappointment filled me at her statement. "Well, yes." Was I missing something?

"You always could have chosen love over power," she clarified.

I tilted my head, still not understanding.

"And restored your angel status."

The weight of her statement slammed into me and my breath caught in my throat. "I could have chosen love to become an angel again at any time." She nodded. "And by choosing love now, I can be restored to angel status?" I scarcely believed it possible. Although it pained me some that I had wasted all these years, until this exact point in time, I honestly never would have chosen a different path. I thought I had chosen the correct one all those years ago.

"What happens now?"

Olivia's eyes glowed white in response to my question. The light wrapped around me, and I cried out. Not from pain, but from the love enveloping me. The light became opaque; I existed in a shell of light. Rhythmic pulsing, pleasant and insistent, synched with the beat of my human heart. It slowed to a stop – was I dying? I didn't believe this had been a trick.

Before the question had fully formed, my heart started again. Slow, even beats. The light thinned and became translucent, before fading away. I stared through renewed eyes at Olivia and Liam. It was difficult to explain. My vision seemed clearer, everything seemed brighter. Even the air smelled better. My gaze flicked between the two.

"Am I an angel again?" I wondered if that meant I had regained my youthful appearance and my hazel eyes.

Olivia nodded and a single tear tracked down Liam's cheek. There was my answer.

"Welcome back, Barbara," Olivia hummed. Even my hearing was different. Crisper, yet softer. Was it like this when I was an angel before? I couldn't remember. The darkness of my demon existence crowded the rest out.

"Thank you," I whispered.

Olivia shook her head. "I merely did what was necessary. You made the choice."

"Thank you, anyway."

"You're welcome. Do you have any other questions?"

I started to shake my head no, then stopped. "Yes! In my premonitions, I saw Liam. I've figured out what that meant." Liam and I exchanged smiles. "I also saw Catherine Rodham. And, I saw her last year. She seems to be very important. Except I'm not sure what the premonitions mean. Last year, I thought she was important in my quest for power in this region." I held my hands up in question. "Now I have no idea."

"She was important in your… quest. Just not for power." Olivia smiled her Cheshire-cat grin. "And she remains important. Everyone is still on the right path and the end is nearly here."

"What does that—"

Olivia dematerialized before I could finish my question. "I guess I'll have to live without that answer." I looked at Liam and he shrugged.

"I have no idea. Archangels don't share the grand plan with lowly angels."

"You're not lowly," I teased while walking to him.

"We're equal now."

"Equally lowly, I guess."

"This has been a crazy ride." Liam took my hands in his, kissed the tops of both. He released them and leaned in for a hug, his fingers twining in my long full locks of chestnut brown hair that fell around my shoulders.

"It has," I whispered into his ear.

"Let's not worry about any grand plans today." He kissed my cheek, nibbled on my ear lobe.

"What should we think about?"

"Getting to know each other all over again," he said, his voice raspy with desire.

"That sounds like an excellent plan," I agreed.

His lips found mine, and I moaned in response. We had centuries of missed love to make up for.

EPILOGUE

Elizabeth Addison and I sat side by side on the familiar blue chairs on the set of *Entertainment Daily*. Her tilted head distracted me from romantic thoughts of Liam. I could tell she'd been wanting to ask me questions since I arrived. I was moderately impressed that she had so far contained herself. Of course, maybe she just wanted to surprise me once the cameras rolled.

I gave her my widest smile, which she mirrored before remembering she wasn't supposed to like me. After all, she wasn't privy to what had happened yesterday. It amazed me that everything happened only yesterday.

"In thirty, Liz," a faceless voice in the dark of the studio informed her.

When the countdown finished, Elizabeth flashed her perfect chicklet-teeth smile at the camera. "Good morning in the Valley! Welcome to *Entertainment Daily*. I'm your host, Elizabeth Addison." She leaned forward in the chair, like a co-conspirator. "I have a special treat for you this morning. As most of you know, yesterday Barbara Knollman won the election for Mayor of Las Vegas. Today, she is our guest." Elizabeth swung her gaze to mine and her smile became predatory.

"Let's get this first part out of the way," the host stated.

"Yes?" I knew where she was going but I wanted her to work for it.

"You look different."

"Hmm-mm. I do?"

"Don't be coy," she said, wagging her finger at me. She meant to be playful, I'm sure. "I know plastic surgery isn't that good, or that fast," Elizabeth commented with maximum snark.

I laughed, my laugh genuine and not rude. Her smirk faltered. "You are correct, Elizabeth. And, I'm not laughing at you. I promise." I took a deep breath. "I am different. That's part of why I'm here today."

"Tell the viewers everything," she encouraged.

"Do you know why I wanted to do my first interview after the election with you?"

"Because I'm the best newscaster in Las Vegas," she answered with a wink at the audience. "In all seriousness, I do not." And to her credit, she actually looked curious.

I nodded. "Because of your *Mythical Being of the Week* segment."

That shocked her. "Really?"

"Yep." I stared directly into the camera and took another deep breath. "I used to be a demon."

"I'm sorry, what?"

"I used to be a demon," I repeated. My gaze swung to hers. "When you first exposed the paranormal underworld here in Las Vegas, we weren't sure how it would go."

"We?"

For a newscaster, I was surprised she was struggling to keep up. "I have the ability to see the future." Elizabeth's eyes bugged. "I foresaw that your report was the right path for us."

"Thanks?"

"At that time, I was still a demon."

Elizabeth eyed me uneasily.

"Don't worry, I'm an angel now. That's why I look twenty years younger."

Gasps sounded from the dark of the studio. Really? *I'm an angel* gets gasps, when *I used to be a demon* didn't. Or was it that I looked twenty years younger. Hmm.

"I'm sure you're wondering why I'm disclosing all of this on live television."

"Among other questions," Elizabeth quipped. I was pleased she'd recovered. We needed her investigative skills for the next piece.

"What most normals don't know is that the head of the city council is also the head of the paranormal underworld for this region. And we have one of the top regions in the country."

I could practically see Elizabeth's mind processing and identifying more questions.

"Everything you've said on your segment, thus far, has been correct. Thank you for helping supernatural beings begin the transition to living fully in the open."

"That's the goal?"

"It is."

"Some of those beings have been pretty destructive."

"Indeed, they have. But, is it so different from a human who kills his neighbor, or a serial killer who takes out many?"

I saw the memory of the serial killing genie from a couple of months ago flash in Elizabeth's eyes. She nodded. "Supernatural beings have more… abilities at their disposal."

I shrugged. "Is it really so different from someone who has a high-powered machine gun, or highjacks a plane?"

She frowned and I held up a hand.

"My goal today is not to hash out all of the challenges of an integrated society. I simply wanted to confirm for your viewers that what you've been saying is the truth, and disclose my role in it in the past and going forward."

Elizabeth held my gaze for a second longer before turning to the camera. "There you have it. An ex-demon, current angel, now holds the dual title of head of the city council and head of the paranormal underworld. The next few months should be interesting, to say the least." She smiled a final time. "Thank you for tuning in – and know that we'll report back every step of the way on this explosive new development."

The camera shifted down, no longer in use, and Elizabeth faced me again. I ignored the murmurings I heard in the studio.

"Thank you for allowing me to be here," I said.

"Are you kidding? I just scooped the biggest story of my lifetime. Of several lifetimes," she crowed.

"I'm glad you feel that way, because I have one more thing."

"More than what you just said?" she asked with a raised eyebrow.

I grinned. "In my visions, I've seen Catherine Rodham repeatedly," I began.

"She doesn't like me so much anymore," Elizabeth admitted.

"I know, but that can change." I leaned closer to whisper. "Another supernatural being told me that Catherine has an important role to play."

"In what?" she whispered back.

"I'm not sure. I believe she's critical to what we're trying to build here."

Elizabeth's eyes gleamed. I had her hooked. "And you want my help to investigate?"

"You're the best. And, you've consistently demonstrated an open mind."

"I'm in. Let's figure out our plan." We grinned at each other.

Turn the page to learn the final truths in the exciting conclusion to the Paranormal Talent Agency series!

Episode Six

The Season Finale

CHAPTER ONE

Television reporters get used to being eyed with suspicion, but usually, those doing the eyeing are human. Not this time. I didn't think. The attractive man had stared at me the moment I entered the café. *Soprannaturale*, where all the nonhumans hung out. I glanced around at the framed pictures of pastoral Italian scenes and classic checkered tablecloths on two-tops scattered throughout the front of the café. Stepping closer to the man, the scent of flowers and earth reached me.

"You smell sweet," I blurted out. "Is that some kind of cologne, or an essential oil you're diffusing?"

The man's eyes widened, then narrowed. "May I help you?"

Refusing to be thrown by his non-response to my question, I smiled wide and extended my hand. "Elizabeth Addison, reporter," I introduced myself, smile faltering when he hesitated. An imperceptible sigh and then his large hand engulfed my smaller one. Breath caught in my throat at the tingles that raced through my body. I snatched my hand back and he smirked.

"Antonio DiMaio. Owner of this fine establishment." His chocolate-brown eyes took in my appearance, a bit bedraggled due to a short rain. Contrary to the public perception of living in the desert, it rained in Las Vegas. And since it was spring, well, it had rained while I walked from my car to the door of his fine establishment.

I attempted to smooth down my short, curly brown hair, frizzy from the humidity, and then ran my hands down the sides of my simple blue shift. Antonio's eyes followed the movement, the smirk morphing into something more complex.

His eyes snapped back up to mine. "May I help you, Ms. Addison?"

"Please, call me Liz," I responded by reflex.

"Then call me Tony."

I nodded. "Tony. I'm meeting Catherine Rodham. Do you know her?"

"Because all supernaturals know each other?" he asked, smirk back in place.

I flushed. "No." A smart retort didn't come to me, because now I wanted to know what type of creature he was. Given my instant attraction, I wondered if he was an incubus. I'd learned from Catherine last year that they could control you by sucking out your soul. Yuck. Though she swore her half-incubus boyfriend Alex didn't do that.

He chuckled, his rumbly voice sexy. "Relax. I'm just teasing you."

Was he *flirting* with me? His comment did not help me relax. If anything, my flush deepened. He ran a hand through his longish wavy black hair and smiled, a dimple appearing on his right cheek.

"But I do know Catherine," he admitted. "She isn't here yet."

"I'll wait for her before being seated." I took the opportunity while I waited to consider his sinewy muscles flexing underneath a simple black shirt and pants. Probably his work uniform. His appearance placed him maybe late-twenties like me, but with supernatural beings, who knew? I desperately wanted to ask what he was, but that had to be a faux pas.

"Did you have any questions?"

My eyes widened. Could he read minds?

"About the menu," he clarified, though I didn't miss the quick smile.

If he was going to flirt with me, then I would be bold. "I do have a question." Our eyes met. "Not about the menu."

He tilted his head. "Ask away."

"What are you?"

"Not fully human."

I shook my head. "That's entirely unhelpful."

"I know."

"Are you flirting with me?"

His eyebrows lifted in surprise. "Do you want me to flirt with you?"

My mouth dropped open, but nothing emerged.

He laughed. "I like you, little human."

I bristled.

He held up his hands in surrender. "It's a term of endearment where I come from."

"Where are you from?"

"Originally Italy."

"When was that, Tony?"

"Nice try, Liz."

"It was worth the shot."

"I have a question for you," he said.

"I'm fully human."

Tony threw back his head and belly laughed. "That's not in doubt."

"How would you know?"

"I know."

"That's mysterious."

He smiled. "As a human," he started, "how did you even know about my café?"

A voice answered from behind me. "I'd like to know that as well."

CHAPTER TWO

"Catherine, thanks for meeting me here," I responded. Hmm, she wasn't alone. Mia Fynn stood to the side of the tall, blond talent agent. "Hi, Mia."

She smiled uncertainly, her bright green eyes wary. "Hi, Liz."

Mia and I had even more history than Catherine and I did; we'd worked together to solve a series of murders, and it turned out to be a crazy djinn (that's a genie to most humans). I'm not sure why they were surprised when I put being a reporter first. It was my job. That's what I did. Still, I knew they felt betrayed that I played an instrumental role in exposing the paranormal underworld at the end of last year. In my defense, we all later learned that this was a good thing. *Why* it was good was part of my current mission.

"Barbara Knollman told me about the café," I explained to the three of them. The new mayor had turned out to be a former demon, current angel, head of both the human city council and the paranormal underworld. That had all blown my mind when I learned it last week. And, then when Barbara made her request… well, that's why I was here. I turned to face the dreamy café owner. Wait, dreamy? No way was I getting involved with a supernatural. I don't care how good looking and flirtatious he was.

"I guess we'll need a table for three," I told Tony.

"Right this way." The three of us followed Tony to the back of the café. I tried and failed not to appreciate his rear assets. My eyes rolled of their own accord at my ridiculousness. We sat in the green vinyl-covered booth he indicated. When my eyes met his, he waggled his eyebrows at me. Did he know I was checking him out? How? Now my reporter-sense was twitching. I'd find out what manner of supernatural he was eventually. Right now, I had more important matters. I finger waved goodbye at Tony and he sauntered away.

"Not that it isn't good to see you, Mia, but why are you here?" I asked bluntly.

Mia laughed her tinkling laugh, shaking her head, green hair moving with the motion. She was a nixie, kind of like a mermaid, though don't tell her that, and could bewitch people with her voice. I knew that firsthand. "Catherine doesn't trust you," she answered and I flushed.

"I was just doing my job."

Catherine held up a hand to stop us from continuing. "It doesn't matter. Why did you want to meet with me, Liz?" Genuine curiosity shown in her blue eyes, so I hoped the truth would pull her in. I knew better than to lie. She was a natural lie detector; I guess you could call that her superpower.

"You saw the interview I conducted with Barbara last week?" Two heads nodded in response. "After the interview, Barbara asked for my help with an investigation." Catherine's expression became more guarded. "She wants me to investigate you, Catherine."

The object of my investigation sighed and Mia glanced at her quizzically. "She's telling the truth," Catherine told Mia. Guess her lie detector could tell I wasn't being deceitful. Catherine held my gaze. "Barbara has hinted that I'm somehow involved with the supernatural underworld since I moved to Vegas last year to start the talent agency."

"You have no idea why?"

"No." I heard the frustration in her voice. "Trust me, I'd love to know. A lot of stuff happened that might have been avoided if I knew." Her expression turned thoughtful. "Barbara still doesn't know? Even though she's been elevated to an angel again?"

I shrugged. "Apparently not. She said you're the key to something big. That's what she wants me to investigate."

"Why you?" Mia asked and I tensed, but her body and expression remained open. That wasn't a dig at me.

"Maybe because I've been covering this story from the beginning?" I laughed. "She did mention my awesome *Mythological Being of the Week* segment on *Entertainment Daily*." I hosted the top-rated entertainment morning show in Las Vegas, and once I unearthed some paranormal secrets, I had found my calling. Audiences ate it up.

Catherine rolled her eyes. "Yeah, that's a great segment."

"Sarcasm?"

"Of course not."

We stared at each other for a beat before she sighed again. "I know you're telling the truth. I want to know what's going on, too. So, I guess we can work together." She bit her lower lip, but I grinned. She might not be happy, but it thrilled me to be on the front line of another paranormal scoop.

"You'll help, too?" Catherine asked Mia, who was already shaking her head.

"I'd love to, Catherine, you know that. But I have a new movie going into production—"

"Say no more," Catherine interrupted her. "If you say I can trust Liz enough—"

"Hey!" This time I cut Catherine off. "No need to be rude."

"I wasn't being rude, Liz."

Mia giggled and a sense of calm wrapped the table.

"Watch it with the bewitching," I warned the nixie.

"Sorry," she said, though did not seem sorry. "I didn't want you guys to get off track." She stared at Catherine. "You'll know if she's lying. I wouldn't worry about it."

"True."

I clapped my hands in delight and the women smiled. "This will be exciting. I can't wait to find out what the heck makes you so important." I mean, yes, she knew if someone was telling the truth or not, but she didn't have *real* powers. I didn't think. Hmm.

The ladies distracted my wandering thoughts by exiting the booth. I hurried to join them.

"I wish you both luck," Mia said. "Please let me know if I can do anything. I'll miss working with you on this."

A pang of regret hit me. We had fun investigating those murders. I genuinely liked Mia. And Catherine, I supposed, though I didn't know her as well. My mouth opened to respond, but thick white smoke filled the area before us.

Blocking the way out.

CHAPTER THREE

Fear filled me at the thought of being trapped in a fire, though my brain was already registering that I felt no heat and could still breathe. The smoke swirled and began to take shape.

"Are you guys seeing what I'm seeing?" Catherine whispered.

I nodded and heard a murmur of agreement from Mia. Noises from others in the café sounded distant somehow. Like there was a barrier between us and them. The smoke, maybe.

The smoke coalesced then cleared, leaving behind a woman. She seemed late twenties with average height and weight. She had long red hair and blue eyes. And wore a jumpsuit of some kind. A pantsuit? But like a onesie. My brain went on a mad scamper to identify her unusual outfit. Then her mouth opened and my brain froze.

"Stop," she whispered. Her wild gaze flicked between the three of us. Like she was trying to figure out who we were.

"Stop what?" Mia asked.

"Stop," the woman repeated. She appeared confused.

"Who are you?" I tried. Her eyes focused on me and then widened.

"Elizabeth Addison," she answered instead.

Something uncomfortable flared at the idea this woman who just appeared in the café knew who I was. "Yes," I confirmed. "Who are you?" I repeated my question.

"Stop the investigation."

My eyebrows lifted. "Stop what investigation?"

"When am I?" the woman asked instead, turning her head to take in her surroundings.

"Do you mean, where are you?" Catherine asked.

The woman lasered in on her. "Catherine Rodham."

In the periphery of my vision, I saw Catherine nod.

"When am I?" the woman repeated.

"April 5, 2019," I answered.

The woman blew out a frustrated breath. "I was hoping to stop your broadcast."

That was clearly directed at me. "Which broadcast?"

"I tried to get to you before the broadcast, but I timed it wrong," she continued like I hadn't spoken. She shrugged. "It's not an exact science."

"What's not?" I asked.

"Time travel."

Said so matter of fact, I almost believed I'd misheard. "Time travel?"

"When are you from?" Catherine asked. Guess her lie detector told her the woman was telling the truth – or at least believed she was. She did materialize out of thin air, so there was that.

"2219."

Silence greeted the date she provided, our brains processing the idea that the woman standing before us had traveled 200 years back in time. To get me to stop my broadcast. Of what? I zeroed back in on that, glad to give my brain something concrete to focus on.

"Which broadcast were you trying to stop? What story did you not want me to tell?"

The time traveler took a step toward me and it was all I could do not to flinch away. Her intensity was intimidating. "You need to stop investigating Catherine Rodham and you need to prevent the integration of the paranormal and human societies."

A nervous laugh bubbled up. "Oh, is that all?"

The woman frowned. "This is a joke?" Her eyes flashed and now I did take a step back.

"No, it's not a joke," Mia jumped in, attempting to smooth things over.

"Your bewitching will not work on me," the woman informed Mia.

"Who are you?" I asked. This was ridiculous. She was crazy or a paranormal, or both, but it was time to figure that out.

"My name is Rowan Walsh and I died in the year 2219."

Catherine, Mia, and I exchanged startled glances.

"I'm sorry," Catherine said, "did you just say you *died* in the year 2219?"

The woman nodded.

"You're not just a time traveler, but a time traveling ghost?" My question squeaked out. This meeting had taken a very unexpected turn.

The woman, Rowan, nodded again.

"And you're here to stop us from figuring me out—" Catherine began.

"Yes," Rowan interrupted.

"And to keep Barbara from integrating human and paranormal societies?" I finished Catherine's summary question.

"Yes."

"Why?" The reporter in me wasn't about to stop investigating on the say-so of an alleged time traveling ghost. I mean, really.

"If you don't, many people will die."

"Oh." Hmm, many people dying wasn't so good. "Are you sure?"

Rowan's blue eyes flashed again, hard like ice, and I shivered. "Yes."

I waited for her to provide details and when she did not, I risked a quick glance at Catherine and Mia. They seemed as much at a loss as I felt.

Screw that. "Rowan, ma'am," I started with a sugary-sweet voice. "I appreciate that you believe all of this to be true. However, it's my job to investigate newsworthy events and people." I held up a hand to stop her from interrupting. "And, frankly, I have nothing to do with what Mayor Barbara Knollman does or does not do with respect to paranormal-human integration." I stopped to gauge her reaction, proud that my voice didn't waver in the slightest.

"That is your final answer?"

"What is this, a game show?" I quipped in response. Catherine or Mia gasped and Rowan's eyes flashed again.

"That is your final answer?" Rowan repeated.

"Yes, it is," I stated. "I will not stop investigating based on a vague statement from an alleged time-traveling ghost."

"Are you sure that's a good idea, Liz?" Mia asked.

"Yeah, maybe we should think about this," Catherine added. "After all, I'm the object of the investigation."

I shook my head. "It's my final answer," I said to Rowan.

"If you stay on this path, you will die in three days," she responded.

"Did you just threaten me?" My voice rose an octave.

"I speak the truth."

"Liz, we should talk about this," Mia insisted.

Against my instincts and better judgment, I took a step toward Rowan and chuckled. "Just checking, but does today count as day one or zero?"

CHAPTER FOUR

Smoke formed around Rowan, obscuring her. We watched, waiting to see what would happen next. When the white smoke cleared, the time traveling ghost was gone. The first eyes I met were Tony's, and he appeared confused. He stepped from behind the takeout counter and approached.

"Can any of you tell me what just happened?"

"What did you see?" I asked instead, curious what was visible beyond the smoke we had seen.

He furrowed his brow. "It all happened so fast. I could see the three of you sitting at the booth. Then you… blurred, I guess is the best word… and when it cleared you were standing here in front of the booth instead. You moved in the blink of an eye."

"Interesting," I muttered.

"That's all I get," he responded, but he smiled.

I laughed. "It lasted longer than a blink of an eye. You missed Rowan, the time traveling ghost."

His mouth dropped open. "I'm sorry, what?"

I explained what had happened behind the blurring he saw – apparently of time and space, how weird was that?

"Well, then, you have to stop investigating Catherine. And, you should probably talk to the mayor about her plans, too," Tony concluded.

I arched an eyebrow. "I appreciate the concern, but that isn't going to happen."

"Is any investigation worth your life?"

I touched his arm, shocked by the thrill that raced through me again. "You just met me, but trust me when I say this. Nobody scares me off a story."

"I don't know," Catherine interjected. "It's not just your life at risk, but countless lives in the future."

"Maybe. According to the woman who just popped in and out of existence," I argued, and glanced at Mia for support.

She shrugged. "I'm not sure. I've been around hundreds of years. It's not as long as you think."

"Okay, playing devil's advocate," Catherine began, "how certain are we that she's from the future?"

"She was wearing the typical *Star Trek* onesie-type outfit," I offered with a smirk.

Tony laughed at my joke, before catching himself with a scowl. Wow, he was really concerned about my safety.

"In all seriousness, I am curious about Rowan and what she said, but there's no way to verify anything. I'm not prepared to stop what I'm doing – or ask Barbara to do the same – on unverifiable information." I looked at their faces; surely someone would see the logic of my argument and support me.

Mia was wavering. She narrowed her eyes in thought. "I suppose we could do some research on anybody named Rowan Walsh, both on the internet and in the magical community."

"Now we're talking," I crowed, glad to have some support.

"I'm not sure how successful we'll be, though, if she's telling the truth about being from the future," Mia warned.

"That's okay, at least we're trying something," I insisted.

"She didn't say she agreed that you should continue the investigation," Tony argued.

I turned to Catherine. "You're the Chosen One, right? Can't you just save me from Rowan, if it comes down to it?"

Catherine fidgeted. "I guess so?"

I chuckled. "I'm just giving you a hard time." I faced the group. "I don't know what will happen, or not. But I don't want to change what I'm doing on the say-so of someone who could simply be a deranged supernatural being. It's not like we haven't seen those before," I added drily.

"She's right," came a familiar voice. We all turned toward the back of the café where the sound originated.

CHAPTER FIVE

A blue-haired, blue-eyed being stood near the hallway leading to the bathrooms and the kitchen. She smiled an ethereal smile as she gazed upon us. I hadn't met her before, but based on Barbara Knollman's description, I knew who she was.

"Please correct me if I'm wrong," I turned to the group, waving my arm in a flourish, "but I believe this is Olivia Williams, archangel extraordinaire."

I had the mad thought of wondering whether she considered us like ants, scurrying, helpful, but ultimately squishable. She turned her magnetic blue eyes on me and I squirmed. I didn't think the archangel could read minds, but who knew?

"We've met," she responded, her voice smooth and velvety. "Hi, Catherine, Mia." She extended a hand to Tony. "You're new."

"Tony," he said, hesitating before grasping her hand. Her blue eyes twinkled at the hesitation.

"It's good you're here, since you're one of the beings who keeps saying I'm so important to the supernatural world. Right?" Catherine challenged the archangel.

Olivia lifted her hands. "I only know what I know," she responded cryptically.

"I'm an empath, nobody special," Catherine argued. "And now, Liz's life and untold people's lives in the future are at risk. Because of me." Her voice thickened with unshed tears and I startled. I had no idea she was this upset.

Olivia placed her hands onto Catherine's shoulders. "You are so much more than you think."

"Wouldn't it be easier if you just told us?" I asked with a sigh.

Olivia wrinkled her nose at me. "Liz, isn't this what you live for? Investigating? Would you really want me to tell you all the answers?"

Her questions stumped me.

"Are you kidding right now?" Catherine asked in exasperation. "No offense, Liz, but if Olivia can give us the answers, I, for one, want them."

I reddened. "Of course, if it can save lives…"

"Unfortunately, it truly doesn't work that way," Olivia said.

"Why not?" Catherine refused to let it go.

Olivia shrugged. "That's not how the universe works."

"The universe works in mysterious ways," I offered with a wink.

"That's not quite what I mean, but that'll do," Olivia concurred.

"Even if it can help us save lives," Catherine said incredulously.

"Catherine, maybe Olivia isn't able to provide the answers we want," Mia soothed.

"Then why are you here?" I asked, not rancorously but out of genuine curiosity.

The archangel laughed. "Changing timelines suggested that you might choose not to continue on this path."

Gasps sounded at the statement, and even I was flummoxed. "Changing timelines? Is Rowan a time-traveling ghost?"

"I'm here to remind you that things are not always as they appear."

"That's not terribly helpful," I responded and Olivia frowned at me. My insides quivered.

"My goal in life is to be helpful, Liz."

"Point taken."

Olivia glanced around before continuing. "It's important you don't lose sight of your goals: investigating Catherine and supporting Barbara's initiatives."

Tony, who'd been silent to this point, chimed in. "I'm with Catherine on this one. Is it worth all these lives to push forward with the investigation?"

Olivia put her hands on her hips and glared at us like we were recalcitrant children. I guess even archangels can get fed up. "This is your choice. Remember though that you do not know what will happen if you choose not to go down this path. It may be worse." Her pronouncement made, she vanished.

"I hadn't thought about that," Catherine acknowledged.

Mia shook her head. "That's probably why Olivia can't tell us much. If we believe that nothing is set in the timeline – or even that there are multiple timelines – anything she tells us could irrevocably change what will happen. Including for the worse."

"What if what she told us made things better?" Catherine argued, but I could see her heart wasn't in it anymore.

"We could talk in circles around this, scientifically, philosophically, whatever. It doesn't matter. We aren't getting additional information from Olivia, or anyone else." I gulped a huge breath of air. "We need to decide what we're going to do."

Thick white smoke swirled before us.

"Oh, no. Not again," I grumbled.

CHAPTER SIX

Rowan glared at us when the smoke cleared. "What are you doing?"

"Talking," I responded.

"The timeline is doing weird things."

"How's that our fault?"

"I'm trying to save my husband and children," she raged.

That threw me. "Oh."

"Oh? That's it."

Indecision wracked me for a moment. "We've been told that your timeline isn't set. Stopping progress won't have the outcome you want." If only I was as confident as I sounded.

Rowan threw up her hands. "If this is the way you want it to be."

"Wait," Mia interjected. "What does that mean?"

"What are you planning on doing?" Catherine asked.

"I gave you the opportunity to make the right decision—"

"According to you," I interrupted. She clenched her fists and I smiled. I never did learn when to back down, or when not to poke the beast.

Rowan appeared confused. "The timeline started to…" She stopped and stared again.

"Started to what?" I asked.

"It doesn't matter. I need to know right now whether or not you are continuing the investigation," she demanded.

Her tone rankled. "I'll take the risk to my life."

"You refuse to stop?"

"As I said before, I refuse to back down. I am a journalist," I declared, a bit pompously, truth be told. "Threats will never stop me." I sensed movement and glanced to my side in time to catch the end of Mia's eye roll.

Rowan lifted her hands above her and closed her eyes. I exchanged uneasy glances with Catherine, Mia, and Tony.

"What is she doing?" Tony asked.

"I don't know," I admitted, bracing myself for what would be coming. Whatever that was.

The tips of Rowan's fingers crackled with energy. She swung around, directing this energy to the café bar. What looked like red lightning jumped from her fingertips to shatter the glass cases. I flinched, throwing my hands up in front of my face, even though the glass would likely never fly that far. The scent of ozone filled the air.

Rowan flickered in and out, like an image being turned off and on, as she became increasingly translucent.

"She's using up her energy," Mia shouted.

Rowan solidified and turned toward Mia.

"Not fast enough," I responded.

Rowan's eyes were lit up from behind, like a candle had been lit inside her skull. She lifted her hands toward the ceiling again. That red energy moved across her fingertips.

"Behind the booth," Tony shouted, and we flung ourselves in that direction. Rowan lowered her hands toward us. Red lightning arced from her. The booth's table fractured and tendrils of smoke rose where the wood burned.

I met Catherine's wide eyes on the other side of the booth. We were smushed up against the bottom of the booth's seats, trying to stay out of the line of fire. "It'll be okay," I yelled to her.

"No, it won't," Rowan roared. She'd stepped closer and stood mere feet from where we cowered.

Energy flowed nearby, drawing my attention. A glance at Catherine and my jaw dropped open. Her eyes looked like Rowan's, lit up from behind. She faded in and out, becoming translucent and then opaque.

"What the—"

Rowan's cry cut off my words. "You will stop or you will die!" Flickering in and out like a flashlight with a dying battery, probably an accurate analogy, she shot off one last stream of lightning. The energy landed where Catherine was. My heart leapt into my throat – until I realized I could see through the talent agent. Her eyes closed.

"Catherine!" I yelled.

Silence filled the café. That scent of ozone crowded out all other smells. Rowan was gone. Catherine had solidified again and lay curled on her side next to a large splintered piece of the table. Tony rose from behind the booth's back, assisting Mia up. She had a nasty bruise forming over her right eye.

I scuttled forward to grab Catherine. I tilted her head up, heaved a sigh of relief when I saw she was breathing. "Catherine? Can you hear me?"

Tony and Mia stumbled around the remains of the booth and joined me beside Catherine.

"Is she okay?" Mia asked.

"Catherine," I repeated. "Can you hear me?"

"Wha—" she mumbled, then stopped. Her eyes fluttered open. "Is everybody okay?" she rasped out.

"Thankfully, yes," Mia answered.

Tony helped Catherine to her feet. Mia and I followed them to a couple of two-top tables. The café had emptied during the attack. That seemed for the best; no collateral damage.

The four of us collapsed into chairs and stared at each other. "That was exciting," I said with a crooked smile.

Mia laughed, as always sounding like tinkling bells. Tony shook his head, but I saw the corners of his eyes crinkle with a half-smile.

Catherine still looked shell-shocked. "I thought you had three days. Rowan attacked us."

"Yes," I confirmed.

She stared at me. "You have to stop the investigation."

"No."

"Catherine's right," Tony argued.

"No."

"Is there anything we can say to change your mind?" Mia questioned.

"No."

"What if I refuse to cooperate?"

"It wouldn't matter, Catherine," I answered softly. "Based on everything we've seen and heard, although my head wants to explode thinking about it, there are multiple possible timelines, and the archangel says we shouldn't stray from the path." I shook my head to stop any of them from interrupting. "Besides, now we have an even bigger question to answer. Though I suppose it's just an offshoot of the original investigation," I mumbled, more to myself than to them.

"What bigger question could there be besides determining Catherine's role in all of this?" Mia asked.

I placed my hands palms-down on the table, sliding my fingers back and forth for a moment, before stilling. "Did anyone besides me see Catherine phase in and out? Just like the ghost."

"What are you talking about, Liz? I didn't phase in and out of anything," Catherine protested. She looked at Tony and Mia for support.

"We were behind the booth," Mia admitted, "so we didn't see anything."

"What do you mean, she phased in and out like the ghost?" Tony asked me.

"Did you guys see Rowan phasing in and out?" I asked in response.

Mia nodded and Tony answered, "She flickered, yes."

"And you saw the way her eyes lit up?" They nodded. "That's what Catherine did too."

Catherine shook her head. "No, there's no way."

"How did you feel during the attack?" I asked.

Catherine suddenly became interested in her cuticles. "I don't know."

"Yes, you do," I pressured.

She gripped the side of the chair and looked between the three of us. "Okay, I felt weird."

"Weird in what way?" I pushed more.

Catherine frowned. "I can't describe it too much more than that." She brightened. "Actually, that's not true. My eyes felt hot. Burning. Sounds and smells faded in and out."

"That would make sense," I said, thinking it through.

"What would?" Mia asked.

"The light from her eyes, whatever it is, must be some form of energy; thus, accounting for the burning sensation. And, the flickering… if Catherine was phasing in and out of our timeline—" I held up a hand to forestall questions I couldn't answer. "—which is only a guess, then it's logical that her senses would do the same."

Catherine snorted. "Logical. As if any of this could be called that."

I laughed. "No doubt." I sobered quickly. "But I don't think I'm wrong. I think Catherine phased in and out of our timeline, our existence, whatever you want to call it."

Catherine had gone an unhealthy shade of white. "What does that mean?"

"I have no idea. Except that there isn't any chance, in this timeline or any others, that I'm stopping the investigation now. Not when it's gotten so interesting."

Mia rolled her eyes again; she really needed to stop

doing that. I wondered what it was about me that seemed to trigger it. I focused on her when I realized she was talking. "—support Liz."

"Wait, did you just say that you support me?"

"Yes, Liz." She smiled at me and then turned a half-frown at Catherine. "I don't understand why you're so important. But, you're clearly more than an empath. And, regardless of the concerns that Rowan has expressed… and trust me, I have my own concerns about the future repercussions… the bottom line is I agree with Liz that we need to help you figure out who—"

"Or what," Catherine corrected with a one-shoulder shrug.

Mia nodded. "—or what you are."

Tony sighed. "I'm not happy lives are at risk." He met my gaze. The frank fear there startled me. "But I agree with Liz and Mia. Catherine, you need to figure this out. And, Liz is right that you don't know that not taking action will help the timeline. Plus, the archangel said to keep going."

Catherine held up her hands in surrender. "Okay, okay, you've convinced me. What do we do first?"

"Mia has professional engagements, so she's out," I said.

"I can get coverage if you guys need my help," Mia offered. "I'd hate for you to be short-handed."

Catherine patted her on the arm. "That's not necessary. You and Liz got the serial killing genie. Now it's my turn."

"And, Tony is going to need to repair the damage to his café, so he'll be a less active partner, too," I continued. "Sorry about that, by the way." He shook his head with a laugh and reached out to squeeze my hand resting on the table. My eyes widened at the tingle his touch elicited; he smiled wolfishly in response.

"You'll make it up to me," he replied.

"Mmm, okay," I mumbled. Mia bit back a laugh and glanced knowingly in my direction. My face flushed and I broke eye contact with Tony. We could deal with our attraction later.

"In all seriousness, though, if you need any help, please ask," he added.

"We will," Catherine assured him.

"That leaves me and Catherine," I concluded. "Which is fine. I have several ideas."

"They are…?" Catherine prompted.

"Tomorrow morning, on-air, we launch the investigation."

"Shouldn't we discuss your plans first?" Catherine asked.

"And give you a chance to try to talk me out of it? Not at all."

"Fair enough," Catherine said.

"What are you planning to say?" Mia asked.

I smiled a Cheshire-cat grin. "You'll have to tune in to find out."

CHAPTER EIGHT

"Okay, spill it," Marilyn ordered. She narrowed her purple eyes (contacts, I always assumed) at me when she delivered the request.

"What do you mean?" I asked, failing, I'm sure, to maintain an innocent air.

"Close your eyes."

I obeyed, and her voice moved closer when she leaned in to work. A brush feathered shadow across one eyelid and then the other. "What story are you doing this morning that they bumped your original story?"

"You'll get to see soon, along with everyone else," I teased her, careful not to move, lest she draw a line across my face. Her tsk-tsk at my failure to enlighten her elicited a chuckle.

"Open your eyes."

I complied, and she cemented my face into place.

Marilyn sighed. "Okay, you're done. Pain in my butt." She glared a final moment, but a wink belied the words and tone. She ran a hand through her spiky platinum blond hair before turning to leave. "This better be worth it."

"It will be," I called after her. In truth, nerves fluttered more than I was letting on. While it was true I had joined Mia last year in tracking down a serial killer who had turned out to be a deadly supernatural being, I personally had never been targeted before. It unnerved me to know that Rowan directed her threat at me. Of course, I still didn't even know if she meant she'd kill me, or if my death would be a consequence of continuing the investigation.

I furrowed my brow and watched the brunette in the mirror mimic me. I smiled, pleased that my lipstick was even and no stains appeared on my front teeth. I stood, smoothing one hand down my bright pink sheath and the other down a single short flyaway curl.

A head appeared in the doorway of my dressing room. She opened her mouth but stopped when she saw me.

"I'm on my way," I informed the production assistant. She nodded and her head withdrew. A final glance at my flawless appearance in the mirror, a reminder to the butterflies in my stomach that this would be helpful, and an exaggerated wink at the newscaster in the mirror. It was show time.

"Good morning in the Valley," I greeted viewers to my morning show, *Entertainment Daily*. "Thank you for spending your morning with us." I perched on a cushy blue chair, legs crossed at the ankles, knees kept together. Demure, yet with my pink stiletto heels, sexy. I loved this combination. The camera closest to me lowered into position and I allowed my smile to slip.

"This morning we start with a story that isn't uplifting and fun, that isn't so positive." I took a deep breath. "Yesterday, a supernatural being told me I would die in three days." I ignored the gasps I heard from the production staff; this was partly why I didn't tell anybody ahead of time what I would be saying. It was a good thing I had such a strong relationship with our producer. I shifted toward another camera. Needlessly dramatic, to be honest, but the public expected it.

"Today is Day Two." Continuing to ignore additional gasps and whispered comments, I explained to the viewers about Rowan's visit to *Soprannaturale*, though I chose not to name the café. This next part would be trickiest; to ask for assistance without throwing a spotlight on Catherine. I didn't care about it being on me. Heck, as a media personality, I loved it. But as it stood, she barely agreed to this investigation.

"According to this time-traveling ghost, I'm slated to die tomorrow. Not if I can help it," I assured my viewers, pleased to hear the steel in my voice.

"Today I ask you for help. There is a woman in town. She is human, but with supernatural abilities. Possibly much more than she ever thought. I am seeking additional information about her." I held up a hand. "Before anyone asks, I'm not divulging her name. Now, I can practically hear some of you asking, How do I know if I know anything about her if I don't know her name?" I smiled and nodded. "Trust me, she's impacting the supernatural energy in Las Vegas. If you have sensed something, seen something, whatever, please get in touch with me. My email is below on the screen, or you can go to our website to access it there. I'm just a human, asking the supernatural world for help. Help me help this woman, and maybe save my life in the process. Thank you." I gave a final smile without showing teeth and waited for the director to indicate the live feed stopped.

I stood, wavered slightly, reached a hand out to steady myself. A blur of well-wishes reached my ears. I nodded in response to words I wasn't truly hearing during the walk back to my office. The ringing of the telephone greeted me before I had taken a seat behind my utilitarian desk. I kept my gaze on my desk, for the first time wishing I didn't have floor-to-ceiling glass surrounding my office. Today it felt way too much like a fishbowl. A different ring cut through the office phone ring. I snatched my cell out of my top drawer.

"Elizabeth Addison," I identified myself when I didn't recognize the number, though it was a Vegas area code.

"Liz?"

I recognized the voice. "Robin?" She and I hadn't had the best relationship, but in the last month or so, she'd broken her blood vow as a demon's minion and rediscovered her witch's magic. She could be a powerful ally – and source of information.

CHAPTER NINE

Blood thrummed through my body and my heart rate beat a fast pitter-patter. But this was excitement, not nervousness. Catherine and I were about to have an audience with the Witches Council.

Did they call it an audience? My knowledge of protocol was sorely lacking. Good thing Robin had issued the invitation.

The witch stood beside us outside the large, squat, metal-gray building off of Industrial Road. She pulled on the end of her brunette ponytail, her brown eyes staring straight ahead.

"Are you ready?" Robin pulled the door open before we even answered her question.

"Yes," I answered anyway. Catherine didn't move. I tugged on her arm. "Hey, are you coming?"

She fixed her unfocused expression on me.

"Is everything okay?" I mean, she was somehow connected to the possible deaths of untold people in the future. But still. This seemed different.

Catherine offered a low wattage smile. "I'm coming."

Robin led us across the linoleum floor, past several hard, plastic chairs, to an unassuming door at the back wall. She rapped her knuckles three times. Within seconds, the door opened to reveal a stunning redhead with a big smile and brown eyes. She enveloped Robin in a hug before addressing me and Catherine.

"Hi, Elizabeth, I'm Jessica. I recognize you from your show," Jessica gushed.

"Call me Liz," I responded.

"Liz. And you must be Catherine."

Catherine nodded though stayed silent.

"Thank you so much for agreeing to see us," I said. "It seemed your area of expertise."

"When we saw your broadcast..." Her smile faltered. "Anything we can do to help you both." She turned, calling over her shoulder. "Please, follow me."

Robin, Catherine, and I followed Jessica down a short hallway. She knocked twice on a door on the left, then eased it open for us to enter.

I gasped at the antique wall sconces and silvery wallpaper that reflected the light.

Jessica glanced back at me with a smile. "We wanted a lovely workplace."

"You succeeded." I almost laughed when I realized I was whispering. The soft gray carpeting kept our steps silent; the overall effect was like a library.

Jessica pointed to folding chairs arranged before a half-circle table with five office chairs opposite. "Have a seat. The others are on their way."

Robin, Catherine, and I sat in the folding chairs; the cushioned seats meant they were much more comfortable than I had guessed. Jessica took a seat at one end of the other set of chairs. I had just wondered how long we'd have to wait when a door behind those chairs squeaked open. Several people filed in. As they sat, Jessica introduced them and they gave smiles or waves.

"This is Theresa," indicating a middle-aged blond with bright purple lipstick.

"Matt," an older bald gentleman.

"Evan," a taller, heavyset man.

"And, last but not least, Marcie," a young blond woman.

When all five council members were seated, Jessica faced us with a blinding smile. "Welcome to the Witches Council. Let's get started. What can we do to help?"

Robin and Catherine looked at me. Guess I was taking point. I stood to address the council. That seemed respectful; maybe they should publish a handbook so people knew what to do. Did the royal family do that?

I focused on the council. "We understand that you watched my broadcast this morning." The councilmembers nodded. "Let me give you the background." I updated them on what had happened since Rowan made her appearance yesterday. Had it only been one day? "As I stated in the broadcast, I die tomorrow if Rowan is to be believed. I'd really rather not," I added with a half-smile. Low chuckles sounded. Some of the tension in the room released.

"We are approaching you to ask if you can provide any information about the time-traveling ghost who calls herself Rowan Walsh; anything about Catherine's role in this; and anything about concerns regarding Mayor Barbara Knollman's plans for integrating the human and supernatural communities." I ticked these off on my fingers.

"You don't ask for much," Evan responded drily.

"I'm a journalist. It's what I do."

"Indeed," he conceded. He turned to Matt. "What have we learned?"

Matt cleared his throat. "After seeing your broadcast, we did some exploring."

"Exploring?" Catherine asked.

Theresa nodded. "Matt, if you don't mind?"

"Please."

Theresa closed her eyes. "My abilities involve an acute sensitivity to fluctuations in the magical energy of the city."

"You can feel changes in the Force?" I joked. She opened her eyes then frowned.

"Liz." Catherine chastised me with the single word.

"Sorry," I mumbled.

"Yesterday, there was a significant fluctuation," Theresa continued. "Unlike any I had felt before."

A chill moved through me.

"There was a huge increase to start."

I opened my mouth to ask a question. Robin's hand on my arm stilled me.

Theresa shook her head. "Then the magical energy dropped back down." She puckered her purple lips in thought. "Finally, it spiked even higher. This is where it became interesting." Her face flushed with excitement. "I sensed two distinct energy signatures. The first was that foreign one that surged and then receded. But, the other one. I'd never felt anything like it. In my entire life," she emphasized.

Blood drained from my face. "What do you think that means?"

Theresa exchanged a glance with Marcie, the youngest-appearing witch on the council, before answering. "Our best guess? The first magical energy surge was Rowan Walsh arriving in our time. The decrease was when she attacked the café. That final surge was her recovery before vanishing…" She stopped with a look at Jessica, who considered Catherine.

"What? What else?" Catherine asked in a whisper.

"We think the larger surge was you," Jessica answered.

"How?" I asked before Catherine could.

Jessica shook her head. "We don't know."

Disappointment filled me. I wanted more.

"Catherine is definitely more than an empath. She clearly is connected to Rowan and most likely is as well to whatever Barbara has seen in her visions since last year. However, we honestly have no idea what or how." Jessica tilted her head for a moment. "To answer your questions. We believe Rowan Walsh likely is from another dimension or timeline, and could be from the future, though we haven't been able to confirm or exclude that conclusion. Catherine absolutely has powers that have either not fully expressed or that she is somehow repressing. And, we don't have any idea the role of Mayor Knollman's integration plans with any of it."

I exchanged glances with Robin and Catherine, could see my disappointment mirrored there.

"Our magic is only so powerful," Jessica said. "I'm sorry we weren't more helpful."

"This was great," I contradicted the redheaded witch, who appeared startled by my statement. "You confirmed we're on the right track and that Rowan isn't just a nutjob to ignore." I blanched. "Of course, that means her threat of my impending death must be taken seriously too. At least we have another day before… something happens."

"What will you do next?" Jessica asked.

"Lunch. Followed by a visit to the mayor's office."

CHAPTER TEN

Tony's gaze found mine the moment I entered his café. Heat suffused me and that knowing smile appeared on his face. Why was it that hot men always seemed to know the effect they had on women? Good grief. I removed my own goofy smile and pointedly turned to face my companions. If I could hear him, I imagined Tony chuckling in response to my action.

"The back booth is still unusable, but the one next to it is clean and available," Tony called out.

Robin thanked him and led us to the booth. I settled into the vinyl seat, choosing to sit so I faced the restrooms and not the front of the café. The damage from Rowan's last visit was still very much in evidence. Someone had cleaned, but the back booth was split in two, the table missing a jagged chunk, and black marred the walls. Smoke? I didn't think it had been that bad.

The three of us perused the menu and ordered veggie sandwiches on ciabatta bread when the waitress came over.

"Is it too early for a cocktail?" Robin joked.

"It's five o'clock somewhere in the world," I responded. We laughed, Catherine a half second behind. "Catherine, you've been distracted all afternoon. What's going on?"

Catherine's wild eyes moved between us, a weird combination of excited and terrified. She opened her mouth, closed it. Flexed the fingers on both hands. Finally, took a quick breath. "Alex proposed."

"Congratulations," Robin enthused.

"Is this what you want?" I asked, playing the killjoy in the conversation. A sensation of being watched returned, and I peered around the edge of the booth to find Tony staring, a peculiar expression on his face.

"I don't know," Catherine answered me.

"Do you love him?" Robin asked.

Catherine smiled, her eyes taking on a faraway look for a moment. "Yes."

I sighed. Could she look more like the stereotype of a woman in love?

"What's the issue then?" Robin asked.

"It's because he's not human, right?" I answered instead and Catherine nodded, eyes filling with tears.

Robin placed her hand over Catherine's on the tabletop. "All relationships have challenges. But, nobody at this table is fully human."

"Speak for yourself," I retorted and then flushed. "That didn't come out quite the way I intended."

Robin shook her head. "It's okay, Liz. We know what you meant."

"Liz is right, though," Catherine said. "Dating a half-incubus is one thing. Marrying a half-incubus is another. I know I'm an empath, and something more, but still…" She frowned. "He's immortal and I'm not. It wouldn't be right for him to give that up – if it's even possible. Does he want to watch me grow old and die? What about me? It's selfish, but how will I feel as I age and he doesn't? Will I resent him his eternal good looks and immortality?" She took a deep breath, stopped the rapid-fire questions. "What should I do?"

"Catherine, you know we can't tell you what to do," Robin answered.

"I'll just play devil's advocate a bit longer," I chimed in.

"Of course, you will," Robin said.

"Can a human and a paranormal have a happily ever after? I think that's the big question," I started, but Robin interrupted.

"Can two paranormals have a happily ever after? Can two humans have a happily ever after? It's the same no matter their persuasion," she concluded.

"It adds an unnecessary complication," I argued.

"Could this be because of a certain supernatural?" Robin teased.

"What? No. I don't know what you're talking about," I stammered.

"Ladies," a deep voice addressed us and my body zinged in response. I looked up and found Tony's warm brown eyes, smelled his earthy scent, and wanted to run my fingers through his black hair. His smile widened. I didn't know what supernatural being he was, but I increasingly believed it was one that could read minds.

Tony set our sandwiches on the table. A chorus of thank-yous sounded. He shifted from foot to foot. Was he nervous? I tilted my head. "Was there something else?"

"Would you like to have dinner with me?"

Catherine bit off a laugh, but Robin didn't bother to hide her grin.

"No," I responded without thought, startled by the question.

My response didn't seem to faze him. "Because you don't think we have a future?"

One eyebrow rose in question. "How do you know that? Is this table bugged?"

"I have excellent hearing," he answered and wagged his ears at me.

"How did you do that?"

"I have skills."

"I bet." My ears burned at the double entendre. Tony smirked. An idea hit me. I mirrored his smirk, satisfied when his dropped a notch. "Yes, I'll go out with you—"

"Wonderful," he interrupted.

I held up a finger for him to wait. "I'll go out with you on one condition."

"Name it."

"Really? That could be dangerous. You don't know how my mind works."

"I'm getting an inkling."

"I'll go out with you if you tell me what you are." I sat back, pleased with my creativity. Robin choked on her water. Catherine's eyes widened. But Tony's smile broadened.

"You have a deal. Meet me at Fleming's on West Charleston for dinner at 7 and I'll tell you. You're not a vegetarian, right?"

"Um, no." I vaguely remembered that Fleming's was a steakhouse.

"See you tonight." He sauntered back to the café's bar, somehow no doubt aware of my appreciation of the view.

"That was different," Robin said.

"What do you mean?" I asked, shooting a look at Catherine when she laughed.

Robin held up her hands. "Don't get defensive. I've never seen him ask anyone out before. That's all I'm saying."

Hmm. I pushed that thought from my mind and focused. "Finish eating so we can head to Barbara Knollman's office."

I hoped the angel-turned-demon-turned-angel would have something useful to provide.

332

CHAPTER ELEVEN

I wanted to drive to the mayor's office, but since my Audi R8 didn't have a backseat to speak of, Robin drove us in her black VW Jetta compact sedan. It rode well, I could admit, but nothing beat being behind the wheel of my vehicle.

But I digress.

Mayor Knollman's secretary admitted us to the swanky office overlooking Main Street. Barbara stood when we entered. Her smile lit her face. Since being… elevated, I thought the word was, back to angel-status, she had regained an ethereal beauty. She no longer pulled her brunette hair back in a severe bun, her teeth no longer appeared small and sharp, and her fingernails no longer looked like talons. Plus, she looked decades younger. Turned out angels were much more attractive than demons. Who'd have thought, right?

"Welcome, ladies. Please sit." Barbara indicated three overstuffed leather chairs opposite her imposing solid wood desk. She retook her own seat and the smile dimmed. "I believe I know why you're here."

"Because you had a premonition?" I quipped, and she shook her head.

"I did, but not about you visiting. Robin called me." Barbara smiled.

This startled me for a moment. I hadn't realized they'd mended that particular fence. It was only a month or so ago that Robin was still Barbara's minion, and when Robin refused to kill her now-boyfriend, Jackson, Barbara tried to have Robin killed in retaliation. It was all very cloak-and-dagger, to be honest.

"You had a premonition?" Robin asked.

"Yes. Not about Catherine," she clarified. "About integration and protection of supernatural beings."

"What did you see?" Robin asked.

"It was typically vague, but showed the human and supernatural worlds as united. It also showed my role. I plan to introduce new legislation that will become the standard across this country for human-supernatural relations."

"That's fantastic," Catherine said.

"When are you introducing it?" I asked, my mind already wondering if I could get her on my show, or maybe even the evening news, to discuss this legislation.

Barbara chuckled. "Tomorrow night, and yes, Liz, I'd like some air time. If you can squeeze me in."

I grinned. "You know I can. I'll have my producer contact you. We're a little busy, as you know."

Barbara's smile slipped. "Yes, I'm aware of the deadline."

Anxiety whipped through me at the direct reminder of my looming death. I smiled wider to hide the discomfort. "We'll figure it out before that. I still have over 24 hours."

"Good luck. Let me know if I can do anything."

"We will—"

"Actually, Barbara," Catherine interrupted me. She stared down at her fidgeting hands for a moment. "I don't know how your ability works, but can you... direct... a premonition?"

Barbara's brow furrowed. "I'm not sure I understand. Do you mean control a premonition? No, I can't."

"Can you think about a topic to prompt a premonition?"

Barbara placed her hands on the desk top. She nodded, her fingernails tapping out a rhythm.

We remained quiet while she considered the question.

"I haven't directly tried before, but I've had times where a premonition followed thinking about a topic, so it's possible."

"I'd very much appreciate if you could try to find out something about me, my future."

Barbara nodded. "Let me give it a whirl." She closed her eyes, allowed her arms to lay loosely at her sides in the chair.

I tried to look at the others with my peripheral vision, afraid to move lest the spell be broken. Not a real spell, of course, the spell of wonderment. I felt a laugh bubble up and realized that my anxiety was increasing. What if we didn't like what she told us about Catherine's future? Worse, what if I ask her to do the same for me, and she sees nothing because I'm dead? My heart rate sped up at these thoughts. With supreme effort, I shut them off and focused on Barbara. I noted that her eyes moved rapidly beneath her closed lids, almost like she was dreaming. I hoped this meant that she was seeing something helpful. Barbara frowned and Catherine gasped. That couldn't be good.

Barbara's eyes snapped open. It was interesting to watch her orient herself to her current surroundings. The awareness increased until she smiled at us.

"That was amazing," she said.

"It worked?" Catherine asked.

"It did." Barbara inhaled deeply, perhaps arranging her thoughts. "I saw you, Catherine, and Rowan, the time-traveling ghost. You were both frowning. Fear and anger saturated the premonition. It was definitely not a happy meeting."

"What were they doing?" I asked.

"That's where it becomes vague. They were in a room together. Perhaps a ballroom? Some kind of larger space, it seemed. But, dark, as if there weren't any windows, and few lights had been turned on. They'd been arguing, I believe. Then the image became fuzzy. The best way to describe it is that mist swirled around."

"That's all," Catherine said, voice tinged with disappointment.

"Not quite. I thought the vision was complete and I was seeing it fade. But I don't think that's correct. It appeared that Catherine and Rowan were fading in and out, of existence or of our timeline. Which makes sense for the ghost, depleting her energy and all that." She frowned at Catherine. "It doesn't make sense for you."

I was already shaking my head at Barbara's conclusion. "That's already happened," I explained. "That happened yesterday."

"Not possible," Barbara countered. "I don't see the past, only the future."

"It's not possible that your powers have changed?" I challenged, and she tilted her head at me.

"It's not."

I suddenly felt like a tiny bug about to be squished. She'd maintained a few of her demon mannerisms.

"I don't understand," Catherine muttered.

"It's simple. It's going to happen again." Barbara shrugged at what to her was obvious.

Catherine paled. Robin patted her arm. "It's going to be okay."

"Thank you for the information, Barbara," I said. "This has been illuminating." Barbara chuckled at my formality. I stood and faced the others in the chairs. "It's time we revisit with Olivia and find out what else the archangel knows."

CHAPTER TWELVE

Catherine called Olivia, who agreed to meet us at Catherine's condo, only a few blocks from Barbara's office. Robin snagged a parking spot just outside the building. I glanced at the sky as we hurried across the street. Dark billowy clouds overhead threatened rain. I sniffed and decided it smelled like rain. Maybe we'd get a small squall. We entered the foyer and Catherine waved at the guard… doorman… security. I wasn't sure what she called him.

The elevator brought us to the 20th floor and Catherine led us down a short hallway to her door. "Does anybody want a drink?" Um, yes, we did. "Have a seat while I grab them."

Robin and I sat at the wooden dining table. I swiveled my head, taking in the space. Just a studio, but high ceilings and amazing floor-to-ceiling windows made it seem bigger. I loved my little house, but this wasn't too bad either.

Catherine set wine glasses in front of us. "All I have is white right now. Hope that's okay."

I lifted my glass. "A toast. To figuring out Catherine's importance and keeping me alive." Our glasses clinked. A knock sounded. "Perfect timing. That must be Olivia."

Catherine hopped up and went to the door to let Olivia in. Catherine grabbed a glass of wine for the archangel on the way back to the table.

"Thank you for agreeing to meet with us," I started. "Random question first. How come you didn't just materialize in here?"

Olivia laughed and shook her head. "That would be rude. This is a private home and nobody is in danger."

"Not at the moment, anyway," I quipped.

"What can I do for you ladies?" Olivia asked.

All eyes turned to Catherine who toyed with a cuticle. If she kept that up, she'd be a bloody mess. She chugged a large swallow of wine before answering. "We've met with the Witches Council and Mayor Barbara Knollman to gather more information. We've confirmed some of what you told us. There's something different enough about me to mess with the magical energy of the city." Catherine chugged another swallow of wine. "I'm going to have another run-in with Rowan, and neither of us will be happy about it." She looked at me and Robin. "But we aren't getting any details." Frustration saturated her voice. "We aren't getting anything we can take action on."

"So, you decided to try me again?"

"Yes," Catherine said.

"I've already told you everything that I can," Olivia reminded us.

"That's not good enough," Catherine snapped, and my wide eyes met Robin's. I didn't think I'd ever heard Catherine get angry before.

Olivia's eyes darkened for a moment, then they cleared and she smiled. "I'm afraid it is what it is."

"More riddles." Catherine's hand tightened around the stem of her wine glass. Robin reached to place her hand over Catherine's.

"Everyone is doing the best they can," she assured the upset empath.

"Are they though?" I asked. Catherine had a point. I stared at the archangel. "Please give a straight answer. Do you know something you're not sharing? Or are you really in the dark as much as we are?"

Olivia reflected my stare. She didn't answer.

My brief show of nerves faltered with her continued silence. She couldn't send me to hell for being difficult. Could she?

Olivia's expression softened. "I like you, Liz."

"Thanks?"

"You never hesitate to say what you're thinking."

I shrugged, ears burning with the compliment. Or at least, I assumed it was a compliment.

"I wouldn't say I'm as in the dark as the three of you, no. Neither would I say that I know exactly what's going to happen. Timelines can be tricky. It's not always clear what will happen in one versus another."

My head throbbed. I held up a hand to stop her. "Are we a primary timeline?"

Olivia chuckled. "For you, you are."

"Riddles again," Robin sighed.

"Ladies. I'm not trying to be difficult. It's as I said before. Based on what I can see, you are on the right track."

"How is this a track? We don't know where we're going," Catherine spat out.

Olivia turned her speculative gaze on me again and I squirmed. "Interesting."

"What?" I asked.

"You're about to get a very clear direction."

"What does that mean?" I asked uneasily. "The last time we got a clear direction, Rowan attacked us." My eyebrows shot up. "That's it, isn't it? Rowan's going to attack us again." Robin gasped. Catherine chugged more wine.

Olivia shook her head. "That I cannot answer."

"I'm right," I crowed. "I know I am." I sobered. "Although I don't know why I'm happy about that. Last time, she nearly turned us into barbecue," I groused.

Olivia laughed. "That is all I have for you. Good luck."

Our responses were said into the void as Olivia winked out of Catherine's dining area.

"That was fun," Catherine mumbled.

"No, this is good," I disagreed excitedly. "We just have to be ready."

"I think we need to make sure the two of you aren't ever alone," Robin said.

Catherine and I exchanged glances. We nodded our acceptance.

"I'll stay with Catherine for tonight," Robin said, "after we bring Liz to her date with Tony." She grinned.

Mention of my date released tension in the room, for everybody except me. I responded with a tight smile. Was I making a mistake? The journalist in me said no, because I'd find out about another supernatural being. The woman in me… I decided not to think about that just yet.

"What happened to supernatural-beings-and-humans-can't-have-a-future?" Catherine teased.

"Have you decided whether to accept Alex's proposal?" I responded with a wink.

Robin snorted. Catherine reddened.

"Okay, this has passed the point of usefulness," Robin concluded, though with a smile. "Liz, are you ready to see Tony?"

I stood with a sharp nod. "Yes, I am. Let's go."

My mind swam as we took the elevator to the foyer. Kaleidoscope emotions filled me. Excitement. Dread. Elation. Trepidation. Desire. My heart hammered in my chest. I might have had mixed emotions about humans and supernaturals, but one stood out above the others. Longing. The intensity surprised me, but the thought of Tony's protective nature, sweet personality, and, of course, hotness brought out such a sense of longing. I could only hope the evening lived up to my internal hype.

CHAPTER THIRTEEN

Tony stood outside Fleming's, looking suave, but uncomfortable, his broad shoulders trapped in a dark, pin-striped suit, no tie. We'd had enough time, and Robin and Catherine had been willing, to swing by my not-exactly-on-the-way house so I could change. Now I was glad I did. Robin pulled her car alongside the front and I opened the door.

"Looking good, Tony," she called out to him. He smiled, though his eyes quickly found mine.

"Thanks, Robin, Catherine. I'll see you later." I closed the door on their quiet chuckling.

"You look wonderful." I walked to his side, looked up into his brown eyes. The heat between us was obvious.

"You're beautiful," he responded, his gaze drinking in my fitted, knee-length, purple dress showcasing my curves. "Are you hungry?"

"Oh, yes," I breathed out.

Tony waggled his eyebrows at me and I laughed, breaking the sensual tension. "Let's go in, then," he said. He held the door open so I could enter.

After giving his name to the hostess, we followed the young woman in a black cocktail dress to a booth on the opposite side of the dimly lit restaurant. We slid onto the red vinyl, maybe leather, seats around the table. Dinnerware and cutlery, including a rather large steak knife, sat atop the crisp white tablecloth. The hostess assured us our waitress would be right over.

Heat radiated off of Tony. I didn't think it was just attraction. He seemed to run hot. As in, a high temperature. My silly thoughts led me to giggle.

"What has you so entertained?"

Let's get to it. "You. I was thinking that your body temperature sits higher than most."

"Interesting observation," he responded. "Why do you suppose that might be?"

I pondered the question. "Because of whatever being you are?"

He nodded. "Have you guessed what being yet?"

"Nope. I've thought about your intensity, your size, your hearing. Your smell." I inhaled deeply, enjoying the earthy scent of him. "Your scent." His eyes dilated and I fidgeted.

"That doesn't suggest anything specific?" he teased.

A thought niggled my brain but left before I could grab it. I shook my head.

"What do you smell?"

"Floral, unspecified, though. Earthy, like after a rain."

He tilted his head.

"What?"

"Most people can't smell what you're smelling."

"Why do you suppose I can?"

"I don't know," he said slowly. "But, a deal's a deal. You met me for dinner, so I'll tell you what I am. Though I hadn't thought we'd jump right in with it," he admitted.

I laughed. "I'm a journalist for a reason. I want to know everything, and I don't wait very well." Tony joined my laughter for a moment. He broke eye contact and reached for his water glass. His hand trembled. "Are you nervous?" I asked softly.

He drank half the glass in a large gulp. Set the glass back down and smoothed out nonexistent wrinkles in the tablecloth. "I am," he said. His eyes met mine. The naked fear there shocked me. "I haven't gone on a date in a long time. But, there's something about you."

"There is?"

"You're intelligent, beautiful, tenacious, stubborn."

"Those last aren't always considered positives."

"I don't want an easy, passive woman by my side."

"If you want a challenge, I'm sure I'm up for that," I quipped.

"I don't want to scare you off. Especially knowing your concerns…"

"We can take it one day at a time." And I meant it. "What are you?"

"I'm a shifter."

That took a second to process. "A werewolf?"

Tony belly laughed, drawing the eyes of couples at nearby tables. He held up a hand in apology, leaned in closer to me. "Not every shifter is a wolf. Try another animal."

My brain couldn't think of another animal. But a shifter made perfect sense with what I'd seen so far. A realization hit. "That's how you could hear me at your café."

"I told you I have excellent hearing."

He waited for me to figure it out. "Tell me what you are," I begged.

"I'm a were-panther."

My eyes widened. "That's so cool." I reached out to cover his hand with my own, enjoying the body heat combined with the heat of attraction. "Is that what I smell? A sleek black kitty."

"Panther," he corrected with a wink.

"I'd love to see that one day," slipped out, and he tensed.

"Maybe one day," he allowed.

Discrete coughing drew our attention; the waitress had arrived. Tony ordered for both of us – steak well done for me, run-it-through-a-warm-room for him. I wrinkled my nose at his choice and he gave me a one-shoulder shrug.

"It tastes better to me."

The waitress left.

"Where are you from?"

"Italy."

"You have such a slight accent. I couldn't place it."

"I've been in the US for some time."

Nerves fluttered. "How long?"

Tony chuckled. "Don't worry. I'm not as old as some of your friends."

"Some of them are hundreds of years old." My mind still had trouble processing that. I wasn't even thirty yet. I couldn't imagine Mia's over 200 years. Or Barbara's 400, I think it was, maybe 500 years.

"I'm not in the plurals yet," he said.

My eyebrows rose. "100 years old?"

"Thereabouts."

I shook my head. "It's seriously not fair how you supernaturals get to live forever but still look so darn young."

"I won't live forever. Shifters aren't immortal."

"I guess that's a good thing," I responded with a nervous chuckle. "However, I'll still grow old while you continue to look like this." I waved my hand up and down. There was a teasing quality to my comment, but Tony didn't miss the harsh truth underneath.

"It's no different than some of your other friends' relationships: Catherine and Alex, Evie and Ryan, Mia and Jacob. It's like one of them said. All relationships have challenges. This would just be one specific to a human-supernatural relationship."

At his repeated use of the word relationship, I grew more certain that I wanted that with him. His eyes dilated again, and he placed his other hand on mine so it was sandwiched between his.

"How do you do that?" I asked.

"Do what?"

"Seem to know what I'm thinking?"

"I don't. Know what you're thinking."

"Yet, your responses suggest you do," I countered.

He gave a lazy smile. "Your body tells me what you're thinking."

My body? A flush crept up my neck.

"Like right now."

"What do you see?" I whispered.

He shook his head, eyes holding mine. "Your physical reactions are easy for me to sense. I can hear everything from the tiniest change in your breath to the racing of your heart. Smell the release of hormones."

I pulled my hand from his and sat back. "You can smell me?"

He looked perplexed. "How is that any different from when you said you liked my scent?"

Another nervous chuckle bubbled to the surface. "Oh, right. That makes sense." I gave a shy smile. "I think I understand more now. Tell me about Italy."

"Those pictures in my café?"

"Yes?"

"I took those as a teenaged shifter sixty years ago."

My mouth dropped open and I snapped it shut. "Tell me everything."

And he did. Tony regaled me with stories of his youth in Italy, his parents' decision to move to America, their decision ten years ago to return to Italy. When our steaks arrived, we paused long enough to scarf the delectable food. Soon the restaurant was closing and it was time to leave.

Tony stood, offered a hand to assist me out of the booth. His warm skin caressed mine with just this bare touch. We held hands traversing the restaurant, releasing only when he held the door open again for us to leave.

I suddenly laughed and he looked at me askance. "I just realized that Robin gave me a ride here, so I need to call her for a ride back."

"You know I can give you a ride."

"I know." I felt like a nervous teenager after a first date. Would he kiss me, should I let him? But, with a grown-up twist. Would I, should I, invite him in? Except I was staying at Catherine's tonight, so that wasn't even an option. Confusing disappointment flooded through me.

Tony stepped closer, used a finger to lift my chin. "Liz, relax. We can go as slow as you want. You don't have to invite me in." His eyes danced with merriment and I shook my head.

"That'll take some getting used to," I muttered. A smile broke across my face. "But, thank you. I knew you were a gentleman. And I like you, so…"

Tony leaned down.

My lips parted to accept his kiss—

"Time's running out," a harsh voice interrupted.

Tony and I sprang apart before our lips touched. My brain, already getting a workout this evening, had trouble comprehending what I saw. "Rowan?"

"Elizabeth. I told you what would happen if you didn't stop investigating. Yet, you spent all day doing exactly that."

To my surprise, the ghost sounded exasperated by me. Well, she wasn't the first and she wouldn't be the last.

"I'm on a date, Rowan," I pointed out, like I could reason with her.

"I'm aware of that." Her blue eyes darkened. "Since concern for yourself or my future family didn't seem to make a dent, I'm trying a new approach."

Fear shot through me. "What do you mean?"

Rowan dematerialized and then rematerialized, next to Tony. We turned to her in surprise. Rowan wrapped her arms around Tony, who growled. Just like a panther would.

Tony's skin rolled, the bones moving beneath. As if they were trying to reshape themselves. His brown eyes flashed an impossible shade of green. Hair sprouted then retracted along his limbs, his face. He growled again, his body becoming almost liquid with the changes he was trying to force. I realized he was trying to shift just as Rowan shot me a triumphant glare. The two became translucent and vanished.

"Tony!" I screamed into the dark night.

CHAPTER FOURTEEN

Tony was gone. Rowan had taken him. These thoughts swirled like a maelstrom in my mind. What was I supposed to do? The sound of a door opening drew my attention. I turned back toward the restaurant. A middle-aged man with a trim beard stood there, mouth agape.

"Are you okay, ma'am? Did I just see… what I thought I saw?"

I blinked, focused on the man. "If you just saw a ghost kidnap my date, then yes. Yes, you did."

If it was possible for the man's mouth to fall open even more, it did with my explanation. "Do you need help?" He asked the question, but the terror in his eyes made it clear he wouldn't know what to do if I said yes.

"No, thank you." I approached him, slowing when he tensed. "There's nothing you can do," I assured him. "Go back inside. I know who to call."

Nodding his head like he had a broken neck, the man retreated into the restaurant. "Good luck," floated past me as the door closed. The lock turned.

I pulled my cellphone from my purse and autodialed Catherine.

"Hey Liz, I'm surprised to hear from you," her voice answered. "Figured you'd get a ride here from Tony." I heard Robin's laughter in the background.

I couldn't find my voice.

"Liz?" Catherine's tone sharpened. "Are you there? Is everything okay?"

I shook my head before remembering she couldn't see me. "No," I whispered. "Tony's gone. Rowan took him."

"What? Did you just say Rowan has Tony?"

"She showed up at the end of dinner. Yelled at me for continuing the investigation. And took Tony because she knows I like him." I explained how Rowan materialized and dematerialized.

Catherine and Robin held a mumbled conversation. "We'll be there in fifteen minutes."

The call ended, leaving me alone with my thoughts. If I hadn't accepted the date with Tony, he wouldn't have been kidnapped. I was cool with risking my own life, not someone else's. Although Rowan had pointed out that I ignored her plea to save her family. My heartbeat thundered through my body. Was she right? Did I only care now that someone I had feelings for had been taken?

No, that wasn't accurate. Rowan's tale of the future may or may not be accurate. And, Olivia insisted that I stay on this path. I was right to keep investigating Catherine. I had to be. But if Tony was hurt because of it—

Stop! This wasn't helping me or Tony. I needed to think. Where could Rowan have taken him? Barbara's premonition showed Catherine and Rowan in a cavernous, windowless room. Could that be where Tony was? Or was that a separate future incident?

Frustration thrummed through me. I tapped my foot on the concrete. The cool wind blew across my skin, lifting my short curls away from my face. My eyes closed. I heard tires on pavement and then a horn. I opened my eyes to see Robin's Jetta.

"Do you think she took Tony to where Barbara saw Catherine and Rowan's showdown?" I greeted the women upon entering the backseat of the car.

Robin pulled away from the restaurant. "I don't know. That's a good question. Could give us a place to start investigating."

"Can you guys think of a large space without windows, though?" Catherine asked, the tip of her right index finger tapping her chin while she thought.

"Most theaters would fit the bill," I said. "Or maybe larger business meeting rooms at some of the casinos. Or even rooms at the convention center." My voice had taken on a gloomy tone with so many options.

"Oof, yeah, there are lots of possibilities," Robin responded. "How would we even go about investigating them?"

"And do we have the time for that?" Catherine asked.

"We have no idea. Bottom line is we don't know Rowan's timeline," I said, sharper than I intended. "Sorry. Frustrated. It would have been nice for Rowan to give us a clue."

"Why would she?" Robin asked.

"What do you mean?" Catherine asked.

Robin slowed the car to a stop at a red light and turned in her seat to look between Catherine and me. "Why do you think she abducted Tony?"

"To force us to look for him, I assume." I lifted my hands in question.

"But, why?" Robin asked again, facing forward to watch the road. The car shifted when the light changed to green.

A lightbulb went off. "Oh, I get it."

"What am I missing?" Catherine asked.

"Rowan likely has no real intention of hurting Tony. She's trying to stop my investigation into you, Catherine."

Robin nodded. She slid the car into a street parking spot across from Catherine's building. I gathered my purse to exit the vehicle.

Outside in the wind, I raised my voice to be heard. "My guess is that she hopes to distract us from investigating long enough for the timeline to change in her favor."

The three of us hurried across the street to the building. Catherine waved at the security guy behind the desk and we continued to the elevator past the mailroom.

"How will she know the timeline has changed?" Catherine questioned.

I frowned. "I don't know. Based on movies like *Bill & Ted's Excellent Adventure*, any changes in the timeline automatically take effect simultaneously across the entire timeline. So maybe she somehow will know." Uncertainty tinged my voice but Catherine and Robin were smiling.

The elevator pinged at the 20th floor.

"I love that that's your reference for time travel knowledge," Catherine said with a chuckle.

"It's all I have," I responded with a wry smile.

Robin and I followed Catherine into her studio loft. "Drinks?" she asked.

"Definitely," I responded, heading for the maroon couch facing the floor-to-ceiling windows. At night, the view from here of Fremont and the Arts District was cool. I sat, crossed my legs, wished I had pants, remembered I had some in my bag in the other room, decided I didn't care enough to get up to change.

Catherine placed three glasses of white wine on the coffee table, then she and Robin sat on either side of me. We reached for the glasses at the same time, eliciting chuckles.

"What do we think?" Catherine asked.

"Our theory is that this is purely a tactic," Robin summarized. "Rowan won't hurt Tony. She's just holding him to stop you until the timeline changes sufficiently for her to know she's saved herself and her family."

"But, if she saves herself in the future, she won't have to come back to the past," Catherine mused. "Would she just vanish?"

The three of us swallowed large gulps of wine.

"Time travel is by far too complicated," I said.

"Rather than getting stuck on the semantics, or physics, or whatever," Robin continued, "let's figure out what we're going to do."

"Great," Catherine agreed. "What are we going to do?"

We burst into laughter, that innocent but huge question somehow breaking the tension that had been building since I placed my call to Catherine.

"Oh my," I blurted out, then stopped. The ladies waited, but I wasn't sure if I should say the next part. I hesitated.

"What is it, Liz?" Catherine asked.

"Are you guys aware of Tony, what he is?" I asked.

"Yes," Robin answered, though Catherine appeared confused. "I assume he told you." Robin directed this at me and when I nodded, she turned to Catherine. "He's a shifter, a were-panther."

Catherine drank another gulp of wine. "Cool," she mumbled around the liquid.

"He started to shift when she grabbed him. He was still shifting when they dematerialized."

Robin and Catherine stared at me. "Hmm," Robin said, though declined to elaborate.

"What?" Catherine asked. Understanding dawned as the realization hit.

"Is Rowan guarding a panther, a human, or a half-shifted were-panther?" I asked what we were now all thinking.

Catherine raised her eyes to the ceiling. We waited. She looked back at us. "Does it matter? I don't think it does. He's a powerful being. He'd want us to do what we needed to do."

"You're right," I agreed. "And what we need to do is show Rowan that she can't force us to do things her way."

"What do you have in mind?" Robin asked.

In answer, I jumped from the couch and headed for the dining area table where I'd dropped my purse. I fumbled for my cellphone and pulled it out. I scrolled for a specific number. Catherine and Robin had followed, now stood next to me.

"Who are you calling?" Robin asked.

"Your favorite person," I joked. Her brow furrowed while she tried to think who I meant.

"It's kind of late for a social call," the voice on the other end said, but without rancor.

"Good evening, Barbara," I said.

Robin rolled her eyes. "Barbara and I are good now," she whispered.

"Sorry for the late call." I met Catherine's and Robin's eyes with a grin. "Any chance you'd be up for a last-minute interview tomorrow morning? We need your help."

CHAPTER FIFTEEN

"Good morning in the Valley," I greeted my viewers per usual. "Today we have a special report and will be delaying our original story about local author Brian Bunter's new book until later in the week. Instead, Mayor Barbara Knollman will be in the studio to discuss her exciting new proposed law. After the break." Sweat broke out despite my antiperspirant. I didn't get nervous doing my show, so I knew the real cause. Today's interview. I turned to my subject, sitting with no visible discomfort or anxiety in the stuffed blue chair next to mine.

"You seem amazingly calm," I said.

Barbara smiled. "I have nothing to be nervous about, Liz. This is the right path."

I harrumphed. "Must be nice to be an angel with precognition."

She laughed.

"Back in five," a voice came from my ear bud. I faced the nearest camera and readied my smile – and steadied my nerves.

"Before I turn the interview over to the mayor, a quick recap for viewers who may have missed yesterday's show. Two days ago, a time traveling ghost from the future arrived to tell me I would die in three days. She demanded I cease my investigations into a certain supernatural being here in town and cease my support of Mayor Knollman's initiatives. Spoiler alert, I didn't." I winked at the camera before adopting a serious countenance.

"Today is Day 3. If this ghost is correct, today is the day of my death." I ignored gasps I heard in the studio. Not helpful. "But you guys know me. You've been watching me for years now. It's not in my nature to quit. Plus, this is bigger than one person." I faced Barbara.

"You and I are on the same page here," I said. "We understand there are humans and other beings who want to stop progress, for whatever reasons."

"Yes, we do understand. And they are wrong."

"To the point as always, Mayor." I chuckled and gestured toward her nearest camera. "The floor is yours. What is your proposal?"

Barbara smiled into the camera. "Good morning. Today has the potential to be historic. This afternoon I will propose new legislation that will be the first step toward allowing supernatural beings, such as myself," she reminded viewers, "to fully integrate into society. Meaning, we won't have to hide." She frowned. "Now, I can hear – well, not literally, that's not my supernatural skill – the objections of some of you." She tilted her head. "What are the dangers? What are the protections for humanity? These are legitimate concerns," she conceded.

"Let's look at it another way. We have always existed. We have always lived among you. What my legislation will allow is for us to do so in full view. To ensure all are protected, my proposal includes creating a Working Group to research and make recommendations for managing expectations between humans and supernaturals. Part of that will involve developing a direct working relationship between the paranormal underworld governing body and the city council. Since I am the head of both organizations, I imagine this will be fairly painless."

Barbara glanced at me. "Did you have any questions, Liz?"

"How will appointment to the supernatural governing body work? Will there be voting? Will humans be able to vote for supernatural representatives?"

"Those are all excellent questions. The purpose of the Working Group will be to answer them. That may not be a satisfactory answer right now, but this is the best way forward. I am not a supreme leader," she said with a chuckle. "Nor am I going to demand certain treatment for those of my kind. The Working Group will have representatives from multiple constituency and supernatural groups, appointed from within each and without interference from the others. This will allow for a diversity of opinions and suggestions for the best ways to move forward with integration.

"These are exciting times. Las Vegas has an unprecedented opportunity to be on the front lines of progress." She turned back toward me. "Thank you, Liz, for this opportunity to address the city."

I nodded and turned to the camera. "You heard it here first, folks. Las Vegas will blaze the trail in human-supernatural relations. Tune in tonight when we'll give you the results of this historic vote."

The producer counted us off the air in my ear. I faced Barbara again. "Thank you again for coming on. I know it was for your benefit too, but it's time to bring this to a head. Without me losing my head."

Barbara's brow furrowed. "I hope it didn't put you in too much danger."

"I was already in danger," I responded with a shrug. "Now we see if taunting the ghost worked."

CHAPTER SIXTEEN

Taunting Rowan had been a calculated risk on our parts. Catherine, Robin, and I figured that the ghost would see what I was doing and identify that we were deliberately taunting her. We hoped she would refrain from coming after me or harming Tony because she would assume that would play into our hands somehow if she did. But, a side effect of her unreleased anger might be a buildup of her own energy. And that, our biggest hope, would be something we could track and home in on.

Thus, we found ourselves back on Industrial Road visiting the Witches Council. Catherine, Robin, and I sat facing the five witches on the council.

A space had been made between us and them, bigger than before. I'd called Jessica prior to my show, and she'd promised to have everyone assembled in time. She'd delivered.

"Welcome," Jessica said. "I've brought the other councilmembers up to speed with the plan and we're ready to go."

"It was quite ingenious," Theresa added. "I could sense the magical energy change as the show went on."

"We should be able to pinpoint the highest concentration of that energy in the city," Matt assured us, running his hand over his bald head.

The witches stood and we scrambled to follow suit.

"You'll notice we've already pulled chairs out of the way to allow room to create the circle," Jessica explained. She approached us, carrying a bag, presumably of supplies for whatever spell we were about to cast.

"We'll conduct a finding ritual," Theresa said, reaching into the bag to pull out four candles. She spoke as she placed and lit each candle in the corners of the space. "These are to help cleanse the energy and call the corners for the ritual." She glanced around at the assembled people. "We have more than enough witches to channel the elements for the ritual, so we'll use those of us with the stronger relevant magic. Given my sensing abilities, I'll take point." She seemed to direct this explanation more at us than her fellow councilmembers, but they nodded when she finished.

Theresa placed and lit a red candle. "Robin, I know you're not a member of the council, but since you're able to control energy, including lightning, you will pull the energy of fire." Robin stood next to the candle and closed her eyes. She murmured under her breath.

I already knew how Robin had summoned and directed a bolt of lightning to kill the witch that Barbara had sent to kill Robin's boyfriend last month. An involuntary shiver went through me at the thought of that much power. And, yet, Catherine was the one who was impacting the timeline. I refocused on the scene before me.

Theresa placed and lit a blue candle. "Marcie, with your feminine energy and emotion skills, you will channel water energy." The young blond stood beside her candle, closed her eyes, and joined Robin in softly chanting.

Hmm, what could 'emotion skills' be? Catherine could sense others' emotions and Mia could manipulate others' emotions. At which end of that spectrum did Marcie's abilities reside? She looked so young and innocent to possess a skill like that.

Theresa placed and lit a white candle. "Jessica, with your purity of spirit, you will channel the energy of the air." The redhead took her place beside the candle and joined in the quiet chanting.

Purity of spirit perplexed me. Weren't they all what were known as white witches? Wouldn't they all have pure spirits? This whole process fascinated me.

Theresa placed and lit a green candle. "And I will channel the energy of the earth herself. This will allow me to narrow my focus on the sensed energy to a specific location on the planet – ideally, where Rowan has taken our friend."

Catherine and I, along with the other members of the council not involved in the ritual, remained outside the invisible circle watching. The chanting stayed indecipherable and then stopped. Theresa's eyes opened.

"Thank you, goddess, for your support of our circle. Thank you to each of the elements. We focus our intent on finding our lost friend. Show me the location of the energy spike from this morning."

Unlike the earlier rhythmic quality, Theresa's request was surprisingly matter-of-fact, almost conversational. My gaze wandered across the faces of the others in the circle. Their eyes remained closed, though they stayed quiet.

Theresa's eyes widened for a moment and then closed again. I saw movement under her eyelids like she was dreaming. Was she having a vision? This was so cool.

In concert, all four women's heads dropped, chins resting on chests. A simultaneous deep inhale, exhale, and their eyes opened. Smiles blossomed across their faces, mirrored by the other members of the council not taking part in the circle. Catherine and I exchanged a confused glance. Did it work?

"It worked," Theresa explained to us, as though reading my mind.

"Where is he?" I asked. Please be in town. In our own time. Unharmed.

The four women blew out their candles before Theresa answered. "He's okay, in our time, and still in Las Vegas."

"Thank goodness," I said with a palpable sense of relief.

"He's downtown," she continued.

"The Strip, Arts District, or some other downtown." I ticked off the possibilities on my fingers.

Theresa smiled. "He seems to be in a wedding chapel in the Arts District."

"That'll be perfect for you, Catherine. You should call Alex," I quipped, and she paled, shooting me a not-very-nice look. What can I say, I crack jokes when I'm nervous.

"There are a lot of wedding chapels in the Arts District," Robin pointed out. "Any chance you could narrow that down?"

"Yes. Other than a small altar for the vows, the room was nondescript, so my best guess is a chapel that is currently closed," Theresa said.

"Could be one that's defunct," Jessica offered.

"Or one that's undergoing renovations," Catherine mused.

"It also sounds like one that's not theme-based," I said. "Anything else that could help us eliminate?" The thought of calling hundreds of chapels made my stomach hurt.

Theresa shook her head. "No, unfortunately."

Tension in the room spiked with this statement.

"I have an idea," Catherine said, blue eyes sparkling. "I forget the full name, but there's a wedding association group here in town. If a chapel is closed for renovations or has recently shut down entirely, they most likely would know about it. We just need to call and ask them."

"That's brilliant, Catherine." I pulled out my phone to google for association names. "Which one of these is it?" There were several listed in Las Vegas and Clark County.

Catherine frowned. Her eyes scanned the listings. "That's it," she said, pointing at my phone. She snatched it from my hand and pressed the hyperlink. "I've got this," she said, walking toward the far corner of the room for quiet and privacy.

"Okay, then." I faced the others. "What's our plan once Catherine figures out which chapel it is? We're not going in there, guns blazing."

"This is the wild west," Robin said with a grin.

"Not that wild," I countered with a chuckle, then sobered. "We don't know what condition Tony will be in when we arrive, so we need to plan for no assistance from him." The others nodded. "Theresa, since you sense energy, would you mind coming with us?"

"Of course."

"Robin, we may need your summoning power," I warned.

"I'm ready."

"Marcie, with your 'emotion skills'—" I arched an eyebrow at her. "—it may be necessary to reason with Rowan."

Marcie gave me an enigmatic grin and nodded.

"I, unfortunately, am a useless human," I half-joked, "but my focus will be on getting Tony."

"No doubt," Catherine ribbed me as she rejoined the group. "We know you want to get him."

I rolled my eyes at her. "And?"

"I've narrowed it to three possibilities, all within a few blocks of each other, centered near Bonneville."

"Robin, you'll drive. Catherine, Marcie, Theresa, and I will go with. The rest of you stay here on standby, in case we need anything," I directed.

"Sounds good, General Addison," Robin teased me.

"Neither Tony nor I are dying today. I don't care what Rowan the time-traveling ghost has planned." The hairs on my arm rose with the tension in the room. "Let's go."

CHAPTER SEVENTEEN

The drive to Bonneville Avenue from Industrial Road was under ten minutes. With only three places to check, I hoped we'd locate Tony and Rowan in under an hour. "You know, if this was a movie, it'd be the last place we look," I joked. "To heighten the tension."

The others laughed. "Maybe we should start with the one we'd check last, try to subvert that ending," Theresa suggested with a smile.

"Too twisty for me – we'll stick with going in order from closest to farthest," Robin said. "After all, I'm driving."

"I've decided to say yes to Alex," Catherine blurted out.

Theresa and Marcie appeared confused, but Robin and I whooped in pleasure and expressed our congratulations.

"My boyfriend proposed," Catherine explained to the councilmembers. They added their congratulations.

"What tipped the decision?" I asked.

"I thought about everything we've been through, how nothing is certain, and when you're in love… you shouldn't let it go or live in fear."

An image of Tony's grinning face flashed in my mind. "Yeah, that makes sense." I felt Robin's eyes on me. "Yes?"

"Does this change anything for you?" She smirked.

I twisted in the front seat to look at Theresa and Marcie in the back with Catherine. "Previously, I've expressed that I didn't think humans and supernaturals could have a future," I explained to them. "I may have been mistaken." I ran a hand through my hair. "To say I'm feeling ambivalent would be an understatement."

"How did your date with Tony go?" Robin asked. "I mean, before Rowan kidnapped him," she amended.

A flush crept across my face. "Really well. I like him. We're going to go out again."

"That's wonderful," Catherine said. The others murmured their agreement.

"That's why I can't die today, and neither can Tony," I stated.

"We're at the first chapel," Robin announced. She pulled over to the side of the road.

Everyone faced the small white building. Even from the car, we could see a sign posted on the pink door. It likely said closed for renovations.

I shook my head. "I doubt this is it. Too small, I think. Didn't Barbara say the room was large, cavernous even?"

"She did," Robin agreed. "But premonitions aren't an exact science," she reminded me.

"Do you sense her energy?" I asked Theresa.

"I don't."

"Are you sure?" Catherine asked.

"She's not here."

"On we go to option number two," Robin declared and eased the car back onto the road. She drove up the street a few blocks. Before she'd even parked, Theresa was nodding her head.

"I sense Rowan," she said. "If Tony's with her, he's here."

Catherine poked me in the shoulder. "Looks like it's not going to be the last place we check."

"Guess we're not that interesting of a movie," I quipped.

Everyone laughed, dispelling the apprehension in the car. We stared at the building. It was a two-story house, painted white with red accents. Pretty. Looked like a nice place to get married. I opened my car door, prompting the others to do the same.

The five of us stood in front of the car, surveying the house further.

"Still not cavernous," I commented.

"Not an exact science," Robin repeated.

I smiled. "Let's go get my mate."

Mate? The word slipped out. I strode forward before anyone could comment. The sound of shoes scuffing on the concrete followed me from the street up to the door.

"They're definitely in there," Theresa whispered.

"Time for boldness," I said with false bravado and tried the door. It was unlocked and swung open to reveal a dark, dusty interior. "Here we go."

CHAPTER EIGHTEEN

The five of us crowded together in the foyer, listening for sounds in the converted home. Silence. Someone cleared their throat.

"Should we split up?" Catherine whispered.

I swiveled my head to take in the wooden stairs leading to who-knew-what upstairs, the two rooms on either side of the foyer, and a dark hallway leading to the back half of the home.

"That would make it faster," I began, "but, that always spells doom in the movies."

"Keeping with the movie theme, I see," Robin teased.

"We'll stick together," Catherine said.

Murmured agreement met the statement. I felt eyes on me and took charge. "We'll check the room on the left first." I strode in that direction, a quick walk of maybe five feet.

Our group stopped in the doorway. A basic chapel, with rows of folding chairs and a small raised altar, greeted us. Empty. We saw no places to hide, for either a manifested ghost or a shifted were-panther. They weren't here.

We backed into the foyer. I glanced up at the stairs. Would she have tried to take him up there? She wouldn't have to physically maneuver him. The ability to materialize and dematerialize made that a moot concern. I wondered whether to check from the back of the house, searching clockwise to end with the room on our right, or move from front to back, which would make the room on the right our next location.

Theresa spoke as I stepped toward the room on our right. "Rowan's energy is rising. She knows we're coming," she whispered.

My anxiety spiked, sending butterflies in motion in my belly and the blood coursing in my veins to thunder. The moment of truth. "Be ready." Marcie shifted to stand next to me, Robin behind her, with Catherine and Theresa bringing up the rear.

I flung the door open, like ripping off a band-aid. My feet carried me forward without thought and the others spread out beside me. We stood in our row of five, taking in the scene before us. We'd found Rowan and Tony.

Rowan stood at the altar, as though waiting for her bridegroom in her utilitarian jumpsuit. Pain sliced through me when I remembered that in her time, her husband and children were dead. Her red hair was like a fiery halo and her blue eyes flashed. Tony lay on the floor before her, in his panther form. He was magnificent, sleek black, eyes closed. Red glowing strands of energy wrapped around him.

"What are those?" I whispered, though Rowan's smirk told me she heard me too.

"I don't know," Theresa answered. "They're throwing off significant energy, with the same vibration of the ghost." Rowan's smirk slipped slightly, suggesting Theresa was correct in her analysis. Tony became translucent and then solidified again.

"Did you see that?" I squeaked out. "What's happening to him? Tony," I called out. He opened his eyes, seeing us for the first time. But not really. I saw no awareness. "Tony?" I whispered. He phased in and out again.

"Those are strands of time energy," Catherine suddenly said.

"They're what?" I asked, cutting my eyes to hers.

Wide eyed, she shook her head. "I have no idea. It just came into my head."

"I think I can control them," Robin said, under her breath.

Rowan's smile fell completely. "Enough."

All eyes returned to her.

"I know you held that broadcast to get at me," she said. "And I knew you would come."

"We're here now. What's next?" I asked. To my surprise, Rowan appeared near tears.

"None of this is what I wanted. I don't want anybody else to get hurt. I just want my family back," she whispered.

"Let Tony go," Marcie stepped forward and urged her. "Come with us to talk to the archangel. She can reassure you that your future isn't set in stone."

Rowan wavered. Marcie took another step forward. "I… no… I," Rowan stuttered, her eyes locked on Marcie's. "Stop! He's mine. I need to delay you longer. The timeline must change." Rowan's voice became frantic. She took several halting steps toward Marcie and Theresa, who had stepped to the left away from me, Catherine, and Robin.

"Her energy is depleting," Theresa said, voice barely above a whisper.

The rest of us were bewildered until it hit me. "Marcie's convinced her we're already rescuing Tony," I said in awe. Gasps met my explanation. Oh, but that meant we needed to actually rescue him now.

With a nudge to Robin's arm, I nodded in Tony's direction. He continued to phase in and out. "Now," I whispered. "While Marcie has Rowan… distracted." Robin and I raced to Tony's prone form. His eyes met mine; I swore he recognized me this time. Energy surged through me. I nodded at Robin, who placed her hands above Tony and closed her eyes. Her fingertips began to glow. We watched in fascination as the red energy bands surrounding Tony flowed up into Robin's hands. When the last wisp entered, Robin directed her fingertips toward the ground and the energy flowed below and dissipated. Panting, Robin turned to us.

"I've grounded the energy. We can grab him."

Tony stood on all four paws, blinking rapidly at us, trying to get his bearings. Robin appeared correct. The crackling energy bands were gone. I stepped toward him, grasped his snout between my hands and kissed his nose. Our eyes met and I chuckled. "You didn't think you'd get out of our second date that easily, did you?"

Tony's eyes danced in merriment and he chuffed at me, then licked my cheek. His tongue felt rough against my skin, yet sent a thrill through my body.

"Time to go," I whispered. Catherine, Robin, and I led Tony past the pews, down the center of the chapel, as if a wedding had concluded. Marcie and Rowan were still locked in... whatever it was Marcie was doing on the other side of the pews. Theresa stood between them and us.

When we reached the door, Rowan's head swung toward us and our eyes met. "Get him out of here," I shouted to Catherine. Robin remained by my side, ready to call more energy if needed. Marcie stared at Rowan, likely attempting to reengage her mind manipulation.

"No! You must stop. Why must you refuse to do what is right?" Rowan turned to face me head on, took several steps forward, the edges of her fingertips beginning to crackle. Catherine and Tony were right behind me, at the doorway to the chapel. Steps from safety.

One day I'd learn to manage my smart mouth. Today wasn't that day. "We've won. There's nothing you can do to stop us."

Rowan raised her hands and red energy arced from them, aiming straight for Catherine.

CHAPTER NINETEEN

Action without thought to consequences rarely ends well.
I saw the red energy arc from Rowan toward Catherine and
without thinking, I dove in front of the empath. The energy
from the ghost slammed into me with the burning pain of
a thousand suns.

Okay, maybe that was an exaggeration but not much. I
slid to the floor, my body in flames. I patted at myself to
douse the flames and realized I wasn't on fire. It just felt
that way.

"Ow, ow, ow," I said, shocked to discover my words
were barely audible. I had thought I was yelling.

A distant voice swam nearer. "Liz! Are you okay?"
Catherine's mouth was next to my ear, and I recognized
that we had fallen together.

But I didn't care too much. Everything was becoming
fuzzy. Fuzzy pain.

I wanted to laugh at the oxymoronic thought, but no longer had the energy.

Something rough touched my cheek and my eyes flew open. Hmm. I didn't know I'd closed them. Images swarmed before me. Tony. Tony licked my cheek. Aww, just like a big kitty. I tried to reach my hand out, but it didn't respond to my command.

Growling penetrated through the fog. That was Tony too. Was he trying to speak to me? I was so tired. And everything hurt so much.

Maybe a quick nap would do the trick. From somewhere in the recesses of my brain, I remembered what I'd learned from television and movies. When severely hurt, if you fell asleep, you died.

The realization sent a shock wave through my body, dulling the pain long enough for me to snap my eyes open again.

Tony stood before me, but facing the other direction. I heard him growling, a constant low rumble. Rowan stood, slack-jawed, staring in our direction, shaking her head. Was she worried my mate would attack her? Was that his plan? Or was he standing guard?

Whimpering reached my ears. Was that me, or Tony? He turned his head, piercing green eyes grabbing mine. He whined again. I could see the human intelligence in there beside the animal. So amazing. I was glad I lived long enough to see it.

With a sigh so small, I doubted anyone noticed, my brain accepted that I was dying. The fiery pain had dimmed to almost nothing. But that seemed to be because I couldn't feel my extremities any longer.

I dropped my head, hoping to catch a glimpse. To see if I even still had extremities. Maybe Rowan had blasted them off, and I was just a stump. That thought ought to terrify me, but didn't.

Hmm. A huge burned gash ran the length of my torso. Good grief, no wonder I thought I was on fire. I wanted to touch the charred edges of my chest, but my arms still weren't responding.

This was what dying felt like. My eyes closed.

Slap! What the—

Someone had smacked me. My eyes fluttered open again, awareness returned. Tony still stood in panther-form, looking back at me, then toward Rowan, back at me again. Catherine's arms came around me, her voice murmured words in my ear that I couldn't comprehend. Robin, Marcie, and Theresa faced Rowan. Robin had her arms raised, as if about to attack. But, why bother? Rowan had won. She'd killed me. The investigation wouldn't go forward.

The timeline would change, just as Rowan wanted. I didn't care anymore. I wanted to sleep. My eyes closed again. Just a little nap. So brief it'd be like it never happened.

Catherine's arms tightened around me and then there was nothing—

CHAPTER TWENTY

Images brightened in my mind. Hmm, was this the last gasp of my brain? Or was I not dying? This seemed like too much awareness for death. But what did I know? I saw Tony, the witches, Catherine, running forward, backward. It was like a movie on fast-forward, then reverse. I frowned. Or tried to. I wasn't sure if my mouth was responding anymore either. Pain flared, then receded, vanished entirely. What on earth?

My eyes widened. The world *was* on fast-forward, then reverse. I glanced down when I felt Catherine's arms tighten, then loosen, then seem to vanish. Holy heck! Her arms *were* tightening, loosening, then vanishing. Her words in my ear came again, then stopped, then came again, but different. Since I hadn't understood her to begin with, I couldn't be sure, but based on what I was seeing, I'd be willing to bet her words were reversed too.

I continued to watch as Catherine's arms phased in and out. I continued to watch as the beings before me zoomed forward and backward. I continued to wince then recover as the pain flared then receded.

Was I in purgatory? Was I stuck in some kind of ghost loop? Destined to relive my dying moment forever? I'd read that in books before, figured if someone created it, in this new world of supernaturals, it was probably possible.

The world froze.

I tried and failed to move, but rather than chalk it up to dying, I assumed I was frozen too. But, why could I hear my thoughts? Why weren't they frozen? This would make an amazing story to tell later.

Catherine's arms tightened around me then loosened.

My eyes closed then reopened. I had the thought that Rowan had won; the timeline would change the way she wanted. Yet, this thought appeared apart from me, running parallel to my current thoughts observing it. Whoa. That was so meta.

Robin's arms were raised as if about to attack Rowan. Marcie and Theresa stood on either side of her.

Catherine's voice murmured in my ear. I again noted my thought that I couldn't comprehend her, running parallel to my observational thought about noticing. She moved backward to stand before me. She was still phasing in and out like she was having trouble staying in our time and/or dimension. My head jerked to the side like someone had slapped me, but then her hand was there on my cheek and my head moved. As if I slapped her hand with my face.

The truth stunned me. Time was moving backward. Yet my thoughts remained enough to observe it.

My eyes closed as time returned to the moment before Catherine slapped me. My eyes opened and looked down to take in the huge burned gash that ran the length of my torso. I had the thought that this was what dying felt like, wanting my arms to respond but they didn't, wanting to touch the charred edges of my chest.

The thought that I was a stump ran through my mind again, my head lay on my chest, trying to determine whether I still had extremities. Then the thought that I couldn't feel my extremities any longer. Dimmed pain began to flare, a breathed out sigh instead of in. Accepting that I was dying.

A thought that I was glad to see Tony's intelligence, then backward into meeting his eyes and seeing the human intelligence beside the animal. He whined again. His electric green eyes moved away from mine and I heard him whimpering. Wondered if that was Tony. Meta-me found this whole reversal fascinating.

Was Tony standing guard or planning to attack Rowan? She stared at me, slack-jawed, then looked away. Tony's growls reached my ears, a constant low rumble. He stood before me, but facing the angry ghost.

Now that I'd realized time was flowing backward, I wondered how far we would go. Back to where Rowan's energy arc hit me? And then what? Move forward again? The thought that I'd spend eternity reliving the most painful moment of my life forever hurt my brain. Was this what it was like for a ghost stuck in a murder-loop?

I re-heard my thought that if you fell asleep when severely injured you died, then my eyes closed. I needed a quick nap. Everything hurt so much. I was so tired. I wondered if Tony was trying to speak to me, then his growling penetrated through my brain fog.

My hand wanted to reach to pet the big kitty, but it didn't respond. Tony's tongue licked my cheek. My eyes closed. Something rough touched my cheek.

Lack of energy prevented me from laughing while I relived my thought about the fuzzy pain. Everything was becoming fuzzy. But I didn't care too much. The meta-me found it interesting that some of this scene flowed the same forward and backward.

I recognized that Catherine was behind me, her mouth next to my ear. "Liz! Are you okay?" Her voice swam away.

When I thought I'd yelled, I was shocked to discover my words were barely audible. "Ow, ow, ow," I repeated.

My body felt like it was on fire. I patted myself to douse the flames, realized I wasn't on fire. I had the strange sensation of sliding *up* from the floor to a standing position. The initial thought of being hit with the burning pain of a thousand suns recurred. And, damn, even in my meta-state, that hurt all over again. But I was still moving. I knew where this would end. My body slid sideways as I reversed my dive in front of Catherine. Rowan's arcing red energy reversed from my chest. So bizarre to see it like it was arcing from me and not to me. It returned to Rowan's hands. The eyes in her face burned with hatred. No, that wasn't right, I realized. It was desperation. That threw meta-me for a moment.

As the energy disappeared into Rowan's hands and she lowered her arms, my mouth moved. Oh, yeah, I had forgotten about my smart aleck comment.

"We've won. There's nothing you can do to stop us," I said backwards.

The world froze again. And then started back up.

Oh no, I'd have to relive the pain again.

Rowan raised her arms to attack, but Catherine was already moving. She leapt toward me and we crashed to the ground as the energy arced harmlessly into the doorjamb behind us. Nobody was hit. Catherine jumped to her feet before I even had time to be awestruck that somehow she reversed time and saved me. Her voice thundered out of her.

"Rowan! Enough. Stop."

And, amazingly, the desperate, time-traveling ghost did.

Everybody halted what they were doing. We all stared at Catherine. Given the looks on the others' faces, I wasn't the only one who just experienced the reversal of that scene. I spoke for all of us.

"Catherine, what the heck just happened?"

CHAPTER TWENTY-ONE

Catherine glanced between all of us, a look of uncertainty on her face. She opened her mouth, closed it.

I jumped into the quiet. "Dang, woman, what did you do? What are you?"

The empath responded to my questions with a quick shake of her head. "I don't know."

"Time went backward. You saved me," I said.

She nodded. "How?"

We all looked around at each other, even Rowan. Nobody had an answer for Catherine. A growl drew my attention and I ran to Tony. I knelt before him, taking his snout into my hands. Those green eyes saw into my soul; that was how it felt, anyway. I kissed the tip of his nose. He chuffed at me, then turned and padded out of the room.

"Tony?" I stepped to follow, but stopped when Marcie shook her head.

"He needs a minute."

Understanding dawned. He needed to shift back into his human form. Hmm, would he be naked when he shifted? A flush crept up my neck at the direction of my thoughts. Hey, that's what happened in the shifter books I read.

Unidentifiable sounds from outside the room reached my ears. What was Tony doing? When he walked back into the room, I couldn't stop the chuckle. He smirked at me.

"Enjoying the show, Liz?" His voice hoarser than normal, perhaps because of the shifting.

"I am," I confirmed. My eyes traveled the length of the now-human shifter. He wasn't naked. It was even better. The noises I'd heard had been him removing a window covering – very *Gone with the Wind*. Tony stood before us with a sheet wrapped, toga style, around his waist, crossing his chest, and over one shoulder. It was a good look on his lithe frame. I wanted to fan myself, but resisted the urge. We exchanged a heat-filled glance. He walked to stand beside me, energy pouring off of him.

Theresa cleared her throat. "Not that this isn't interesting, but what now?" She pointed at the ghost.

All heads swiveled to Rowan. Tears streamed down her face. She shook her head. "I don't understand what happened."

"You killed me," I told her bluntly. "Then Catherine reversed time to undo your damage."

"I don't want to kill anyone," Rowan whispered. Her arms hung at her sides. "I want my family back."

That familiar pain of loss sliced through me at her words. "This isn't the way to do it."

"Maybe I'm wrong?" she asked.

I nodded. "Yeah, I think so."

"What do I do now?"

"I have no idea. We'll help you figure that out." I smiled, and she returned a shy one. I spun to Catherine. "But you… what the heck?"

"I think I know what happened," Rowan answered my question to Catherine.

"You do?" Catherine responded.

"You time traveled," the ghost said simply.

Catherine's mouth fell open. "But… I don't… I've got nothing."

"How is that possible?" Robin asked.

Rowan shrugged. "That I don't know."

"Barbara Knollman said from the moment you came to town that you were important," I reminded Catherine, who blushed.

"Is this what she meant?"

"I have no idea," I answered with a laugh. Adrenaline that had coursed through my body from my near-death experience had made me giddy. "You're going to save the world."

"Not exactly," came a voice from the doorway.

"You do that on purpose, don't you?" I teased the archangel.

"Wouldn't it be boring if I walked in like everyone else?" Olivia Williams responded with a wink.

"Can you explain what Catherine did?" I asked.

The blue-haired, blue-eyed archangel belly laughed. "Of course."

CHAPTER TWENTY-TWO

Catherine, Rowan, Robin, Marcie, Theresa, Tony and I waited semi-patiently for Olivia to deliver on her promise of explaining Catherine's apparent new skill. Time traveling. Who knew?

"First, let me congratulate all of you," Olivia began. "You've done it." She beamed at us.

"Done what? Have we fixed whatever went wrong in Rowan's timeline?" I scratched my head, more like a nervous tic than to show my confusion.

Olivia walked to Rowan, took the time traveling ghost's hands in her own. "Yes," she answered my question, but kept her eyes trained on the ghost. "You have."

Rowan's watery eyes widened and she whispered, "They have?"

Olivia nodded. Rowan threw her arms around the archangel. "Thank you, thank you, thank you." Olivia patted the ghost's head, like comforting a child, before detangling from her.

"It's time for you to return to your own time," Olivia told the ghost.

Rowan grimaced. "You mean, cross over? 'Cause I died."

Olivia quirked an eyebrow. "That's not true anymore."

"It's not?" I asked before Rowan could.

Olivia gestured for me to stay out of it and directed her answer at the ghost. "It's not true anymore," she confirmed. "When I said that the timeline had been changed, I meant completely."

"My family?" Rowan asked, voice trembling.

The archangel nodded. "You're all alive. That's all I can say."

Rowan took several deep breaths. She waved a hand in front of her face but it didn't stop the waterworks. Tears fell and she hugged herself. "I don't know what to say." She looked at the group of us. "I can never repay you."

"I'm glad we did this without anybody dying this time," I quipped, fear rippling through me at my remembered death, though the memory faded more with the passing of time.

Catherine rolled her eyes at me, but said nothing.

"Are you ready?" Olivia asked Rowan.

"Wait!" the ghost exclaimed.

"What?"

"Can you send me back after you explain what Catherine did?"

Olivia's mouth fell open. I guessed it took a lot for someone to surprise her.

"It's just," Rowan continued with a small shrug, "I've never seen a human, even with supernatural abilities, move time back and forth like that." She grinned. "Please."

The archangel chuckled. "Sure. I can do that." Olivia approached Catherine, who dropped her eyes. "Look at me." Catherine complied. "Do you believe you time traveled?"

"That would seem to be the case," she side-stepped in her answer.

"It's not quite accurate."

"It's not?" I interjected again. Olivia ignored me this time.

"What did I do?" Catherine whispered her question. "What am I?"

"You are a descendant of Kronos," Olivia began.

"Wasn't he the God of Time?" Theresa asked.

Olivia nodded. "Yes, he was."

"Catherine's a Goddess?" I asked this incredulously. The empath in question paled. Olivia shook her head.

"It doesn't work like that."

"Thank goodness," Catherine blurted.

"You are genetically a descendant," Olivia clarified.

"What does that mean?" Catherine asked.

"Your role is to keep the timeline on track."

"No pressure there," she muttered.

"When you moved time backward to save Liz, did you consciously choose to do that?"

"No. I didn't even know I could."

"Then what happened?" Olivia asked the question, but I frowned, uncertain where she was going with this line of inquiry.

"Everything felt wrong when Liz died and I had the thought that I needed to fix it." Catherine shrugged. "It all happened so fast."

"In the moment of stress, knowing the timeline was going off track—" Olivia started to say.

"Because Rowan was never supposed to be here," I wondered aloud and Olivia frowned at me for my continual interruptions. I grinned at her. "Sorry."

"Your power activated in that moment of realization," Olivia continued to explain to Catherine. "It didn't matter that you didn't know what was happening."

"I've been in life-threatening situations before. I've had people I care about be in life-threatening situations before—"

"Aw, does that mean you care about me?" I interrupted.

"I'm reconsidering my position on the matter," Catherine said, rolling her eyes.

"Or is it something else that you can't tell us?" I asked Olivia.

"You were partially right, Liz. Rowan was never supposed to be here. But, it was also because it needed to be something messing directly with the timeline to spark the development of the power. Like a trial."

"To see if I was worthy?" Catherine asked.

"Something like that." Olivia tilted her head. "Going forward, you'll become even better at recognizing when things are going sideways and you'll be able to consciously choose to intervene."

Catherine audibly swallowed. "I will? Now that really sounds like a lot of pressure."

"I'll guide you."

"Oh, thank goodness," Catherine breathed.

Olivia turned back to Rowan. "Are you ready now?"

"Yes." The ghost faced us. She appeared stricken. "I want to apologize for all the pain I caused." She looked at me. "Even if some of it was only temporary." Her fingers fidgeted in front of her, clasped together. "I didn't know what else to do. When I discovered I could direct myself elsewhere in time as a ghost, I had to try. I had to save my family." Rowan began glowing. "And I did. Thank you for everything." The ghost flickered, phasing in and out of our dimension, timeline, however Olivia would describe it. With a final wave at us, Rowan winked out of our existence.

Olivia copied Rowan's wave at us. "That's my cue to depart. I'll be in touch," she said to Catherine. "Oh, Liz?"

"Yes?"

"What have you learned from this?"

I frowned. "Don't mess with Catherine?" The empath smacked my arm and the archangel shook her head.

"Try again," she said dryly.

I pondered her question. What was I missing? The heat still flowing off of Tony distracted me for a moment and I gazed at him. He raised his eyebrows. Did he know what the archangel was asking? I turned back to Olivia, lifted my hands in a gesture of helplessness. "I don't know."

Olivia smirked. "Let's just say that you and Tony are more compatible than you might think." And with that obscure pronouncement, Olivia winked out of our existence too.

"That wasn't vague at all," I grumbled.

"We'll give you guys a moment," Catherine said, with a knowing look at us. She and the others filed out, several smiling or waggling their eyebrows at us. When they were gone, I faced Tony.

"Am I the only one who doesn't understand what Olivia was hinting at?"

"Probably."

I slow nodded. "You know what she meant."

"I do."

"And you're not going to tell me."

"I'm not."

"How come?"

Tony didn't answer. He brushed my jaw with his fingers, the touch sending shock waves of pleasure through my body. I curled my fingers around his, holding them in place. Our breath commingled. He stepped back from me, an acute sense of loss filling the space he'd occupied.

"I need to find the answer on my own," I speculated, and he nodded.

"Do you still have reservations about humans and supernaturals?" he asked.

"Yes," I admitted, shame over the answer flooding me. "No matter how much they like and are attracted to each other."

Hurt shown in his eyes, but also compassion and understanding. He gave a sad smile. "At least you admit you find me attractive."

I laughed at the unexpected comment and took a step forward. "Attraction has never been the issue," I assured him. "Time to process. That's what I need," I concluded. "Can you give me that?"

"You know where to find me," he answered. With as much dignity as a man wrapped in a faux-toga could muster, he left the room.

I stood alone and contemplated everything I'd seen, felt, and learned in the past – what? 30 minutes?

When we first met, Tony had been shocked I could smell his cat. Olivia had said he and I were more compatible than I knew. My mind raced. I was fairly certain she didn't mean I was also a shifter, though I poked at my skin anyway.

"Is there an animal under there?" I asked the air.

Receiving no answer, I laughed at myself. All I had right now was my incredible attraction to the sweet, funny, hot, loyal man Tony had shown himself to be in the past few days. Had it only been that short a time? Would that be enough, without knowing the big secret everyone else knew?

The answer rose within me and I smiled. Before I could call Tony to share my revelation, my phone rang.

"Hi, Barbara," I answered. She reminded me that tonight was the vote on the human-supernatural integration bill. "I'll be there as soon as I can get a ride."

CHAPTER TWENTY-THREE

A quick drive from the Arts District to our more-or-less "proper" downtown, and the driver let me off in front of the two-story government building housing the city council. I entered and headed for the marble stairs to the second floor. The preliminaries appeared finished as I snuck in and sat in the audience, wincing when the seat squeaked.

Within the elongated half-circle of elected officials' seats, Mayor Barbara Knollman sat dead-center. Her councilmembers fanned out on either side, every seat taken. No abstentions tonight, I imagined. This was a hot-button issue. Opposite them sat all of us, the audience. Not as filled as I would have expected in the 500-seat occupancy room, but probably a lot more than a typical meeting held. In the center between the audience and the councilmembers was a podium with a microphone. A man stood before it, not speaking. I noticed a line of people behind him. Wow, was this all for the integration bill?

A hand touched my shoulder and a voice whispered in my ear. "Hey, Liz. Long time, no see. I guess you got the call?"

"Hey, guys," I whispered back with a low chuckle, as Catherine, her boyfriend (fiancé?) Alex, Robin, and Marcie filed into the row behind me. Evie the 1920s vampire, her actor boyfriend Ryan, Mia, and her detective boyfriend Jacob had joined them. I gave the group a little wave, noticing the disappointment I felt that Tony hadn't gotten the call, too. Or maybe he needed to check in at the café?

"Thank you all for coming," Barbara's voice cut through my thoughts. "I'm glad to see we have a good turnout for today's historic vote. Most of you know that this afternoon I informed my fellow councilmembers of my intention to introduce new legislation tonight. I wanted them, and the voting public, to be aware of my intention and not feel blind-sided.

"As some of you also know, I went on a local morning show to discuss components of the proposed legislation. I won't repeat that here, except to summarize that the legislation is not the be-all-end-all on the subject. It's an opening round to start the conversation of how to legally integrate human and supernatural societies." She took a sip of water. I knew she couldn't be nervous and figured this was her way of letting the audience catch their breath.

"Before the vote, I'd like to open up the floor for opinions on the proposal. I see folks have already begun lining up." She gestured to the line at the podium. "If you wish to join the queue, please do so." The first gentleman in line stepped up to speak.

"Thank you, Madam Councilwoman," he started, though his voice bounced around the room with strong reverberations. He backed his mouth away, apologizing. "I would like to voice my opposition to the proposal as not having enough safeguards for the human population."

With that salvo, we were off. About a dozen folks spoke, more for the legislation than opposed, I was pleased to see. But, amidst the rhetoric and overblown conclusions, I worried we'd lose the purpose of the legislation.

I made my way toward the podium. Whispers reached me as members of the audience recognized me and commented on my movement. Several folks still in line offered to let me go ahead of them but I declined. That would defeat the purpose of a speech on equal treatment.

When it was my turn, I stepped to the microphone. Barbara lifted a single eyebrow at my presence. "Good evening, councilmembers, concerned citizens, fellow members of the press," I began. "For those of you who do not know me, and for the record," I continued, with a nod toward the woman manning the recording equipment. She smiled up at me. "My name is Elizabeth Addison." I spelled my name. "My job is as a newscaster. For that reason, you may question why I am here, providing my opinion on legislation I will continue to cover." My throat tightened, and I pulled back, coughing to clear it. "I am here, not as a member of the press, but as a citizen of the great city of Las Vegas." A few hearty claps greeted my statement.

"For the past year, humans have learned more and more about the so-called paranormal underworld. Some of that has been negative. A serial killing genie and incubus; homicidal vampire; murdering demon; deadly witch-for-hire; and just this week, an angry time-traveling ghost." Voices tittered at that one. "Don't worry, she's better now," I joked. Laughter rolled through the room.

My gaze traveled up and down the council table. "But those bad apples shouldn't spoil the bunch, to use a trite phrase. Would we want humanity to be judged by the killers among us? Of course not. What I would like for the councilmembers to remember — and the humans who spoke today against the proposal — is that when we keep anyone in the dark, treat anyone like second-class citizens, it goes against everything we stand for.

"This proposal allows us to explore how we live in peace. This proposal allows us to determine what is necessary to manage expectations for beings with, essentially, superpowers. This proposal is a step forward, allowing all beings equal treatment under the law." I waited for the spontaneous applause that erupted to stop.

"Thank you very much for your time, councilmembers, and I hope that you vote with your conscience." To more thunderous applause, and a few boos, I retook my seat with my friends, only half of whom were human, I realized with an internal chuckle. A few more citizens spoke for and against the proposal. Then it was time for the vote.

A hush settled over the room. The seven members of the council, including the mayor, leaned forward to speak a single word when their names were called. As each "aye" rang out over the crowd, tears pricked my eyes. The proposal passed unanimously. I heard the doors at the back of the auditorium open, most likely as members of the press raced out to film quick shots to notify their viewers of the proposal's passage.

In the room, a motion was made to adjourn, it was seconded, and the meeting ended. Just like that, they had charted a new path forward. Exciting times to be a citizen, a member of the press, and a potential romantic interest of a supernatural.

People rose and began filing out. I caught up with Catherine.

"Well?" I asked, raising an eyebrow.

"Well, what?" She played dumb.

I laughed. "Fine, don't tell me."

She leaned forward, her lips an inch from my right ear. "I told him yes. We'll announce wedding details when we make them."

With a squeal, I threw my arms around her and gave a thumbs up to Alex, who just shook his head with a laugh. Those involved with the Rowan event knew, but others glanced at me in confusion.

For the first time in my life as a newscaster, I didn't desire to explain. It wasn't my story to tell.

I had my own story to tell in the morning. And I had a lot to say.

CHAPTER TWENTY-FOUR

Marilyn cocked an eyebrow at me. "You seem nervous, Liz." She leaned forward to apply blush to my cheeks. "What gives?"

"I'm going out on a limb with this morning's show."

She smirked. "Don't you do that every other day or so?"

I laughed. "Touché." My eyes closed so she could apply the setting powder over my entire face. When she finished, I continued. "But, seriously, this one is more… personal."

"Oh? Maybe I'll watch then."

"Don't put yourself out," I said. She laughed.

"Have a good show." With that, she left the room. I confirmed I looked camera-ready and then headed for the studio. The production assistant hadn't come to get me yet, but I was ready. In every sense of the word.

"Liz, I was just coming to get you," the PA said when I met her in the hallway.

"Let's rock this thing," I responded, and we continued to the studio.

After taking my seat on the familiar stuffed blue chair and crossing my legs, I watched the teleprompter above the camera scroll backward and forward to finally land on my opening for the show. Not that I needed it. Not this time. I had my entire speech memorized. I hadn't been exaggerating when I told Marilyn this one was personal. Even when I'd invited the murderous genie into my home for an interview – that hadn't gone quite as planned – that was still business. This would definitely veer into personal.

The countdown to the start sounded in my ear. I cleared my throat and prepared to speak.

Camera rolling sounded in my ear bud, I opened my mouth, and nothing came out. With a deep breath, I nodded as though this was business-as-usual and tried again. Words emerged. Thank goodness.

"Good morning in the Valley! Welcome to *Entertainment Daily*, Las Vegas' most watched morning show. I'm your host, Elizabeth Addison." My smile dropped for a moment. "For those viewers keeping count, I'm still alive and today is Day 4. If you remember, several days ago, a time-traveling ghost bent on changing the future told me I had three days to live. That worked out pretty well in the end." I gave a quick summary of what had happened.

"Once we saved the future," I said with a chuckle, "it was time to take steps to put us on that path. I'm pleased to report, for those who missed the sweeping coverage last night, Mayor Knollman's integration legislation passed unanimously at the City Council meeting last night. Congratulations, Barbara." I cleared my throat again. Here came the challenging part.

"Last night, I voiced my support for this legislation. It was both political support and personal support. Over the course of the last year, I've made many supernatural friends. They've saved my hide, figuratively and literally. They deserve equal treatment."

I could hear my blood thundering in my brain. I hoped I didn't have a stroke from the nerves. "My friends know that I've expressed concern that humans and supernaturals were too different, the challenges too great to overcome, to make a romantic relationship work. Well, they may have an extra layer of challenge, but I've seen it work." I winked at the camera, hoping Catherine and Alex were watching the broadcast.

"And I've recently met a very special supernatural. If he's still willing to take a chance on an insecure, uncertain human, I'd like to have a chat." My mouth felt like I stuffed it with cotton balls, and I wished I'd thought to put a cup of water on the table beside me. "We'll take a break for some words from our sponsors and be right back."

The rest of the show passed in a blur. Everyone congratulated me when I left the studio and walked past the cubicles to my glass-walled office. I closed the door, sank into my desk chair, and with a tremulous breath, withdrew my cellphone from the top drawer. A text message.

Please come by the café when you have time.

Heart in my throat I replied. *On my way.*

CHAPTER TWENTY-FIVE

Butterflies had taken flight in my belly. I took several deep calming breaths before opening the door to Tony's café. Why was I nervous? He'd dropped enough hints of his interest and I finally got my priorities aligned. This would be fine.

Tony's eyes lit up when he saw me, and I knew I'd made the right decision. He stepped toward me as I crossed to the counter. "Hey there, stranger," I greeted the were-panther.

"I saw your show this morning," he responded. He started to rest his arms on the countertop, reversed motion, and stepped around and out toward me. His familiar heat rolled off him, warming me.

"What did you think?"

"I liked it."

"I'm glad."

Tony took my hands in his. "What changed?"

Squeezing his hands, I grinned. "I got out of my own way," I quipped before answering for real. "Seriously? I thought about how I feel when I'm around you." He smiled lasciviously and I shook my head with a chuckle. "I considered how I feel when I'm not around you." His smiled dropped. "I thought about your reaction when I could smell your cat—"

"Panther," he corrected, but his smile was back in place.

"Panther," I agreed with a good-natured eye roll. "I considered what Olivia said about our compatibility." My eyes met his, unshed tears blurring my view of him. I blinked to clear the image. "When you were hurt," I swallowed as the remembered pain passed through me, "I thought of you as my… mate."

Tony gasped and tightened his grip on my hands. "What does all that mean?"

"I'm not certain. I'm not a shifter, but I can sense the shifterness of you," I teased him. "It doesn't matter if I'm human. I want to be with you. None of the rest of it matters."

Tony's eyes dilated and he leaned toward me, releasing my hands so he could cup my face. He feathered delicate kisses on my forehead, my cheeks, my nose (that triggered a giggle from me). We'd only met four days ago; it was like the insta-attraction in a romance novel.

But it was real.

His chapped lips found mine. Gentle at first, then with more passion. Energy zinged through me and my arms wrapped around him, pulling him closer. My heart swelled with… surely not love yet, but something similar…

I pulled back and smirked.

"What?" he asked, his sexy voice pitched low.

I stood on my toes, leaned forward again. My lips stopped an inch from his ear. "If you know what Olivia meant, will you tell me now?" I whispered.

Tony chuckled. "I wasn't positive until you said you thought of me as your mate," he began to explain, his eyes shining with that same undefined feeling. "You carry shifter genes—"

"No way," I interrupted in an exclamation that drew the attention of the few people in the café who weren't already watching our performance. My head dropped onto his shoulder. A flush crept across my face.

He lifted my chin to regain eye contact. "Yes way." He beamed. "And you probably can carry shifter offspring."

After I picked my jaw up off the floor, I responded to his bombshell. "That's a conversation for another time."

"Indeed."

I placed my hands on his chest, reveling in the warmth and strength pulsing under my palms and fingers. "Guess this is the dawn of the Age of the Supernaturals."

"That's not dramatic at all," Tony teased. "Like this is a television show."

"Don't you want there to be a season two?"

"You mean, after this exciting season finale?"

"Exactly. This doesn't have to be the end. We want people to tune in again."

"I'm not sure I could take the excitement," Tony said drily.

A giggle bubbled up. I wrapped my arms around his middle again, looked up into his amazing chocolate brown eyes. "How about being my date for a friend's wedding then?"

His lips closed on mine again and his nod moved my head in concert. I tried not to giggle, but another escaped around our clasped lips. "This is going to be so much fun," I whispered.

"Yes, it will, my mate."

EPILOGUE

I told myself I wouldn't cry, but tears formed when I saw Catherine in the open doorway of the chapel room, in her simple white knee-length fitted sheath, blond hair falling loose around her shoulders. Elvis stood next to her, guitar at the ready. He strummed the strings, and the two began to walk down the short aisle.

A hand took mine, and I glanced into Tony's face. He leaned over to kiss my cheek. We both turned to watch the bride continue down the aisle, the good-looking young Elvis singing a love song. I shifted my gaze to Alex, looking sharp in a black tuxedo, standing at the altar with the wedding officiant, a tall, thin, older man with an engaging smile.

Catherine reached her groom. Her blue eyes mirrored the happy tears in his green ones. Alex took her hands in his. The grins on their faces sparked many in the audience.

"Friends and family, welcome," the officiant began. Although, to be accurate, it was mostly Paranormal Talent Agency friends. I chuckled when I realized how many of us had found love, thanks to Catherine accepting the job opportunity of starting the West Coast arm of the Peterson Talent Agency here in Las Vegas. And how many of us weren't even human.

"We are gathered here today to witness the joining of Catherine and Alex." I wasn't big on ceremonies, so my attention drifted. I glanced around at the group sitting in cushioned folding chairs arranged like pews.

Vampire Evie, her 1920s blond bob in place, snuck looks at her human boyfriend Ryan, his auburn hair in need of a trim. Nixie Mia, her green hair in an elaborate French braid, held hands with her human boyfriend Jacob, his close-cut blond hair not in need of a trim. Robin and Jackson, human witches, their heads resting against each other. And, even Barbara and Liam, 500-year-old angels, recently reunited.

I refocused on the couple at the altar as the officiant reached the question-and-answer portion of the ceremony.

"Do you, Catherine Rodham, promise to love and trust Alex, in sickness and in health, in adversity and prosperity, for better or worse, so long as you both shall live?"

"I do." She smiled, happiness radiating off of her. I'd swear she was glowing. Now that we knew she was descended from a god, maybe she was.

"Do you, Alexander Moore, promise to love and trust Catherine, in sickness and in health, in adversity and prosperity, for better or worse, so long as you both shall live?"

"I do." He blew her a kiss and she giggled.

"Do you have the rings?"

Catherine and Alex answered yes. Mia and Jacob handed the rings over, unadorned platinum bands.

"With this ring, I thee wed," Catherine spoke softly.

"With this ring, I thee wed," Alex echoed.

And then the moment we were waiting for.

"By the authority given me by the State of Nevada, I now pronounce you man and wife," the officiant intoned. "You may kiss your bride."

Alex scooped Catherine up in his arms – not easy to do when she was so tall – yet delivered a chaste kiss. His lips moved, and I wondered what he was saying, but glad that they would have those whispered words to themselves.

Elvis began playing something fast, and the newlyweds walked back down the aisle to where Catherine had entered. They beamed as they passed their assembled friends.

All brought together by the Paranormal Talent Agency and leading the charge into the Age of the Supernaturals. Catherine and Alex disappeared through the doorway. Elvis stopped walking but continued singing. We in the audience waited with bated breath. The newlyweds reappeared back in the doorway, we whooped our appreciation, and then everyone was standing, hugging, declaring ecstatic congratulations to the couple.

We'd all done it.

Happily ever after.

THANK YOU!

Thank you so much for supporting my work and reading this collection. I truly hope you enjoyed reading it as much as I did writing it.

If you liked the book, please consider leaving a review online.

Just a few lines would be great. Reviews are not only the highest compliment you can pay to an author, they also help other readers discover and make more informed choices about purchasing books in a crowded online space. Thank you so much in advance.

If you didn't like the book or have concerns, please email me directly at
heather@heathersilvio.com

ABOUT THE AUTHOR

Heather has written fiction and nonfiction; she is also an actress and licensed psychologist. When she isn't working, she channels her inner flapper as a 1920s jazz and blues singer.

Visit https://www.heathersilvio.com for more information and to sign up for her weekly newsletter.